THE **HEART** LADDER

ELIZABETH MACBAIN

URBANE
Publications

urbanepublications.com

First published in Great Britain in 2016 by Urbane Publications Ltd
Suite 3, Brown Europe House, 33/34 Gleamingwood Drive, Chatham, Kent ME5 8RZ
Copyright © Elizabeth Macbain, 2016

ISBN 978-1-910692-06-6
EPUB 978-1-910692-07-3
MOBI 978-1-910692-08-0

Design and Typeset by Julie Martin
Cover by Julie Martin
Printed and bound by CPI Group (UK) Ltd, Croydon, CR0 4YY

URBANE
Publications

urbanepublications.com

FSC

The publisher supports the Forest Stewardship Council® (FSC®), the leading international forest-certification organisation.
This book is made from acid-free paper from an FSC®-certified provider. FSC is the only
forest-certification scheme supported by the leading environmental organisations, including Greenpeace.

For Ba and Unc.

May you find each other again, in time.

ACKNOWLEDGEMENTS

I would like to thank my husband, for your love and your unending faith in me; my son, for your beauty and light, and my unborn child for the happiness you are sure to bring. My sincere gratitude goes to my wonderful mum for the countless hours of babysitting you gave me so that I could complete this book, and for being the inspiration that you are.

Finally, I wish to say a big 'thank you' to Matthew Smith at Urbane Publications for taking a huge chance on my first novel, before it had even been written, and to all of those people in my life who continue to believe in me when, at times, I forget to believe in myself.

CHAPTER **ONE**

AND THERE SHE WAS.

Leather-booted and pregnant, her green eyes following the baggage carousel as it meandered on its usual course, seeking out her holdall. The young woman pulled her shawl around her shoulders, her hair barely contained under her pink crocheted hat. *Gee, it's nearly as cold as home,* she thought. Despite this, she looked unseasonably bright there, amidst the gray scale transience of the airport arrival lounge, and the business men who frequented it. There was a frisson of excitement amongst those standing closest to her, brought on by her presence. She was an *other*; yes, a female, and a different sort of girl. An unmarried one. She was aware of them looking, despite her protruding belly, of which she felt so conscious, yet also unashamed. She let her mind drift away from those around her, and back to the previous day; the day she had left her life.

She could still smell the city and hear its comforting sounds as it breathed its life into those who inhabited it; like a concrete organism coloured by little humans who busied themselves within and upon it, going through all their little dramas while the sun rose and set and the lights flashed and the horns honked.

The invisible threads which had tied her there felt looser now, and there was a thrill within her of the unknown, which had dazzled her sadness into submission, at least for now. Everything she needed she carried within, or it was in that bag, the one she was waiting for; the remnants of her 23 year old life

THE HEART LADDER   7 crammed into tiny spaces, like the memories which bounced around her heart.

She suddenly spotted her holdall, and tried not to race around and grab it. *No-one would steal it anyhow*, she thought. It was such an old thing, of no consequence or value to anyone else. As she watched it go round, her eyes collided with a man who was looking directly at her. He was not dressed like the others, he was scruffy and unkempt. Unperturbed, she returned his gaze and he finally looked down, turned and walked away: an outcast just like her. She reached out for her bag and turned to face the world. She couldn't wait to get outside now, out of the stifling airport and into the English air, breathed by so many for so long and filled with possibility.

There was no queue for international passengers, and she placed her passport down on the counter. The man looked up at her.

"Name?"

"Faith Anderson," she replied, and smiled. He returned the passport to her outstretched hand, and that was that. She managed to barely squeeze through the turnstile and then she walked through the airport foyer as if she owned the world. Finally pushing through the exit, she spun around once and threw her hat up in the air, like some kind of college graduate on his last day of grad school. She climbed into the nearest black cab and told them her desired destination. It sped off and, just like that, she was away.

Once on the train, Faith watched the dreary city disperse until she began to see little vegetable patches in people's gardens, and then some more trees and natural spaces, until eventually her window was filled with the greens and browns of the countryside. She had little idea where she actually was, geographically. Somewhere north of London. But she knew where she was going. An old lady sat across from her knitting, and there were only a few other people in the carriage.

Every now and then, the lady smiled and Faith smiled back. She didn't know how to begin the conversation, just as she hadn't really known what to say to the cab driver on her way to the train station. He'd chatted away in his cockney accent, and Faith had tried to decode it. Even through the rear view mirror, he'd managed to do that thing some guys do where they can't help but look at your breasts every three or four words. It was only afterwards that it occurred to her it could have been her condition he was eyeing, after all.

In the sky, she spotted some kind of bird hovering, still, like lake water, waiting to dive. She thought about those primal needs to consume and to pro-create. Could that be all we were made up of? Needs; desires; survival. Faith didn't want to believe that her coming here was an entirely selfish act. For the most part, she wanted to build a future for her baby, one where he or she could shine without the dull ache of the past to tarnish this brave new world. She rummaged around in the outer pocket of her bag and pulled out her watch, a battered old Timex, and saw she had about a half hour left of the journey. She took out her notepad and opened it at a list of names. She looked out the window for inspiration and wrote, *Sky*.

Faith was going back to a place she had left behind long ago, but it was a place of childhood, captured in her memory like an old photo or home movie: a piece of nature so well-explored and yet so exciting. She vividly remembered building a den in the space between a hole in a tree and the hedge, using piles of leaves and bracken, in which she would curl up for what seemed like ages, shivering from the thrill of being undiscovered and yet aching for someone to get close, so she could watch and listen to their secret moments, whilst they were left unable to know hers.

She remembered her aunt's cracked-looking hands as they showed her how get out all the little runner beans from the pod, popping them out like candy and feeling like it was a little gift from the earth. She had always had a bottle of Ellnet hairspray and a tub of Atrixo hand cream by the bath, magic potions which Faith was desperate to try and yet also knew it wasn't time for yet. Sitting on the train now, Faith wriggled her toes inside her boots, imagining the soil rubbing between them as if she were back digging holes in the ground at the back of the cottage where she'd thought fairies had lived.

The announcement of their imminent arrival at the bigger station, from which she would have to catch a local train, interrupted her thoughts, and she put her shawl back on and checked her purse. The old lady sat across from her smiled and said, "Are you visiting someone?"

"Oh dear, is it so obvious I'm foreign?" Faith asked her.

"Oh I'm sorry, no, but you just…look like someone on a little adventure," said the lady.

"Thank you," she replied, laughing. "I'm actually on a pretty big adventure."

A few hours later, and after one change of train, the smaller three carriage contraption, which reminded her a bit of the juddering subway she'd so often frequented in NYC, pulled into the small town of Hayfield. She gathered her things, and stepped off onto the platform, with significance, as if this step was the first of many towards something new. No-one else had alighted here. There was a mist and a real bite in the air, more so than when she had arrived at the airport further south. She walked up to the ticket office but she couldn't make anyone out. She peered in, and just as she did so, a hand in a fingerless glove wiped away the steam from inside. She gave a start but the face behind it surprised her with its warmth, and its femaleness. The woman who looked back at her had a round face which wore a kind expression under thick greying curls. She smiled and Faith noticed she had a couple of teeth missing.

"Sorry duck," she said, with a strong accent. She sounded to Faith's ears, like she said 'duke' and she couldn't make sense of that at all, so she chose to ignore it.

"No, it's okay," Faith said loudly, feeling like she needed to speak up due to the Perspex between them. "I need to get to Whiston Cottage, I believe it's about a 10 minute drive but I don't have a car. I guess I'm kinda stuck."

"Oh yes," the lady turned away as if she was looking for something. There was an interval in which Faith wondered if she was just being ignored, but finally the lady turned back to her, holding a folded letter.

"You must be Faith Anderson? The American?" The lady grinned as if pleased with herself.

"Wow, yes I am, how did you...?"

"Here's a note from Charlie, Charlie Simpson."

Faith looked at her blankly, but she took the note and opened it. It read,

Welcome to England, Ms Anderson. We took the liberty of hiring you a car, which you will find at the front of the station. It's just a little run around but should get you to your destination fine. The keys are in the ignition. There's a pub in the village called the White Hart Inn where we have reserved you a single room for tonight. We hope this will be to your liking and not too noisy. We trust your journey went smoothly and look forward to meeting you tomorrow.

Yours, Messrs Simpson and Jones, S and J Solicitors, Hayfield.

Faith couldn't believe she hadn't even thought about where she would stay that night; idiot! She had left New York in such a hazy state that she'd imagined herself arriving at the cottage today, like a drifter finally reaching his destination, but of course she didn't even have the keys yet. She wondered if this was an English thing, to think of everything, and decided it must be to do with politeness. She wanted to thank Mr Simpson there and then but resolved to get him a present tomorrow before the meeting. Suddenly, she realised the lady behind the counter was looking at her, waiting.

"Thank you," Faith said, smiling and waving the note at her. Then she turned to go.

"Everything alright, duckie?" The lady asked her, almost as if she didn't want her to leave.

"Oh, sure, thank you. I have a car outside, apparently," Faith said, leaning down so she could address the woman properly. "Thanks again for your help."

The window had steamed up somewhat, even in this short interval, but she thought she saw the lady wink and then heard her say, "Take care, then me duck."

Duckie, she realised, as she walked through the old oak doors and onto the station foyer, was how the woman had addressed her. *Me Duck?* She couldn't ever remember her aunt calling her that, but maybe Denise hadn't always lived here, or just hadn't picked up the local accent. Faith spotted a beige car, a tiny thing, parked at an angle across two spaces, but it didn't matter as there were no other cars there. It was iced over and when she tried to open the door, she had to give it a yank as the coldness and frost had made it stick. Once open, she realised she was at the passenger side, and walked around. Things were different here already, she thought. She climbed in and adjusted the seat and wing mirror. It was a squash to get her belly behind the wheel. She tried not to remind herself of the last time she'd driven, several years ago and in a friend's Chevy Caprice; about three times the size of this one and an automatic. She hadn't needed to drive much in New York, so this was going to be an experience. After several tries, the engine kicked into life although it didn't sound too happy about it. It was then Faith realised she hadn't asked the station lady for directions to the pub where she was to stay that night. She was about to get out when she noticed a piece of folded paper sticking out of the glove box. She pulled it out and opened it, and someone had drawn a small but neat map; Messrs Simpson and Jones, she presumed. *They have thought of everything.*

After a hair-raising but thankfully short journey, she found herself sat in the White Hart Inn, with her hands wrapped around a cup of tea. She had asked for coffee but they had none. She'd better get used to that, she thought, amused. Still, it seemed fitting: an English pub, an open fire, the low murmur of some of the locals, gathered around the bar and the crackling of the embers breaking the pattern every now and then. A man, the landlord she presumed, approached with a bowl of soup and a bread roll, which she devoured within minutes. When had she last eaten? On the plane, perhaps. Her stomach had felt too knotted with nervous excitement to eat, until now when she found herself famished. She felt a stab of guilt at not looking after herself, and as if the baby knew, it gave her a kick just to drive home the point. *Okay honey,* she said, stroking her belly discreetly with her free hand. *Mommy will do better from now on.* With a wave of emotion, she realised it had been the first time she'd referred to herself as a mother. Her new identity or the threads of it, which had begun to weave themselves together. She thought of her LP's and Carole King's 'Tapestry'. She would have to fish it out and find something to play it on once she got the keys to the house. She wondered what picture her life would form, what pattern might materialise, and wished it to be full of bright colours and joyful scenes.

The next day, Faith found herself sitting in a cold office opposite a man, perhaps only 10 or so years older than herself, who wore a grey suit and bright green cravat. He had not called her *duck,* but very formally addressed her as 'Ms Anderson', until she had implored him to call her Faith, saying it made her feel old to be addressed so importantly. He had agreed. She had not slept well. Something had gone on in the bar downstairs, of which her room was directly above. She had heard shouting and the sound of a glass breaking. *Where am I?* She wondered, inwardly laughing at the fact that she'd seen – or rather heard

— more action in the first few hours of being in this small town than she had in the past month when she lived in New York. But after that, her mood had shifted and she found her thoughts scampering across her mind like wayward mice, looking for scraps of familiarity to grab onto and feast upon and yet finding them too sparse to make connections. Her dreams were troubling; of the woman from the station, only this time she had pointed teeth, like a vampire, and she dreamed of her new home, although in the dream it wasn't Aunt Denise's cottage but an English mansion such as you saw in those black and white films of Brontë novels; cold and dark and lonely. On top of that, the baby had decided to position itself right under her ribs so she could not find a position that was comfortable. Nevertheless, she had run herself a hot bath that morning, pouring in her shampoo to create bubbles that, although short-lived, gave her some feeling of luxury, until she got out into the freezing air and had to sit by the electric fire to warm up. She shook off the dreams and made the best use of her limited supply of make-up so that she looked, sitting now as she was in S and J Solicitors, half-respectable, having ditched her crocheted hat and mini-skirt and found a mid-calf length, teal- coloured dress of her mother's to wear.

"Faith," said Mr Simpson, whose name she knew was Charlie, but she didn't know whether it was polite to address him so. "You should know that the cottage will need some repairs. Your aunt specified these in her will, along with an apology for not seeing to them herself."

"Are they serious?" Faith asked, imagining a derelict structure and buckets strategically placed under dripping holes.

"No, nothing serious," Charlie said, smiling faintly. This changed his face so that he looked younger and less stuffy. As if he knew that, he returned his expression to a neutral, yet kindly, one. She wanted to ask him if they practiced that in solicitor's college or whatever, having sometimes to be bearers of bad news. "The side door is stuck so doesn't open, but you still have the use of the front and back. There are a few broken panes of glass in the kitchen and I believe the shed is pretty much falling down. If you'd like us to arrange the repairs, I'd be happy to pass on your details to a local firm. They're very reliable and – "

"That's okay," Faith said, cutting him off. His mouth was still open, half-forming his next word. "Oh, sorry," she said. "I forget my manners. What can I say, I'm American!" She held her hands out in apology but felt slightly embarrassed. "I mean, that's very kind of you, but I think I'll check it out for myself. Maybe they're things I can live with, if Aunt Denny could."

"Of course." Charlie handed her the deed and asked her to sign on the dotted line. She felt a whizz of nervousness rush across her neck as she did so, and she looked at the keys before her. Her own house. She and Jacob had talked about it one day, but she never thought she would be doing it now, and in England, and alone.

She looked again, down at her signature; it looked childish next to his sophisticated scribble underneath. Raising her head, she must have looked uneasy because he asked her if she was alright. She nodded.

"Oh, I got you something, just to say 'thank you', for all your help. Jeez, I don't know what I'd have done without that little car yesterday!"

She reached down for the small plant which she'd managed to find that morning on a small market garden stall. She'd also gotten herself some vegetables for her first dinner that night, trying to make up for her lack of nutrition the previous day. Looking at it now, it looked a little bit pathetic.

She handed it to Charlie and his cheeks washed over crimson.

"I was just doing my job, of course."

"Oh well," Faith felt a little flustered and wanted to ease his embarrassment. "It felt like it was beyond the call of duty, you might say. I'm just grateful. It's a big thing to arrive in a strange country on your own. Not strange, I mean, foreign is a better word." She stopped talking as she realised she was babbling but it seemed to have put Charlie at ease, distracting from his own awkwardness. "It looks good on your table but I won't be offended if it goes in the trash," she said, smiling.

"That's kind of you, thank you." He smiled and reached out his hand. Faith realised their meeting was over. She wiped her hand on her dress without thinking and leant over to shake his.

"Thank you, Charlie. Mr Simpson." They shook for perhaps a little too long, and he looked at one moment like he would say something more but nothing came. Faith left the office, the keys jangling in her purse and a feeling of freedom coupled with isolation that she never quite managed to shake off in the weeks to come.

Faith felt in conflict about the space she felt, suddenly. Sometimes she revelled in it, and other times, she wanted to escape. For the first month, having been so used to the city sounds drifting up to her window, she found it hard to adapt to the country silence. One night, she awoke up to what she felt sure was the sound of a woman being attacked: this horrible screaming, high-pitched and frantic. She looked out of the bedroom window through a crack in the curtain, but couldn't see a thing. It was the first time she had realised how truly alone she was, and that she hadn't bought a flashlight yet. *Charlie Simpson even suggested to me to get one in case of a power cut but I guess I hadn't really believed him,* she thought. And then, it stopped suddenly. She couldn't make out any shapes in the dark. Faith was awash with shame and yet a survival instinct kicked in which kept her frozen to the spot. She knew if she saw something in the paper the next day she would never live with herself for not investigating further. It was only when she told her nearest neighbour, a farmer called Jack about it, that he had set her mind at rest, telling her it was a fox's bark. Not only that, but he launched into a tirade about the animal having eaten three of his chickens. It was the longest conversation they'd ever had. At first, Faith had not been able to believe an animal could make that sound, but sure enough a few weeks after this, she heard it again, right outside the window. The baby was nearly due and gave her a few strong kicks, hearing it too and responding.

Underneath all the nature was the loneliness which crept up on her, like bony arms of ivy wrapping themselves around stone until before you know it, they're part of the brickwork, intrinsic and entwined, offering no comfort. She got polite 'hellos' in the village but no-one seemed to want to know where she had been or why she was there, although they had known Denise. She began to wonder if they thought that the cottage was a house of unusual women; strange females, who chose to be alone and were secretly casting wicked spells or doing rain dances in the middle of the night. Faith had never understood that male conviction that if you're not with one of *them* you're obviously unhinged. She began to walk in the garden at night. Once she had faced her fears of nature, and realising that the terrifying sound had an innocent origin, she became obsessed with encountering a fox in person, in its own night-time habitat. She would buy a bit of meat from the butchers and leave it at the step and wait. She had no job to get up for, and she couldn't get comfortable in bed anyway now she was so big. When she sat on that step in the darkness it felt as though she was in some kind of other world; a magical world she created, one in which she wasn't scared anymore. She would sit very still. Inside Faith's belly, the baby would go still too, waiting.

One night, it happened. She was staring ahead and her eyes had adjusted to the dark, so that she could see the shapes of each bush and the small tree by the gate. The moon was nearly full and it shed a gentle glow on the ground. She saw a shape materialise to her right centre and she didn't move a muscle, but searched it out with her eyes until it moved a little closer. It was a beautiful animal; it moved tentatively and made no sound. Its tail was like gossamer, floating in the air. It looked at Faith and stared for a moment. She tried to summon all her most benevolent energy to send somehow, telepathically to this creature that there was no need to be frightened, that she wasn't a threat. They were still, like this, for what seemed like many minutes. Then it twitched its whiskers and walked on over to her. She was sat just an arm's length from the meat, and although it kept glancing at Faith the fox didn't seem afraid. She thought it would just grab the prize and run, but instead it delicately put down one paw on it to hold it steady and then it ripped off little bits gently, casting a sideways glance at her now and then. It ate its meal just there, next to her, so close she could almost touch it. Suddenly, and without a rational explanation, she knew she was having a boy. Just like that. The baby gave her a wallop, as if to say: *That's right, Mom. Here I am.*

– – –

The truck bounced over rough terrain and the heat from the bodies around him was stifling. Jacob kept his head down and his hands in his pockets, not wishing to look at the faces around him, which stared vacantly as if they were ghosts. One guy, a Texan by the sounds of it, had struck up a conversation with his black neighbour, who turned out to be from Detroit. They were having such normal conversation, Jacob thought, nothing out of the ordinary. A part of him wanted to shout them to 'shut up', but he held it in. No point making enemies of the guys you might be protecting, and who might hold your life in their hands someday soon. Basic training had been shorter than expected; after all, they had heard on the sly that US troops wouldn't even be fighting anymore. Nixon was withdrawing the draft and they were just the last unlucky suckers to end up out there. Still, around them in that jungle there was a war going on, no matter what anyone said.

During training, he'd sat down night after night to write Faith but things had been weird when he'd left. It was like they'd both frozen up; like they wanted to put their love in a capsule and not let it be tainted by this goddamn war. He managed a short note, and sent her a photograph this journalist guy who was tagging along had taken of him and a few of the other guys.

The thing was, he thought bitterly, all of them knew they didn't really need to be here; that one swing from fate's pendulum would've gotten them out of this mess. When talk of the draft ending had begun, it was like all around young men were holding their breath. They'd all seen what happened to the vets when they came back; how they were treated, how they were blamed. Jacob had even been one of them to look at these men in silent disgust, although he wouldn't admit it to himself now.

And all the while though, hidden somewhere in his heart, Jacob had felt real uneasy, as if he and Faith were just too happy – like they didn't deserve it, that life. Then he got his draft letter and something inside had died, just like Carole King said. An inevitability had taken over.

The men couldn't see where they were going. The chains holding the back of the truck in place rattled over each bump, like a reminder they were trapped there now.

When the engine stopped, he shook himself out of his daydreams and watched some of the guys around him do the same. One guy, who had a guitar on his back, smiled at J but the guy stood next to him gave Jacob a look that said "Don't invade my eye line", that kind of thing. It was tense. The men walked down the wobbling platform onto Vietnamese soil and just like that, they were doing their duty. Around them, they could see torched areas of jungle, the remains of villages, and amongst these, temporary shelters for the soldiers still serving there. Jacob and his detail were pieced together and then put into helicopters that were headed to Black Virgin Mountain. It was his first time in a chopper, and he held on so tight to the bar next to him that his knuckles went white. *What a pussy,* he thought to himself, but tried to stop the thoughts thereafter; those that said something bad was going to happen; that this would be the end of him.

On their way, Jacob could just about see through his dirty window some brightly coloured gates. As they swung by, he could make out a statue of the Buddha. It made him wonder if that was a good omen; that they might be protected somehow. He had no religion to speak of but it felt good to imagine someone or something might be on your side. He looked around to see if anyone else had spotted it but it was so quiet, save the chopper's infernal buzz that he wouldn't be able to make himself heard should anyone want to listen. He said to himself, out of sight of the men, *it's a good sign. It's a good sign.*

The camp was sparse and looked temporary but he was informed it had been there for years, although nowadays there were only half the allotted number of soldiers now, with the war effort dwindling. The men were briefed that their main focus would be to maintain communications and signalling. Jacob was bunked with five other men, who'd been assigned to his team. Because he'd had some education and gone to college, he'd been picked out to act as an officer, even though he had no experience of being in a war zone or what it might entail. He'd wanted to go back into his shell and yet here he was being told he had to make some kind of leader of himself. The men hauled their packs off in silence and it was like no-one knew how to start a conversation. Jacob made a point of asking where each guy was from, and that seemed to break the tension a little. In the mess tent, things relaxed a bit and he started to learn who these guys were, although not one of them gave him his real name, but some variation of it or some other nickname. He realised he didn't have one himself so shakily introduced himself as Officer Miller. A couple of the guys looked at each other in such a way as they were thinking, *Check this guy out, he thinks he's better than us just cause they assigned him some role that doesn't mean shit anymore.* Jacob wanted to say to them how he didn't want to be singled out, but he knew that would make him sound weak. He could hear Faith's reassurances in his head, echoing with her rich voice, with its hint of New York and the way she smelled when she had said it to him before they'd parted, said it softly into his ear: *It won't be for long, just ride it out*, she'd told him. *You can weather the storm.*

Over the next few days they familiarised themselves with the camp and were shown the centre of the base, which comprised several cabins filled with transmitting equipment. Along rows of wooden benches, yanks sat alongside South Vietnamese soldiers, training them how to use the equipment for when the army would up and leave. Jacob wondered what these local guys thought of the exit; of the miles of destruction in their country and to what end? So that they could be left with the fallout?

Training at the base was technical and mentally challenging at first; getting to grips with technology that they'd never seen before. Some of the men even said they'd rather be out fighting than this, but Jacob didn't believe them. Every now and then, a unit would be sent down into the jungle to repair an antenna or replace some cable. Usually four or five would leave and usually they would all come back. Sometimes with injuries, which would kick the base into action, and out of its inertia. It was like some of the guys here had a death wish. Jacob realised some weeks into his stay that a few of his company were sneaking out at night and going down into the trees to stalk the so-called enemy, or wild animals or even each other, just for the kick of it. He had discovered there was a steady supply of uppers and downers going round the base, and some of the soldiers who'd been here for a while had gotten accustomed to that state of being. They couldn't accept, either, that they weren't supposed to be acting as soldiers anymore; that soon, they would probably be going home. Jacob had tried some of these pills once and even gone out with a couple of men from his team. They'd camouflaged themselves against the night and for all that buzzing in his head, he'd felt as though he was playing war games like he had when he was a kid. The tension of it, that blackness and the unidentified noises around them, and then the idea that there might be a real enemy round any corner; one that still wanted them dead; well it had gotten too much and he'd had a full-blown anxiety attack. Skinny Bobby – the young guy who had given Jacob a smile on the truck on the way – had found him and dragged him back to the base, putting him to bed like some child. He'd never said anything to the others and Jacob silently thanked him for it, even though they never spoke of the incident after. He'd avoided the pills after that, although sometimes would've killed for a joint and could smell it sometimes at night on the base.

A few months in and they'd all got into some kind of pattern and felt like they knew what the hell they were doing there, and

Jacob was told they had to go on a recon mission to replace a broken station deep into the jungle. To his relief and also slight shame, another Commanding Officer had been drafted in to lead and a couple of seasoned corporals joined them for the muscle. One of these was a crazy looking guy with a tattoo on his neck, who knew the territory. Although he knew the guy to be unhinged, Jacob felt some relief at having some muscle on their side. That made seven of them altogether, which Jacob couldn't help feeling was overkill for what they had to do. *Still, safety in numbers,* he thought. They set off early one morning, lightweight packs on and expecting to return by nightfall the following day. Earlier, one of the guys from another unit had brought Jacob over a letter and his heart had jumped when he saw the familiar hand. He'd stuffed it into his chest pocket. As they made their way down the steep mountainside, the view from the walk was filled with green and the patchwork of fields, and illuminated by the most elegant sunrise Jacob had ever seen, which sent rays of light streaming off their gun metal and buckles on their packs. As he breathed in the smell of vegetation and watched the steam rise off the trees below, Jacob could almost believe that they would get out of here, out of this country and back into the arms of the ones they loved. An hour later they stopped for water and to check they were on course. He leaned his back against a tree, took the envelope out of his pocket and ripped it open. He started to read.

— — —

It was a good while later, in a conversation with her new friend, Judy, that Faith found herself revisiting the events of the previous year. She had kept in touch, by letter, with her friend Moll in New York, but slowly the letters had dwindled down to one every couple of months. Faith found she had little to tell her friend and found Moll's accounts of life in the city would fill her with an unhealthy nostalgia that she couldn't handle. She knew this was selfish, but she couldn't help but resent Moll and the rest of her friends for leading normal lives. They still went to parties; they didn't have babies and baggage. Their lives sounded care free, and Faith felt ten years older. Sometimes she imagined herself being an old lady in the cottage, like Aunt Denise. Would Daniel have his own children? Would they come to visit her? Would they love Grandma or would they shy away from her withered kisses and her house that smelled strange?

All of these ifs and buts got her nowhere, but she couldn't help herself. So when Judy asked her one day over a Campari and lemon, sitting in Judy's beautiful back garden, where Daniel's father was, she found herself thinking of Jacob and clinging onto what might have been.

"He was fighting in Vietnam. He was called up in the very last draft, would you believe? Anyhow, I hadn't heard from him really, in a long while. I was pregnant, you know, and then I had this government letter out of the blue, telling me he was MIA."

Judy looked at her blankly.

"Missing in action," Faith explained, taking a sip of her drink and unable, for a few seconds, to hold her friend's gaze.

Judy leaned forward, "Oh my god, Faith. How awful. And you were pregnant at the time? How far along?"

Faith felt as if her face had lost its colour suddenly. She felt a little nauseous.

"If you don't want to talk about it…I'm sorry, I shouldn't have asked you." Judy put her hand on her friend's arm.

"No, no" Faith shook her head. "It's not that, it's – "

She looked over to the blanket to check on Daniel. He had just woken up but was very quiet, looking up at the sky and moving his little hands as if to clutch at things that weren't there. She took a breath and said, "About 6 months or so." She stirred her drink with the pink plastic stirrer and watched the pips of the lemon as they followed the circular motion she had created. At that moment, something she had been grappling with had been defeated, at least for now. She locked it up in a box inside, and resolved to throw away the key.

"So they never found him." Judy said.

"No, he had an awful injury too. His company looked for him but never found his body so they think…well, either it was taken by the enemy or that the storm…"

She couldn't find the right word.

"I understand," said Judy, and looked at her friend for a long time. Faith shut her eyes briefly, to let the sun wash over her eyelids. When she opened them, her vision was slightly blurred. Judy was still looking at her, but then her face broke out into a smile.

Still," she said, holding up her glass. "There's the future."

They clinked glasses.

"Yes," said Faith. "To the future."

The two women finished their drinks in one go and began to laugh.

CHAPTER **TWO**

IT WAS NEARLY CHRISTMAS, and the windows of 'The Blank Page' were lined with condensation. Inside the shop somewhere, a radio was on, and a female voice was singing along to Chris Rea. The walls were lined with wooden shelves, and filled with books in varying states of disarray. On the counter, near the cash register, was a rather pathetic looking silver tree.

Dan yawned as he looked once more at the historical section, wondering how to slot in the latest local history effort between the latest Bill Bryson and 'Pompeii', or if the latter title should even be in the history section, since it was really fiction.

As he pondered, his colleague Fiona wandered over with a cup of coffee in each hand.

"Anyway Dan, you won't believe what happened to me last night…" she said, with a grin.

"Go on, Fi…" he said, relieved to have a distraction.

"Right, you know how I was supposed to go round to Bill's and, you know, we didn't know what was going to happen, i.e. we thought he might try and seduce me…" she giggled excitedly.

Bill was the latest of Fiona's conquests and Dan thought he sounded like a dickhead, not least because he had a girlfriend of four years who he lived with. He knew it was pointless drawing attention to this, however, as Fi had her 'up for a challenge' look about her, which *really* meant: 'Don't challenge me'.

"Yes…" He took a sip of his coffee and regretted it, fanning his mouth. She laughed and imitated the gesture.

"Stop taking the piss. What about this Bill?"

"Well," she continued, "I decided that he's not right for me." She paused and blew on her coffee. "I mean, I think he might be a bit of a cock, actually."

Dan felt a surge of relief and an almost irresistible urge to say 'obviously', which he managed to contain by fiddling with the key ring he was holding in his other hand.

"OK," Fi carried on, "so I went home, and decided to make a little splif to celebrate, and go to bed early for once…"

"This isn't one of your better stories," Dan interjected.

"No stupid, let me finish, so I went to sleep and then, I don't know what time it was but it was pitch black, I kind of woke up, but not really…I felt like I was awake but I couldn't move and it was like my eyes were open but shut.."

"What do you mean?"

"I can't explain it, but anyway then I," she paused, to adjust her voice to a dramatic whisper, "*had a vision.*"

"What kind of vision?"

"An American Indian man spoke to me, he told me to be careful!"

Dan hid his smile behind his cup, gesturing for her to go on.

"OK, well there was this green light everywhere, and his face, and he looked so wise and powerful, you know, and the words kind of appeared around him…not writing but, you know, I was aware of the words…'Be Careful'."

"Wow, hmm, where do you get your weed from again?"

"Oh shut up," she replied, hitting him on the arm. "What do you think it means?"

He shrugged, "Maybe it means you should be careful?"

Fi, missing his sarcasm completely, shrugged back and picked 'Pompeii' off the shelves.

"What's *this* doing here?" she asked, and headed off for the fiction section.

Dan put his hands out in a gesture of 'search me', and felt in his pocket for the shop keys. It was 9.55am, time to open up and let in the throngs of customers, he thought sardonically.

Undoing the bolt on the door of the bookshop and flicking on the window spotlights, Dan tried not to think about why these moments with Fi were the best moments of his day, why he had stayed in this job for so long, and why, despite his best efforts, he couldn't imagine sharing his first cup of coffee of the day with anyone else. He picked up the few books that he hadn't shelved, slotting them in, not caring enough whether they were in the right place or not. He could hear Fiona clattering around in the store cupboard. She had left her cup on the wooden steps they used for reaching the highest shelves. He took their cups into the back, through the 1970's beaded curtain, where there was a sink unit, a microwave, an old desk with a box of invoices on it and an ancient looking laptop covered in sticky notes.

At 9.59am, the bell on the shop door tinkled, but neither Dan nor Fi heard the man walk in, and they certainly didn't notice the chill that entered the building a moment after that. It was Fiona who, wandering back into the shop with a huge box of till rolls, collided with someone and, thinking it was Dan, shouted "Jesus!" and dropped the box onto the man's right foot. He cried out in pain and reached down, clutching the end of his boot and hopping on the other foot.

"Oh my goodness, I am SO sorry," Fiona said, as she realised she'd injured a customer. "I am so sorry," she said again. "Are you okay?" She rushed over to grab the wooden steps and encouraged him to sit down on them. At this moment, Dan walked out of the back having heard the commotion and raised his eyebrows at Fi. She glared back and rolled her eyes.

"Would you like a cup of tea?" she asked the man, who still had his head down towards the floor as he rocked gently on his other foot. He nodded as she backed away and hastily turned towards Dan, pulling him with him into the office at the back.

"You're so violent, I've always said that about you," he said, teasing her.

"Fuck off," she said, angrily. "Go and speak to him while I make a cup of tea, or he might escape!"

Dan smiled. They were so desperate for customers these days that they had even developed a routine – part good cop bad cop, part straight and funny man – to ensure whoever *did* come in would make a purchase. Unfortunately, fracturing toes had not been part of the original act. He went out to the man who, Dan could now see, looked to be in his late 50's. He was wearing a hat that immediately reminded Dan of the singer from Dexy's Midnight Runners, and a battered old army jacket.

"Hi there, I'm so sorry about my accident-prone colleague. How's the foot doing?"

The man looked up and Dan saw a face that was less rock star, more weather-beaten. *A face with a story*, his mother would have said. The man broke into a smile and he shook his head.

"I'm really fine now, it was just a…bit of a shock," he said, as he dusted himself off and stood up. Fiona came out of the doorway with a large mug in her hand.

"Gosh, I am really sorry," she gushed. "I put a large sugar in for a speedy recovery.

The man gave her a large and forgiving grin, and took the cup from her.

"Thank you, I take two so that just sounds perfect." Fiona lingered and Dan looked at her as if she should go on.

"So," she said, waveringly, "can we interest you in any literature? Or have we scared you off now?"

He laughed; a gravelly laugh, and then broke into a mild coughing fit. Fi and Dan looked at each other and then back at him.

"I'm okay, too many cigarettes…" he replied between coughs. Once recovered, he looked at Dan and said, "*You* can probably help me."

Fiona realised she was no longer needed. "So sorry, again…" she said, and went off to look busy.

– – –

Dan looked again at the man before him and shook his head.

"But…how did you find me?" he asked, not able to take it all in.

"Well, your mother left a forwarding address with a friend of hers who I finally managed to track down through the internet," the man, who was called Jacob, continued quietly.

"But she said you were lost…in the war in Vietnam…are

you saying she lied?" Dan's voice was stricken.

Jacob touched his arm.

"No, she didn't lie," he explained. "I was missing, but then I was found by a patrol a few days later, just in time. I was really lucky." He looked away sadly.

"When I eventually got back to New York your mother was gone, but I didn't want to look for her – I figured she was gone for a reason."

Dan pulled out the chair from behind the counter and sat on it, slumping; his eyes puzzling into the mid-distance.

"But I…I don't understand why you've come?" he asked. "Why now?"

"Because I wanted to know my son," Jacob said, his voice faltering. "Because I think maybe we could be friends?"

"You don't even know me," said Dan, looking up at this somewhat dishevelled man standing before him. "More to the point, I don't know you? How do I know you *are* who you say you are?"

Jacob smiled. "I agree it's a lot to take in, all at once. I'm sorry to do this to you while you're at work." He looked at his watch. "How about a drink after work? What time do you get off?"

Dan found himself agreeing to meet Jacob at 5.30pm at the Water Fall in the market place. The man had expressly requested that he, Dan, not tell his mother about their meeting. After he had left the shop, Dan sat for a minute and rubbed his forehead. *Head fuck,* he thought, and shut his eyes. He always hoped for uneventful Mondays. His nerves somewhat shattered and the remnants of a hangover still dancing around his psyche, this felt like way too much to take in. Fiona, who had been on the phone to a customer, walked through to find him sitting there.

"Dan?" She touched his shoulder and he shook his head and opened his eyes. She listened as he told her what the man had said. She asked questions that Dan had wished he had, so they made a list of things he needed to speak to Jacob about.

They talked about how life can change in a heartbeat; how just an hour ago everything was normal. He didn't tell Fiona that the man had limped out of the shop. He knew she'd already feel guilty about her clumsiness, but he secretly hoped she hadn't done any permanent damage. That would not be a great start to this…thing, whatever it was.

Dan tried to go about his daily business without watching the clock, curbing his nerves with a quiet humming, and distracting himself with the latest invoice from the wholesaler. Every five minutes or so, he found himself staring out of the shop window, wondering what would happen now.

— — —

Several hours later, Jacob was sitting at the small and slightly greasy Formica table of the greasy spoon cafe, drumming his fingers on its surface and trying to think of something he could say next. Outside in the market square, there was a marquee advertising some novelty act from Bangkok, and the temporary ice rink held a few teenage couples and a handful of families, mums and dads clutching at their offspring with strained looks on their faces. *Winter fun*, he thought, drily. Near the town hall, several skateboarders were attempting tricks on the three benches while their friends looked on in admiration. He couldn't help staring out at these young people and wishing he could be one of them. His legs just didn't work very well anymore, and his cough kept him from exerting himself above a light stroll. Dan arriving with their drinks interrupted his thoughts, and the younger man sat down opposite him with a friendly smile.

"How's your foot?" asked Dan. "Fiona says 'sorry'."

"Oh, it's fine, really. That leg's a goner anyway so no harm done."

Dan laughed, a little nervously. There was an uncomfortable pause.

"Well, I guess you're wondering what made me come and find you...?" Jacob said. Dan now noticed he had a slight accent.

"You could say that," he replied, breathing out through his teeth. "I'm pretty shocked, to tell you the truth. I didn't even think I had a dad out there anymore." He looked across at Jacob, expectantly.

"No, well, that's kind of my fault," said Jacob, quietly. "Like I said, I didn't know what to do when I got back from 'Nam and found out your mother had moved away. I didn't even know about you until a few years ago, when a friend contacted me who I hadn't heard from for years. He was really embarrassed as you can imagine..."

Dan looked at him and studied his face for signs of dishonesty but he couldn't read between the lines, which formed crevices around the man's eyes and across his forehead. Now he realised that Jacob's eyes were wet at the corners and he suddenly felt a surge of pity for this man, whoever he really was.

He took out a pack of fags and pulled one out, offering one to Jacob who took one, but said sadly: "'S'why I've got this damn cough." They both took a drag and looked at one another. Jacob smiled. Dan thought about where to go from here. He had wondered about this moment before but now it was here, he didn't know how to talk to this man. Jacob cleared his throat and began,

"I'm sorry it's taken me so long to pluck up the courage to find you."

Dan took a sip of his drink. "It's okay," he said, graciously, "you probably had other things going on." He realised this statement was a bit pathetic, or rather, implied that this was a bit of a poor excuse so he said, "I mean, life, and stuff!" He laughed awkwardly, because this sounded even more pathetic.

"Hmm, well, it never seemed like the right time, if I'm honest," replied Jacob.

Simultaneously, Dan thought this a pretty lame excuse and felt a stab of paranoia, like he needed to question this man further.

"You don't have much of an accent anymore, where have you been living?"

Dan knew he was sounding like he was checking Jacob's credentials, but he couldn't help feeling a little unimpressed with the man sat before him but something was niggling at him about the whole thing. The pity he'd felt moments ago was turning and the beginnings of a power trip was rearing its ugly head, like when you suddenly turn on the younger kid who everyone bullies despite befriending them the previous break time.

Oh man, Jacob thought. He was being tested. He'd expected as much.

"Well, don't take this wrong, but I've been in Britain for a while, in different places. It just was easier to try and blend in and I guess I just lost the accent."

Dan nodded, unconvinced. "I s'pose that's plausible," he said, although inside he was unsure. He looked out of the window and noticed a couple with a teenage daughter; she was pirouetting ahead of them, looking around for their approval. They would pause in their conversation and clap encouragingly at each spin she did. He looked at Jacob, who had been watching the scene with a subtle smile.

"I guess that's how we learn to love," he said.

"You mean parenthood?" Dan responded.

"Yes," Jacob said firmly. "I never had the chance."

"Are you saying it's mum's fault? That she kept you away?" Dan had put his coffee down on the table and was holding a packet of sugar, pressing it into different shapes with his fingers as he spoke.

"I'm not saying that, no, definitely not. Your mother did what she thought was best. "And really," he continued, "I've come to find out about you, what you're up to, how your life has panned out. Maybe we could become friends?"

Dan looked again, out of the window at the family groups and the youngsters, the familiar buildings creaking in the cold, and he noticed that the town's Christmas tree lights had come on. He sighed.

"And I can't tell mum about you?"

"It would destroy her, Dan. Please don't."

He took a deep breath, and it seemed that, held within that pause between in breath and out breath was some kind of destiny moment, like the ones you get in films where people's lives could take a different route. Exhaling, Dan said, as if resigned to an idea not entirely of his liking:

"Okay."

They shook hands, and a little of the tension in the room melted away, as that physical boundary was crossed and a decision had been made. They began to talk again, and ended up sharing a plate of fish and chips before parting ways. Dan had not asked Jacob where he was staying but he watched him walk purposefully away towards the cathedral. Dan began his journey back home in the other direction without looking back.

– – –

"So, how was it?" Fiona was waiting for Dan when he arrived at work the next day, with a paper tucked under his arm and a bag of croissants he'd bought on the way because he'd snoozed his alarm too long and missed breakfast.

"Give me a chance!" he said, as he plopped them down on the one chipped plate they shared on a rota system at meal times. He took off his coat and Fiona grabbed it and hung it up on the hook behind the door, at which Dan gave her a bemused smile.

"What service…" he said.

"Well, I'm dying to know what the old man had to say for himself," she said, in a frustrated tone, busying herself making two coffees for them both so they could sit and talk properly.

"When you say 'old man', do you mean it in the literal sense or –"

"Both, for God's sake…" said Fiona, not in the mood for his

efforts at humour. She sat opposite him, clasped her hands firmly around her oversized coffee cup and looked at him expectantly. "Well? Put me out of my misery!"

Dan smiled and suddenly found himself feeling a bit shy, which seemed at odds with how he and Fiona had always shared things: no holds barred.

"I don't think he's that old. Not as old as he looks." Dan said.

Fi shrugged. "Carry on."

"Well, he asked about me, what I was up to, how I spend my days, that sort of thing."

"Boring," Fiona replied. "What is *he* up to? Where's he *been* all this time? And more importantly have you told your *mum?*"

"He absolutely insisted that I didn't, it feels weird, dishonest really, but at the same time it might just...destroy her, or something."

Faith frowned and said, "Is that what you really think? I mean, she doesn't seem the type of woman to just crumble. She must have wondered if this day might come...?"

Dan shook his head.

"I think she always believed Jacob was dead, I think somehow it helped her to believe that so she could move on," he explained, and yet even as he said it he began to doubt its integrity as if suddenly seeing it through someone else's eyes for the first time. "But even if she secretly thought he was alive, it must have broken her heart that he never came to find her...to find us."

He took a sip of his drink and said firmly: "I'm not telling her, Fi."

"It's your decision," she said respectfully. "So...what's he like?"

Dan told her of his first impressions, slightly ashamed that he doubted Jacob's real identity but admitting he'd felt sorry for him. He told her that the man seemed sad but at the same time sure of himself, of his purpose. He talked about emotions a lot, which Dan admitted he had found a bit embarrassing, to which Fiona had uttered some expletive and kicked him on the leg. Dan wondered to her, half jokingly, if all this self-expression was because he was American or whether it was the product of a lonely life, or a bit of both.

"What do you mean 'his emotions'? Did he talk about your mother?"

"Hardly," Dan said, shaking his head. "He kept talking about being true to your heart and he said that was what made him look for me."

"Ooh, he does sound interesting..." Fi said, with an excited look in her eye. "God, you know, when I bumped into him – I shouldn't say this, but it's only you – I kind of thought he was a bit of a...well, sort of a..."

"Tramp?" Dan smiled, but felt guilty for suggesting this about his possible father and for how quickly he too had made a judgement.

"Yes...sorry. I shouldn't judge people like that," said Fiona, voicing his worries.

"Well, it doesn't matter now."

Dan got up and put his dirty cup in the sink, turning to Fi.

"I suppose I just carry on as normal, now...do I?"

Fiona laughed, and pushed her fringe out of her eyes.

"There are no rules for fathers coming back from the dead, so I'm guessing that's all you can do."

— — —

The two men had agreed to meet again the following week, which meant in the mean time, Dan had to visit Faith that weekend without mentioning anything about Jacob. He planned in his head what they could talk about; what subjects might get her enthused so he could excuse his secretiveness by thinking post meeting that the opportunity to mention him hadn't come up – this he knew to be bollocks but he felt it was worth a try.

The shop had had a flurry of custom over that week in the lead up to Christmas and he and Fi had been at the local markets trying to flog old stock, which had been a bit of welcome relief from the tedium of normal life. Jacob didn't have a mobile phone, so they had discussed meeting at the same café again, although Dan felt like he wanted them to get out of town so they could really talk. There were too many distractions and he'd felt like Jacob, on their first meeting, had been evasive. He wanted to pin him down to some facts about his disappearance, although he didn't feel hopeful about getting the answers he wanted. Since their meeting, he had felt a strange dull sadness which he couldn't name. He couldn't identify it as the blues, nor a seasonal malaise. It muffled him like a blanket. He thought about his life until now, and then looking forward. What had he done so far to speak of? What would he achieve in the future? Wouldn't Jacob just lose interest? When he considered that prospect, he felt a twisting in his insides which he knew to be pain, locked up and sleeping until now.

On Sunday at 10.36am, Dan boarded the number 132 bus which took him to the village where his mum lived, alone. It was a pleasant journey once you'd got through the soulless suburbia of the city, which spread out now in brownish lines before him. He had his headphones in, with Eric Roberson singing about changing and he felt his soul lifted up above the outside and all those faces in the street. He shut his eyes and in his head he spread his wings and flew away, into a film where he was the star. He was dancing with a pretty girl and there were no worries or cares, just the next chord and the next break. Rising strings caressed his heart and soothed his worries like a summer's day. When it was over, he pressed pause and took a deep breath, determined to maintain this feeling of peace and happiness. They were going through fields now, and he noticed some kind of bird of prey hovering over its next meal, waiting for the right moment to make its move. *Maybe,* he thought to himself, *that's all I'm doing now – just waiting for the right moment, it's never too late...*

The bus approached his mum's village and suddenly the nerves kicked in. How could he lie to her? He never had been able to, except when she asked him about some of his extra-curricular activities. Even then he just avoided answering, although he suspected she knew vaguely what he got up to; after all, she'd grown up in the 60's.

He fiddled with the catch on the green gate, the paint flaking and the catch sticking, and it gave an almighty squeak when he finally got it open. The sun had started to come out and caught the old sun catcher hanging on the tree by the gate, which hung so low it looked as though the weight of its branches might split the trunk at any time. His entrance had disturbed a group of sparrows, which scuffled about in the hedge while a bolder female blackbird hopped across the lawn a few feet and turned to look at him, as if to say: '*Who are you, and what are you doing in my garden?*'

As always, his mum opened the door before he'd managed to get his key out of his pocket. Her hair was wild today and she was wearing an old kaftan which Dan thought he remembered from when he was a child.

"Hi darling," she said, grinning, and they hugged.

"How long have you had this, mum? You look like a proper hippy," Dan gestured to her outfit.

"And you look tired," she said, putting her hand to his cheek. "Anyway, I'm just having a nostalgic day is all," she continued, sounding more American suddenly as happened with her accent, which came and went with her mood or the weather.

Walking in to the front room, Dan could see what she meant. Strewn across the floor were books and LP's and there was a big pile of clothes in the corner.

"Jesus, Mum you'll have nothing left, "Dan said, sighing "And where has this stuff all been anyway?"

Faith laughed. "Oh, stuffed into my closet and in the attic, I need a clear out."

She pushed the air away from her chest on the word 'out' as if to push away the past. "Hey, do you want a cup of tea? Sorry about the mess, ignore it if you can."

Dan moved some of the books off the couch to make a space

to sit down as his mum went into the small kitchen at the bach. He picked up 'The Art of Being' by Erich Fromm, and opened it up somewhere in the middle, reading a few paragraphs. Closing it, he walked in to the kitchen where Faith was filling her old whistling kettle and she turned to him.

"Mind if I take this one?"

She looked slightly puzzled but said, "Sure…hey, maybe you can sell some in your shop?"

"Mum, it's not a second hand shop, it's like a proper book shop with new books."

"I know, I know! Couldn't you just have a little corner where you sold beat up old novels? I'd buy some."

"You'd end up buying some of your own back," Dan said, chuckling, and she pretended to jab him in the ribs with the teaspoon she was holding.

"Besides," he carried on, "it's not *my* shop, I just work there."

"I know, you run it and that man just pops his head in now and then and tells you what to do," said Faith, sighing. "Cogs in a wheel…" she muttered.

"What?" Dan said, although he thought he had heard correctly.

She waved the teaspoon in the air as if to brush away what she'd said.

"Oh, nothing."

"Mum, if you've got a problem with my job or something, just come out with it,"

She looked stunned, "Dan, no, how could you think that? I just meant…it's a shame that you don't have more…."

"Money?" He said, coldly.

"Oh my god, no, since when did you think that mattered to me?"

Faith was visibly insulted and Dan saw her eyes fill up slightly and he felt ashamed. These days, many of their conversations seemed at odds, often taking a turn that left a bad sort of feeling in the air, like things were being left unsaid. Dan believed he was partly to blame, but at the same time, his mum was secretive – always had been, and it got to him.

"I meant it's a pity you don't have the say so to do what you want with it," she continued quietly. "I mean, it's you who's there all the time."

"Yeah, well…." Dan ran out of words.

"Sorry hun," she said, softening. "You probably don't want to talk about work, anyway, I guess."

He looked around the room and spotted some LP's he remembered her playing as a child. "You're not getting rid of those Motown records are you? They could go for a bomb on eBay."

"Take them hun, if you want them, I need to cleanse. I need to look forward not back." She leant back on the couch and looked out of the window ahead.

Dan's mind was brought back to the conversation he'd had with Jacob and he felt a pang of anxiety. He wanted to broach the subject of his father without his mum suspecting anything untoward was going on.

He put down his cup of coffee.

"Do you think it's unhealthy…to live in the past too much?" he asked, tentatively and trying to sound nonchalant, whilst flicking through the book, which was resting on his knee.

"It depends what you find there, sweetheart," she said, her eyes not moving from the garden as if she was really somewhere else.

"What do you mean?" Dan asked, looking where she was looking.

"I mean," she turned to him, "that it no longer exists, just in your head, and your heart, but it's not real anymore, is it?"

"No, I suppose not."

"It tells you all about it in there," she said, "- how to move on and be happy in your own skin."

Dan nearly asked her what she meant and then realised she was pointing at the book on his knee.

"Oh yeah, I'll read it…thanks," he replied, and gave her a weak smile.

They went on to talk about what Dan was up to that weekend, with Faith telling him about her week at the local primary school where she worked. She asked about Fiona, and said not for the first time, "I really must meet her, why don't you bring her over one weekend?" Dan explained, yet again, that they didn't really socialise together at weekends but that he would mention it to Fi when he saw her on Monday.

When 4 o'clock came he stood up and took their cups to the kitchen to wash. Faith looked around at the mess and said,

"Now you've been and we've talked, I don't feel quite so Trojan about this…"

"Then leave it for another day!" he shouted through from the other room.

"But where will I put it now…?" she asked herself.

On the bus journey back, Dan put on his headphones again

and sat back. The sky was darkening and he pulled his winter coat up and adjusted his scarf. An old couple sat a few seats down from him, in silence. He wondered what they talked about when they were at home, and what they'd been like when they were young. He wondered if life had delivered any of their hopes or if they'd just settled for the everyday and let time pass like a gentle breeze, until it etched lines on their faces and eroded their youthful dreams so that they crumbled like cliff tops into a sea of memory.

Fiona was lying across her bed on her front with her eyes shut and her head resting on her folded arms. In the background the floating melodies of Air did their best to soothe her Sunday blues and she pulled the quilt around her a bit more. Her head hurt, and the two paracetamol she'd ingested some 20 minutes before were as yet doing nothing to avail the thumping in her temples. There was a noise in her ears every time her heart beat which sounded like the swishing of the tides, although it wasn't as pleasant as that. On the floor were her clothes from last night and one wedge sandal on its side, the strap broken. She knew if she looked in her handbag, she might gain a few clues as to her whereabouts the previous evening but in the back of her mind she felt thankful that at least she'd got home in one piece.

As Fi lay there, she let her mind wander to the week leading up to this moment, and wondered how she'd ended up here again, feeling like this. She knew that time and a feel-good film, and perhaps a 'hair of the dog' drink would sort her out and she would be okay for work tomorrow. But for now she would have to pretend everything about this was normal, it was what everyone did at the weekend. She was young and single, so why not? At the sound of her bedroom door opening, she opened one eye and felt someone sit down on the edge of the bed. A hand stroked her back and she tensed up.

"You're so sexy," said Neil, who she had met last night and whom she no longer wanted in her flat.

"Don't be silly," she said, quietly. She didn't know whether to move or just lie there, so she chose the latter, feeling like a bitch but unsure of what the best thing to do would be. He didn't move.

"Sorry," she groaned, "just feeling a bit rough, might have to have a sleep now."

She put her head under the duvet.

"Oh okay," he sounded disappointed, which made her feel like an awful person. "No worries." She felt the bed rise as he got up. "Shall I…leave you my number?"

"Yeah sure!" she said.

And then after a few moments, she heard the flat door close, and breathed a long sigh of relief.

Fi dragged her duvet with her into the front room and collapsed on the couch, planning on lying there for a while and then putting the kettle on. She found the remote and put on the TV hoping for some light-hearted non-taxing, reassuring type of programme. Her phone beeped and she fished around for it, knowing it was here somewhere. After much fumbling she withdrew it from underneath her and looked at the screen. A message from her friend Kate: *Rough….*was all it said, with three kisses. Fi texted her back: *Oh my god, me too! That boy just left – I'm such a slag…!* She sent it and waited for a reply. Meanwhile she found an old Peter Sellers 'Pink Panther' film, which reminded her of her childhood. She found herself chuckling at some of the sillier bits. Her phone beeped again and Kate had replied: *Don't be stupid! Just watching TV under duvet, you?* Fi texted back: *Same! Xxx*

She leaned back into the couch and made herself a nest with the cushions. The TV just about fuzzed away the blurriness of the night before and provided a welcome distraction from the darkness that ebbed away at the edge of her consciousness like a melancholy sea. Whatever fun you had, thought Fi, whoever you shared your evenings with, it always came back to this: to sitting forlorn and unwashed on the couch in a fog, to doing your best to curb the blues, to accepting that once more you were alone.

She considered texting Dan but they didn't really speak at the weekend, preferring to do their own thing. Weirdly, their paths had never crossed and maybe it was better that way. She wasn't sure whether it was her weekend self or her working self that was the real Fiona, but she thought she preferred the person she was in the week, in the shop, with Dan. She wondered what he was up to. It was just so bizarre what had happened with his dad – if the guy even was his dad. But if he wasn't, why turn up like that? Fi thought he'd seemed like a warm person, but how come he'd never been to find him before? What had happened to him to make him disappear?

– – –

The five men walked along, one behind the other, sweat dripping off the ends of their noses and running in rivulets down their cheeks. Occasionally someone cursed at the heat, or was spiked by some unfamiliar plant or bitten by some jungle bug. Not one of them had chosen to be there, and boy did that hurt, but it was never discussed. One grubby hand passed a rolled up cigarette down the line to the next guy and someone started to sing. Suddenly in the distance, machine gun fire and a few backs tensed, the man at the front, who they called 'Elmo', checked again that his gun was on his back.

"Chill out El man, you got us watching your back," said the man behind him, and then spat his gum out into the bush.

"Shut the fuck up, Chuck," said a big white guy two men further down, through gritted teeth. He had a large tattoo across the back of his fat neck which showed a woman's vagina, but only when you looked at it the right way. So that was what they called him; 'Muff Neck'.

Some kind of cicada was chirruping, a few joined in and then even more struck up. The noise was directly above them and took over the world for a brief minute. The man who took the rear was large, and imposing. The men called him 'Finch' on account of he was reading 'To Kill A Mockingbird', and he didn't speak much today. He'd gotten a letter from his girl, and who knew what was in it, but he had the look of someone broken.

Earlier that day, some action on the edge of the jungle had taken two of their company in the most gruesome way, and the men had been in some kind of daze after that. They'd lost their Commanding Officer, who himself had lost his leg when a group of Viet Cong snipers took a pop at him from a hiding place so good that even Chuck, known for his gook tracking, hadn't detected it in time. They couldn't stop the bleeding and Skinny Bobby, the youngest of the bunch at 19, had puked his guts up when he'd caught sight of the wound. Finch had carried the man some metres before they realised he'd gone and so he and Muff Neck covered him up with leaves to come and collect him later, or that's what they'd said. Truth was, despite their hand-drawn map, nobody knew where the hell they were, just in some jungle in this godforsaken country where they knew neither the land, nor the lay of it, or what was around the corner or hiding behind the bushes.

Just a quarter of an hour or so after that, they'd had another fright and nearly killed a young girl, who was collecting firewood or something. Elmo had shot at a noise and she'd screamed, clutching her ear where there was just a flesh wound. Elmo had gone over to help her but she raced off, soon hidden in the thick jungle. He was cursing himself and cursing the war and jumping at every little scuffle in the undergrowth. Those cicadas were freaking them out. They were loud as if you had your head in a box of frogs, and Chuck soon started calling out to them to shut their goddamn mouths. The rest of the men tried to get him to stop but he'd had enough and soon he was shouting at the top of his voice, they couldn't even hear him properly though for the din, but it seemed so wrong making noise like that when the VC could be just around the next tree. Muff Neck was now right up in Chuck's face, screaming at him to shut up when Elmo suddenly pulled out his hunting knife, thrust it in the air and screamed a blood-curdling Tarzan-like yowl which shook the shivers out of the trees. And suddenly everything went quiet. It was like that second before a dropped glass hits the floor and smashes into pieces. The men froze like that, like those soldiers in the Iwo Jima statue but with no flag to speak of and Elmo clutching his knife so tight with Finch's hand around his wrist, like they were a still from a movie. Suddenly, a bang. A bomb ahead of them? A twist of metal in the sky? And yet, it came from all around, not just one place. A weird greyness filled the area. The seconds between that and what happened next ticked by slowly. One…two…three…then Bobby found himself lifted off his feet and a huge gushing noise in his ears, he felt himself collide with a branch, or a limb, was it? It reminded him of when you get caught under a wave in the sea, and just for a brief moment he was back in his hometown of Pescadero with his buddies, trying to catch a wave as the cold sea air sliced through his back and nipped on his ears.

Elmo felt his back against a tree, where it hadn't been that moment before, the bark digging into a part of him and a sharp pain penetrating his side. Hadn't he just been turning to Finch telling him to get those suckers to shut up before they got them all killed? Where had his knife gone? It was dark, much darker than before, and just this noise which rushed through him and pinned him to the wood so he couldn't get free. Rain pelted his face as if it wanted to razor right through his cheekbones. Something flew by him, something big, what was that? He shut his eyes, imagining he'd seen the outline of a man, flying. He laughed inside his head.

In the sudden silence, Chuck had finished the word he was on, which ironically was 'quiet' and his breath held in a vice like it was caught in the back of his throat with a pincer-like wind, which hadn't been there before. He felt as though he couldn't breathe but he wasn't worrying about it, because at that moment he was floating along the airwaves like a feather. Jeez, he hadn't felt so light and airy since he was a kid, leaning against the wind with his sister in a cornfield. It was how he imagined it felt to be a balloon, and the feeling of freedom coursed up his spine until he felt a shiver of ecstasy at that moment, like a flashback from the dope he'd had the day prior. Then nothing, as his body broke almost in two on a large piece of rock and on a high like he'd never known, his vacating eyes took a last look at the darkened skies above him, and nature continued on its black course.

Clutching a bunch of bamboo, Muff Neck cursed as he found himself being pulled every which way. This storm had come out of nowhere, and the hell he was being derailed by it after all the crap he'd gone through in this shit-sucking war. When he realised he was done swearing and his grip didn't feel so tight, he shut his eyes and began to sing a song from home. His spit dried like paint on the side of his face and his fingers were slowly pried looser by the crackling rain and the piercing gushes of wind. He felt like he was being torn up like a paper serviette and all the while he sang 'Stand by Me' and danced through his memories with his girl Lorraine in the bar around the corner from his house the last time they'd touched.

Finch was a heavy man, and rather than being transported across the jungle he'd been floored on the spot by the gale force winds that had buffeted through the place where the men had stood a few seconds previously. Unfortunately, Elmo's knife was lodged in his wrist and with the force of the typhoon, his right hand was half hanging off, and he could see the sinews straining at the pressure of it. He puked and he never even heard it come out of his mouth due to the racket around and above him, which even though he didn't believe in either he could only think was the wrath of God or the blazing fury of the devil come to claim their souls. His face was pushed down on the side, and the smell of it came up his nostrils and the retching motion made him shut his eyes. Weird adrenalin was pulsing through his body, and he shook under those branches, which held him pinned to the jungle floor. The torrent which fell was building into a pool of water and it started to seep into his mouth, choking him on each new breath he took.

As little bits of his vomit made their way back in, his shaking became uncontrollable and he knew it for shock. He wished he could rewind and yet he knew there was no going back. His heart and body were broken now, there was no mending to be done and all the love he thought would get him through this damn war didn't mean shit now, because the world had turned against them and they were damned all to hell.

— — —

Jacob sat in the small room, with a notebook open in front of him. Steadying it with his elbow, he wrote falteringly yet with purpose, pausing to gaze out of the grubby window. His room was on the first floor of the old Victorian terrace. It was not salubrious, nor in a nice part of town, and hence he felt like he blended in better round here than anywhere else. It was almost like being invisible, but he had learned that skill elsewhere. It was quite a useful string to have in your bow and one that had served him well over the years.

He was writing about his day. The book in which he wrote was tatty but had clearly once been a fine one, leather bound and built to last. By contrast, he was writing with an orange plastic biro which had been nibbled at the end. He had got this from the landlady when he had first arrived. She too had the air of a person who knew how to be invisible. Jacob wanted to talk to her about it. He wondered if she would agree that the hardest thing was when, sometimes, you couldn't even find yourself again and it was like you'd got lost and could almost fade away; like your life was of no consequence. But he didn't. Now he had found Dan, he felt he had another chance. He could make a difference. He could believe that there was hope for better things.

Sometime later, it had grown darker outside and Jacob sat

reading yesterday's newspaper. It was the kind of intellectual read that you could no longer buy where he lived. There were real articles written by people with opinions based on evidence and high argument. There was controversy. He enjoyed reading this kind of thing. It elevated him from where he felt he had descended. He thought it was good to see that people were talking about society and trying to make it better. He saw words whose meaning he had forgotten and, try as he might, he couldn't bring that meaning back. He made blank spaces in his head and thought of bananas – someone had once said that when memory failed you give your brain something else to focus on and up it pops, the word or the fact you'd forgotten. Bananas. Or maybe it was oranges? He couldn't quite recall. He got up to fetch his drink and caught a glimpse of himself in the bathroom mirror. He looked away, and then back again, as if to test his own reaction to the memory. He noted a slight raise in temperature, a paling, an inward wobble. He shuddered but then kept looking, moving closer to his reflection, as it lingered there. He studied his own face, trying to see it from Dan's perspective. Had he noticed a resemblance? *Perhaps*, Jacob thought. Would Dan believe him when he told him his story? *Perhaps not*, he thought again. *But I must try.*

CHAPTER **THREE**

"I TOLD YOU MATE, I'm having a break this weekend, just me, a few beers and a horror film."

It was Saturday night. Dan was arguing with his mate Tipper, aka Andy, who was doing his best to convince his friend that he wanted to celebrate turning 30. Dan felt his resolve weakening as his friend began to resort to bullying tactics.

"If you don't come, then I can't go," he said, almost whining.

"You're 31 Tip, you're old enough to go to a club on your own," said Dan, sighing and slumping back in his chair. He took a swig of his beer.

"Yeah, but the Freestylers are playing, mate! And the point is that you're 30 now, and joining the ranks of the middle aged party crew!" At this, Dan winced. "Come on," Tipper continued, jabbing his friend in the ribs. "You can't just sit at home on your own, it's just sad."

Dan rubbed his forehead. What he wanted to say to Tipper was how he felt even more sad about the fact that recently he had spent every weekend the same way, crawling through Sundays on his very last legs and almost praying for Monday morning so the come-down hangover hurt would cease and he could pretend to be normal again. He'd wanted to mark this birthday with something different. He'd wanted to wake up in his right mind.

"Dan, come on man, I can hear the cogs of temptation turning in your brain! Plus I have some little ones to keep us going, it'll be a top night mate, you can stay in next weekend and…"

"Alright, for Christ's sake! I'll come…" Dan said, through gritted teeth.

"Excellent excellent," said Tipper, who promptly picked up his jacket and headed for the door. "Pick you up at 9."

Shit, thought Dan, as he heard Tipper slam the door behind him. He got up from his chair and put his beer on top of the pile of dvd's he'd chosen for his personal 'Horror night in', now defunct. He looked out of the window at the weather, and then turned, heading for his bedroom in search of something to wear. Opening the wardrobe, several coat hangers clattered to the ground and he swore at them, and tried to hang them up again but they wouldn't fit. He growled and threw them onto the floor then slammed his flat hand onto the wardrobe door.

Why did he let himself get talked into this, every time? Dan knew now how his weekend would pan out, how it always panned out. He would be cross with Tipper, who would ply him with drugs, which would make him feel better; not just better, bloody fantastic. He would dance in a whirr of lights and bodies, and caress and be caressed by total strangers. Some hours later he would undoubtedly find himself lying in the chill out room of some club with some girl resting her legs on his knee and a guy offering him a joint and that's when he would start to panic. The sound of desperate clubbers shouting 'One more!' would filter into his consciousness and the silence which wasn't silence, a buzzing and whooshing in his ears, would bring him abruptly to the surface of an early morning reality. Tip would be nowhere to be seen, probably snogging some girl, having successfully employed Dan as his prop until he was no longer useful. The lights in the club would be up and everyone looking for the next party so that the next day didn't have to start just then, not yet, please not yet.

Still, Dan thought, *I've said I'll go, so fuck it.*

A couple of hours later he and Tipper found themselves in a hot room with a vibrating floor and lots of bodies moving to the same beat.

"Wicked, man!" Dan shouted into his friend's ear.

Tipper gave him a friendly punch on his arm in response and a smile which turned into a gurn halfway through. He said something but Dan couldn't hear so just grinned stupidly and put his arm around his friend. They jumped up and down together with the rest of the people in the club, moving as one now, like a giant pulse, an undulating wave of energy, everything and everyone bobbing and throbbing in the moment with no thought for before or after or tomorrow.

Dan was at the bar when he saw her. He was buying Red Bull for himself, a bottle of water and a shot of vodka for Tipper. She looked really different and Dan suddenly realised he had never seen Fiona out at night-time. She moved in different circles, preferring to see live bands which she would seek out in the local what's on pages, priding herself on finding a new gem she could tell her friends about. She had her hair down and it rested on her shoulders and, as he looked, she brushed some away from her eyes and held it there as she looked searchingly around the club. She was wearing something turquoise around her neck, a scarf maybe. Dan's eyes juddered and he felt a rush up his spine. He became aware that the barman was looking at him and saying something.

"£7.50 please!" the guy shouted across, at the same time sticking five fingers in the air. Dan shut one eye so he could see the change in his hand. Slowly he counted out what he thought was the right amount and handed it over. When he looked up, Fiona had gone.

He picked up the drinks using all of his concentration to get them back to the spot on the dance floor, where he found Tipper accepting some poppers from a girl in pale blue flares and a brown halter neck. Dan passed him his drink and declined the poppers. He looked around, hoping to spot a flash of turquoise amidst the crowd. A tune he recognised came on and the girl, who was actually quite pretty, took one of his hands and one of Tipper's. They started doing some kind of snaking dance where she went under his arm and Tipper followed and they were all getting kind of giddy and dizzy and as Dan broke away, he was aware of spilling his drink on someone and when he looked up to apologise there was Fiona, looking at him, pointing at the wet patch on her trousers but laughing, her eyes crinkly at the corners.

He gave her a rather enthusiastic hug, aware of sort of crushing her but unable to stop himself. Tipper was dirty dancing with flares girl, whose name turned out to be Hilary, which Dan found funny but he wasn't sure why. Dan tried to introduce Fi to him but he realised he was talking too quietly and anyway Tip just gurned back at them, albeit in a friendly way. Dan tried to ascertain whether Fiona was at all wasted and surmised that she wasn't, and he then began to realise how freaky Tipper actually must look through sober eyes. He felt Fi's breath in his ear and for a moment thought she was going to kiss him but, hang on, she was talking to him, but he couldn't make out a thing she said. He pulled at her sleeve and gestured to somewhere else, somewhere away from the loudness and crazy pilled-up clubbers (of which he admittedly was one).

As he turned he grabbed her hand and she gave him a puzzled smile, but followed. He had a feeling of possession as he pulled her through the corridors of the club and up some narrow stairs. He thought he'd sobered up a bit but suddenly felt another rush and had to stop halfway up. Fiona then went ahead of him and pulled him along to a vacant sofa in the chill out room. She sat down and so did Dan, and then he put his head back and shut his eyes. The music was doing something to his spine, something wonderful. After a moment, he realised he was still holding Fi's hand. He squeezed it.

Fi looked around at the twisting faces. Everyone was having a great time up here by the looks of things. *This* sort of music was more her cup of tea, she thought, concluding that you had to be chemically enhanced to enjoy the heaving, pounding mass that was downstairs, which Dan evidently was. She prised her hand gently away from his, and reached inside her bag for the splif she'd rolled earlier. Checking around the place for bouncers, she lit it and inhaled deeply, sinking back into the sofa and observing the different groups of people they shared the space with. To her left, a group of young girls lay entwined with each other, every now and then lifting their heads to speak and nodding enthusiastically before dropping back onto the cushions. Fi watched as a slightly older man approached them and sat down next to the girl on the end. She squinted up at him and smiled, then closed her eyes again. He started to skin up, which caught the attention of another girl who sat up slowly and grinned at him.

Across the room were some black guys, one of whom she recognised as the DJ she had seen playing when she had first walked in. He was smoking and chatting to his mates. There were a few complicated handshakes and gestures going on. A couple of older women were dancing nearby, in what Fiona thought was supposed to be a suggestive manner, but actually looked slightly odd. No-one seemed to care though; the DJ took a look every now and then but carried on chatting.

The joint began to take effect and she felt that she was now enjoying herself. There was certainly nothing threatening in the air, and Fi let her mind drift to why she had come. She'd needed to see a friendly face; that was all. Dan had mentioned he came to this club sometimes so she'd come out on the off-chance, blagging a student ticket on the door by flashing her ancient NUS card and batting her eyelids. She had texted Bill about meeting and he had sent a horrible text back, calling her his bitch and saying he'd let her know. She hated not being in control; hated being in the dark. She had sent one back saying if he just wanted someone to shag then he should find someone else. No response. She didn't talk to her girlfriends about him because she knew they would roll their eyes and say words to the effect of 'uh oh, here we go again', which she didn't want to hear. She could say that to herself well enough. With Dan, though, she didn't feel she had to explain what she'd been up to in her life or why she was there.

She looked sideways down at his face. Every now and then his eyebrow twitched and his hand, where it rested on his thigh, started to thump perfectly along to the beat. She knew he went clubbing and sometimes she would get a bit of information out of him, but on the whole, she didn't know *this* Dan. Fi put out the splif in the ashtray, and leant back again into the misshapen cushions, soft with the shape of hundreds of bodies, restful and thoughtful through time. She gently rested her head against Dan's and shut her eyes, drifting into the music, weaving in and out of her own memories, her mind like water flowing down over old rocks, trickling and tickling what is hidden.

Suddenly, Fi became aware of a voice, someone's voice, and a strong hand shaking her shoulder. She slowly opened her eyes and screwed them up in the brightness that greeted her. A big bald man looked down at her seriously.

"Time to go, love," he said, brusquely. She nodded and reached round to flatten her hair, and she noticed that Dan wasn't next to her anymore. Her heart sank, but she began to scan the room for him as she gathered her stuff. The splif was no longer in the ashtray but fortunately her handbag was still on her shoulder and looked unopened. In the bright light, people looked dirty and slightly unhinged. She spotted the group of girls holding hands in a chain so as not to lose each other, even though the lights were on. The older guy had gone. Where was Dan? She was being ushered down the stairs and felt she had to go with the flow. Like a group of stunned school children in a new place, startled at their surroundings and wondering what would come next, the clubbers poured out onto the pavement. Disparate and yet still aware of each other, the groups huddled and lit fags and discussed where to next. Fi suddenly felt very alone, and too conspicuous. She had one last look around for Dan and then just as she was about to give up she caught a glimpse of him in a doorway. He was talking to a girl; was it the one she'd seen when she first found him? As she started to walk over, she saw him take the girl's face in both hands and kiss her. The girl wrapped her long arms around his neck and they disappeared from view a little. Fiona turned and walked away, past the queue to the takeaway and into the solitary early morning, her hands resolutely in her pockets as she tried all the way home to think only of good things.

It was Sunday morning. As predicted, Dan awoke in a fog of come-down, unable to move at first. The stale smell he identified as Tipper's spare duvet, which undoubtedly had never been washed. Nevertheless, he felt extremely comfortable and he didn't yet dare look around the room and face the daylight. Reaching out to find his phone, Dan pulled it under the duvet with him as if he was doing some kind of secret research under there. It was 4 in the afternoon. *Jesus.* He braved a peek out and noticed it was getting dark. *Another lost day.* He flicked through his phone for text messages, and saw one from an unknown number which read 'Hey, it's Hilary! Had fun tonight x' Yes, Hilary. She was nice but…something. Not very bright, maybe? Although he didn't think they had talked very much, so perhaps he wasn't being fair. A couple of garbled texts from Tipper and then one from Fiona: 'Hope you got home okay last night – sorry not to say bye, see you at work xxx' Of course, he'd seen Fi! And he'd been off his head. Not so good. Plus he couldn't remember exactly what he had said to her, although he remembered that she had looked pretty; that he had felt pleased to have her on his arm.

Yawning, Dan pushed himself up and looked around the room for his belongings. He could feel that his wallet, which was in his pocket, had made a dent in the side of his hip where he had slept on it. He opened it up to see what the damage was – there were still a couple of tenners in there; not too bad. His coat was on the floor by the pull out sofa bed, where he had spent many a misspent night and early morning. He looked in the battered old mirror above the disused fireplace. Fuzzy. *In body and in mind*, he thought, and grimaced to see the state of his teeth. He grabbed his coat and let himself out of Tipper's front door, closing it softly behind him. On his walk home, he sent a text to Tip telling him to wake up and saying 'Cheers for a debauched 30th birthday mate'.

In the weird afternoon half-light, Dan felt that sense of detachment from life that he only felt when he had lost a whole day. It was as though other people had a secret they were keeping – that in his absence, the world had gone on to greater things; and all of the people in it, except him (and probably Tip as well) had shared an experience together. Now he was awake, they all pretended nothing was going on, but when they looked at him, he knew they were hiding something. He was nearly at the bottom of the hill, and around the corner was his street. He swung into the corner shop to buy some fags, and had a quick look at their DVD collection. He still had the horror film from the previous night but he didn't think his nerves would take it. He picked up an action film from a decade before, and stocked up on crisps and milk.

It was only when he settled down on his sofa that he remembered he had arranged to meet Jacob that day. Cursing, he spent a moment figuring out what to do. Jacob didn't have a mobile and hadn't given Dan the details of where he was staying. *Shit*, he thought, as he pictured the old man waiting with a cup of coffee at their usual table, and looking at his watch. How long would he have waited before leaving? Where would he have gone? Dan felt a stab of pity that knocked him in the heart. What if it had been Jacob's only thing to do that day? He thought about how he could make it up to him when he next saw him and then realised he couldn't make an arrangement with no contact details. *You idiot*, he berated himself, *you selfish idiot*. He took a fag out of its packet and sparked it up, trying to pedal back to that moment the previous evening when Tipper had pressurised him to come out. He wanted to go back and tell himself not to bother; that it would be fun but no more than the next time; that he had important things to do. He would tell yesterday's Dan to grow up, to remember what mattered: to follow his heart. He hoped Jacob would forgive him. He hoped the old man would come to the bookshop to find him. And Dan realised, for the first time, that he would be sad if he didn't.

— — —

"Put it in the Adventure/Thriller section," Dan shouted from the back office.

"It's not so much of an adventure, in my opinion," Fiona called back, indignantly. "It really drags."

Dan smiled to himself and sighed.

"What's it supposed to be like?" He shouted again. "What does it say on the back?"

Fiona was standing in the doorway. "Oh, you're there."

She was leaning against the frame of the door with her hand on her hip.

"'A raucously funny romp through the 18th century," she read, "filled with busting corsets and swash-buckling rumpus...' Honestly, who on earth writes this stuff? It was just like crap porn, you know, with a weak storyline. I'm putting it in the teenage section." She walked off decisively.

"You don't have to read them all, you know," He called after her and then muttered to himself, "Might be easier if you didn't..."

"I heard that!" she called over her shoulder, in mock offence.

They were having their usual Monday, stocking the shelves with the latest deliveries. Neither had spoken of the Saturday night, and Dan didn't really know what to say. He still couldn't remember when they had parted, or what had been said, despite racking his addled brain. She hadn't brought it up so he hadn't either. She had, that morning, presented him with his birthday presents: the 12 inch version of 'Regulate' on vinyl, which he'd been seeking out for ages, along with the rather odd gift of an egg poacher, which he couldn't see the logic behind and wondered if they'd had some weird conversation about the subject in the nightclub.

Dan was feeling rough. He had those jagged edges that could only be ironed out by the passing of time. It was the normality of the shop that soothed him, and the presence of Fiona. That lunchtime, neither of them had anywhere to be so they sat in the office and ate their sandwiches together. Between the small talk, he could tell she wanted to talk about something and he presumed it was Saturday's impromptu meeting.

"Um, sorry about Saturday, Fi," he said, swallowing and wiping his mouth. "I was a bit pissed! What with it being my birthday and Tipper – my friend, did you meet him?" She nodded and gestured for him to continue. "He's a bit of a bad influence. What I mean is a night out with Tipper is always a messy one."

She laughed. "It's fine, Dan. You were fine." But Dan felt she didn't sound wholly convincing. She carried on, "I mean, you were a bit twatted! You held my hand actually."

Dan blushed. "Oh, sorry."

"No, don't be. You led me up to the chill out room and then you promptly passed out."

"Oh shit, Fi, I *am* sorry." Dan said, putting his hand over his mouth.

"It's okay! It was quite funny. So I sat and watched the world go by, fell asleep and when I woke up you were gone."

"Without saying goodbye?"

Well," Fi carried on, "You might have said goodbye, but I was asleep. But I saw you outside with a girl, when I left."

Dan felt a surge of embarrassment. "Oh, yeah, that was…oh god, I can't remember her name!"

"Oh my God, Daniel, who'd have thought it?" Fi said, giggling.

"What?" He said, defensively.

"You're as bad as me!"

They both laughed and then he pointed his finger in the air and said, "Hilary!"

"*Hilary?* What was she, 58? Was she wearing tweed?"

"Fuck off! She was pretty...I think."

"She was *hot* for you," Fi said, pushing his shoulder.

"What do you mean?" Dan said, offering her some of his crisps.

"I mean blokes, it's harder for you isn't it? To pull. If a girl's up for it, you're like 'I'm in there man!'"

"I don't think that's fair, actually. What about you?" He regretted this as soon as he said it.

"What about me?" Her smile wavered.

"Oh, nothing," Dan said, turning to get his drink out of his bag.

"Well," she said, frowning slightly now. "I said, what about me?"

"Just that you...oh, whatever I say now is going to come out wrong. Maybe we should change the subject."

"No, I'm interested to know what you want to say about me."

He shook his head. "Whoa, Fi, don't get so defensive – I'm not saying anything. I just meant that you...you're a bit of an expert. On men."

"I'm a slag? Is that what you're saying?"

"Of course it's not what I'm saying. I mean, you like the thrill of the chase. Don't you? I mean some of the blokes you end up with, they're just..."

"What are they, Dan?" Fi's voice was cut with cold. He knew he was digging a hole now, but he couldn't seem to stop.

"I mean, you're out of their league. Now we're on the subject, that Bill arsehole. He's never going to leave his girlfriend, you know?"

"Who says I *want* him to leave his girlfriend?"

"But he doesn't respect you, Fi. Why can't you find someone who respects you?"

"Hmm, I don't know Dan, maybe you could find a man for me." Fi started to put the rest of her sandwich away and pushed back the stool to get up.

"Fi, please, this is a stupid conversation. I'm paying you a compliment anyway," Dan said, feeling slight panic that she was going to walk out on him.

"Are you? What a charming way of doing it." She took her scarf off the peg.

"Oh, you were wearing that last night," said Dan, his voice slightly raised. "You looked really pretty!"

She put the scarf around her neck and turned to him, her expression softening slightly. "Did I?"

"You really did. You stood out, actually."

"Oh fuck off, you can't even remember!" She let a small smile break and didn't move to go.

"I remember that." He grinned.

She sat back down again.

"Anyway, you cock," she sighed. "I wasn't looking for a man last night, for your information. I just...wanted to go out."

"Oh well, I'm glad you did." As he said this, Dan felt his insides relax, realising the tension which had built up when he'd thought he'd upset her.

"I just...wanted to get out of my flat." She looked down

and started fiddling with her fingernails. Dan waited for her to elaborate.

"Sometimes it all gets a bit claustrophobic in there," she continued, scraping off bits of red nail polish.

"Hmm, well, it is quite a small flat."

"No, I think I mean mentally," Fi said. "I go round and round in circles in my head."

Dan prodded her arm. "I always wondered why you were such a dizzy blonde."

"Oh shut up, that is such a shit joke," She said, hitting him with her fist. "Seriously, mum and dad came over and after they'd gone I couldn't stop thinking about them, how…I don't know." She shook her head. "How…*cold* they are."

Dan had met Fi's mum and dad once. At the time, he couldn't tally the two people in front of him with Fiona. Her mum bore a slight resemblance around the mouth, the difference being that she never smiled. She wore lots of make-up and her hair was immaculate. She would possibly have been attractive if she wasn't so miserable. Her eyes flitted down to your clothes while she spoke to you, as if she was secretly judging you or pricing up your wardrobe. Fiona's dad had seemed halfway between this world and the next. He hadn't looked Dan in the eye once and it was as if he was some kind of peasant that Mr Taylor wouldn't demean himself to speak to. Either that, or the man had serious social issues. He remembered thinking: no wonder Fi had moved out at 16 years old.

"I don't know why they bother coming. All mum does is inspect the furniture for dust, and it's always fucking dusty. She always looks at my stuff in semi-disgust. I mean, when you have children, can you expect them to be carbon copies of you?"

"Thank god you're not!" Dan said, and then felt like he may have overstepped the mark. It was okay for someone to slag off their own parents, but maybe not for friends to so enthusiastically join in. But Fi carried on as if she hadn't heard.

"Don't you wonder what holds people together? Is it love? Or is it habit, or that they back you up in your shitty ways so you don't have to question your behaviour? I don't know."

Dan was quiet for a moment before he spoke.

"I wish I knew. My mum seems so happy on her own, but I know she loved my dad. She's never said anything about anyone else in the time I've known her, but she must have had opportunities."

Fi looked up at him quizzically. "I'm sure. What does your dad say? Are we calling him your 'dad' yet?"

"Christ knows!" Dan replied, laughing. "I know that the war happened and turned things to shit, that he went missing. I just don't get why mum didn't look for him more."

Fi sighed. "Maybe she didn't know who she was looking for anymore. War changes people, so they say."

"Yeah," said Dan, sadly. "Anyway, what excuse can we give your parents for being fuck-ups?"

"You know what? I just think they're not very nice people. I don't want to be like that."

"You never will be," Dan said, reaching over to squeeze her shoulder. "Now, shall we get back to corset-busting or whatever it is?"

"Yes," Fi said decisively. "A swash-buckling rumpus is just what I need to shake my mood."

— — —

Dan's mum had left him two messages: one singing him 'Happy Birthday' from the Saturday night, and saying how she guessed he'd be out partying but to call her in the morning, and the next the previous day, sounding slightly anxious and asking him to call her when he got the chance. He felt guilty and phoned her on his lunch break.

"Mum, I'm so sorry. I had a really late one on Saturday and stayed over at Tip's. By the time I'd got home it was – "

"Dan, it's okay, you're 30 now! You don't have to explain your weekends to your mother anymore," Faith said, laughing. Dan could hear the barely disguised relief in her voice.

They agreed he would come over the following day after work and she would cook him a birthday meal. This was something they had done every year since he'd moved out. At first, she'd said did he want to bring a friend, or a girlfriend, but it had never seemed quite right; he felt weird about asking his male friends and he never seemed to have a girlfriend at the time; at least, no-one he wanted his mum to meet. This time, she asked again, did he want to bring anyone.

"Actually, yeah. I might ask Fiona, you know, who I work with?"

There was a pause on the other end and then Faith said, surprised: "Oh! Are you two…?"

"God, no mum! We're just friends."

"Well please bring her, I'd love to meet her – I've heard lots about her."

"Okay, I'll ask. I'll let you know, yeah?"

The following day, Fi and Dan stood on his mum's front step. Fi had offered to drive but in the end they'd got the bus together after work. They had spent the journey going over their favourite quotes from films and reading through her texts from Bill to decipher just how much of an arsehole he really was.

"Remember, nothing about Jacob," Dan said to her in an urgent whisper.

"Of course," she said, annoyed. "Stop worrying!"

The door opened and Faith greeted them, giving them both a big kiss on the cheek and a hug.

Fi turned to Dan and smiled. He thought that she and Faith would get on but part of him still resisted the cross over between his mum and his friends. Still, this was Fi. It was a bit different with her anyway.

As she walked into the house, Fi complemented Faith on the lovely garden. Faith explained that it really took care of itself, and she went to get them both a drink from the kitchen. On the wall in the hall was a collage of photo's, mainly of Faith and Dan together, and Dan on his own as a little boy. Fiona stopped to examine them. There were some where Faith had held the camera out herself and just about squeezed the both of them in, and others where they looked less relaxed, as if she had asked someone to take the photo for her; she stopped at a picture of Dan, grinning at the camera with his front teeth missing and riding a little tricycle. He had a plaster on his knee.

"My first bike," Dan said, standing behind her and grinning in a slightly embarrassed way.

"I love this one," Fi said, pointing at a black and white image of his mum standing behind Dan on a beach, with her arms around his neck. He was looking up at her. He looked about four years old. She had a large sunhat on and a long beaded necklace, which hung down and nearly reached his chin as he stared up at her. Neither had shoes on, and in the background was the sea.

"You look so *together,*" Fi said, aware that she needed to explain further. "Like a team, I suppose, like nothing could tear you apart."

Dan couldn't help himself but the Joy Division song about love tearing people apart came into his head.

"I love that one too," said Faith, who was standing in the doorway of the kitchen with a tray of drinks.

"Sangria," she said with a cheeky grin. "Hope you like it?"

"Ooh, yes!" Fi replied enthusiastically. Dan was glad they'd got the bus.

A couple of hours later, he and Fi had gone out for a cigarette. Faith was clearing up, having refused all offers of help from Fiona. Dan could tell she was enjoying entertaining, and she and Fi hadn't stopped talking. He took a drag of his cigarette now, and rubbed his hands together in the chilly March air.

"You seem really interested in Mum's life…" he said to Fi.

"Of course," she replied. "You have to admit, it's unusual. She comes to England, what, when she's like 7 or 8 months pregnant with you? That takes guts, don't you think?"

Dan nodded in response. "Plus, someone who lives alone and is content with that…I don't know, I just find that inspiring somehow. She seems, well, self-sufficient, emotionally."

"Yeah, I think she is, pretty much," Dan said. "She never makes any demands on me. I never feel I have to look after her. I suppose that is unusual when it's just the two of us."

"I think it's unheard of," Fi said, and put her cigarette out on the stone bench. Dan passed her the plant pot Faith kept with sand in outside for smokers and she pushed it down until you could no longer see it. When she stood up she wobbled a little.

"Too much sangria," she said, giggling.

"Come on, drunken idiot," Dan said, taking her arm. She shoved him away playfully.

"I'm not drunk! Just merry."

"Yeah, yeah..." They made their way inside.

— — —

Jacob had popped into the bookshop the previous week, and he and Dan had arranged to meet at the café again. Whilst Dan hoped he could persuade Jacob to go for a walk with him, his father had other ideas.

"I wondered if you wanted to go to the pub together," he ventured.

Although he agreed, Dan couldn't help but feel a little nervous about going somewhere he might see his mates with a 'strange man'. He'd have to explain his identity, but how could he if he couldn't even be honest with Faith? They walked towards the Old Mill at Dan's suggestion. It wasn't somewhere his friends usually frequented but even so, he asked Jacob what he should call him.

"Well," he replied, smiling. "Perhaps you could say I was a friend of your mum's? Or even an uncle?"

Dan agreed and they went into the pub and ordered two pints of Guinness. He watched Jacob drink. The older man shut his eyes, as if savouring every morsel of the dark liquid. Dan couldn't help but think this guy was weird. He still thought of him as 'this guy' and he felt slightly embarrassed and awkward in a social situation with someone who was almost a stranger.

"How about some pool?" He asked Jacob. They played a couple of games. Jacob wasn't so bad and Dan made some pretty poor shots. They played best of three. His father asked him lots of questions, which Dan tried to answer whilst at the same time fighting the desire to keep some parts of himself hidden, just in case...Just in case this was some weirdo who had taken it upon himself to make an idiot out of him. *But why would you do that?* Dan wondered. *Some people do get their kicks in strange ways, I suppose.*

Then he started asking about Fiona; how long they had known each other, how she seemed like a good friend. For some reason, this got Dan's back up even more.

"Listen, sorry but I don't see how you can make that assumption. You only really met her for a minute at best. She trod on your bloody toe, for god's sake." Dan took a shot more forcefully than he had been doing. Jacob had gone quiet.

"You're right," he said after a moment. "I don't know her at all. Like you said, I was just making an assumption." They played on in silence until Dan's guilt made him fill it.

"I don't have a girlfriend at the moment," he said quietly. "I don't know why I'm saying that, but I guess I thought you were implying that Fi and I should...you know, everyone else does anyway. But we're just mates."

Jacob smiled. Shaking his head, he said "I didn't mean to imply anything. I'm just curious about your life, what makes you happy. That kinda thing." Dan couldn't help but feel uncomfortable after this conversation. He had a feeling in the pit of his stomach that this was a ridiculous situation and he didn't want to be there. He made some excuse once they'd finished the game, and they both finished their drinks.

"You can stay," he said to Jacob, not wanting the older man to accompany him through town. Jacob said he'd walk with him as far as the theatre. They paced down the busy ring road and said nothing.

When they reached the intersection outside the bus station, Dan motioned that he had to go in the direction of the town centre. They shook hands.

"I don't mean to make you feel uncomfortable," Jacob said. "I'm sure this is a totally bizarre situation for you. But if you want to, I'd like to meet again. I'll try not to be too irritating."

"Of course," Dan replied quietly, feeling ashamed. It was almost as though Jacob had read his mind. They parted ways and Dan found himself wandering past the shops and peering into the steamed-up windows at the remnants of the January sales. He got out his phone and wrote a text to Faith, saying what a good time he and Fi had had at the meal. He wandered into Waterstones, feeling like a bit of a traitor. In the 'Hobbies and Interests' section, he found a large hardback book about clocks on sale for £4.99. He knew Faith had worked in a watchmaker's shop when she was younger, so he bought it for her. He never quite knew what to get her for her birthday so he was quite pleased with himself for thinking ahead. While he was fraternising with the 'enemy', he took the opportunity to visit the history section and found a section of about 15 books on the Vietnam War. Dan had a flick through one that looked more factual than the others and read about why the Americans had joined the war and their strategies. He had not realised that some of the Vietnamese had been enlisted by the US to fight in the jungles, in order to stop the VC from transporting weapons along the Ho Chi Minh Trail. A few paragraphs on, the book explained that these Vietnamese soldiers, the Hmong people, trained by the US were massacred afterwards and none but a handful had survived. He closed the book. Sometimes it was too much to hear about these things. He couldn't imagine having to fight like that; to not know if you would survive from one day to the next. And for what purpose? He wanted to ask Jacob next time he saw him. Suddenly, there was more he wanted to know. Like how does someone survive an experience like that? And what the hell comes after? Did you ever look at yourself and wonder who you were anymore after something like war? He may not be able to understand why Jacob had taken so long to find him, but maybe he could try to understand his experiences along the way; bridge the gap between the past and the future; forge some kind of bond between then and now.

CHAPTER **FOUR**

IT WAS MAY DAY Bank Holiday, and the streets were filled with revellers who had decided to spend their day off in the pub. In the old market square, a beer festival was taking place, and Dan had to fight his way through the hoards of people clutching at their pint glasses as they trudged around exhibiting varying degrees of pissed.

He and Jacob were meeting at their usual spot, but Dan had the idea they might head out into the countryside for a walk. He had no idea if Jacob liked the countryside, or whether he enjoyed walking but Dan felt he wanted to show him some of the great outdoors. Only to himself, he admitted he also thought it might help Jacob to open up a bit more. The atmosphere of the café and the bustle of customers and outside gave them the chance to skirt around the past, with easy distractions prompting his dad to order another coffee or roll another ciggie, and divert the conversation.

Absent-mindedly, he accepted a flyer thrust into his hand as he approached. Thinking it must just be another beer festival offer, he folded it roughly without looking at it and put it in his back pocket, pushing open the door. The blue blind on the door banged on his leg as he walked through, as it always did.

He saw the back of his dad's head, and he found he could picture his face, and as he rounded the table he saw that Jacob wore the same crooked grin. He was just putting out a roll up and had a small coughing fit immediately after saying 'hello'.

"God, Dad, you need to sort that out," Dan said, patting him on the back. Jacob screwed his eyes at him momentarily and then smiled. Once he'd got his breath back, he said quietly:

"You called me 'dad'."

Dan felt suddenly silly and a little defensive. "Well…yeah, so I did. Is that okay?" He realised it was the first time he had used that name and wondered now if Jacob would prefer to keep up the pretence that they were just a couple of guys sharing a coffee and setting the world to rights.

"Of course," He said, grinning. "I liked it."

"Maybe it's a bit weird…" Dan said, backtracking. "After all, we're both adults and we don't know each other *that* well."

"No problem," Jacob said, reassuringly, "It's up to you, Dan."

Dan nodded and pulled out the chair opposite but didn't take his coat off.

"I wondered if you might want to get some air today, you know, head out into the great British countryside…"

Jacob reached for his tobacco tin, lifted the lid and took out a finger full of the rich, orange leaves. In his other hand, he held a cigarette paper. Dan watched as he rolled a perfect cigarette in seconds. It seemed as though Jacob sometimes had to have a fag in his mouth to think. It was frustrating, at times, but Dan was learning to let it go.

He took a deep inhalation and breathed it out, turning his head towards the window.

"That sounds nice."

— — —

THE **HEART LADDER**

They had taken the bus out to Tillersdale, in the opposite direction from his mum's village, since he was paranoid he might bump into her if she was on one of her impromptu hikes with her friend, Judy. The bus had dropped them at the end of a long lane, flanked by trees and on one side a steep verge which you couldn't see the top of. Dan hadn't been here in a long time, but he thought Jacob would appreciate it. The older man had been quiet on the bus, staring out the window at the passing fields with an almost childlike expression. Every now and then he had pointed something out to Dan, as if Dan hadn't seen it before, like a particular type of bird or a distant tower; it reminded Dan of when he was little and on journeys with his mum. He would sit in the back with his walkman on, but she would reach around the chair with her hand and give his knee a pinch, shaking him out of his daydreams. He'd turn down the volume briefly and make the right noises so she was satisfied, and then he would return to his fantasy.

There were few sounds, save the trudging crumble of their boots on the stony lane, and the birds flitting from one bush to the next. Somewhere, the noise of children penetrated the back of Dan's hearing and as they walked on, he spotted where it was coming from. There was a football pitch here, surrounded by trees, and nature encroached upon it from every angle. Rhododendrons thrust their lush purple flowers towards one of the goals, as if pointing the players in the right direction; an old oak tree grew at the very side, like a motionless and wooden referee. As they got close, Dan saw that the children played with no trainers on. Someone had painstakingly mowed the grass but left the whole surroundings untouched. The two men stopped to watch the game for a minute or so. Jacob mumbled, "I've never seen that before."

When Dan asked him what he meant, he replied, "I've never seen a football pitch like that before," but he seemed to go quiet after that.

Dan didn't know when or how to broach the subject of Jacob's past, or even his present, so to him there was what felt like an expectant silence, although his father seemed unaware of the discomfort and was looking intently at all the trees he passed, stopping to touch a flower here or examine a leaf there.

"Dad..." he said, when they reached a wooden bench by the side of the beginnings of the stream, which ran through Tillersdale gradually widening and expanding and, eventually, turning into the River Dove at its outlet further down the valley.

Dan gestured to the bench and so they sat, side by side. "I wondered if we could talk. I mean, properly. I don't mean about me. I want to know more about your life up until now."

Jacob was quiet, and Dan felt he had offended him somehow.

"I mean," he continued, "my life is pretty boring. Here you are, back from the dead in a manner of speaking, and you never really tell me what your life's been like, not in any detail."

Jacob drew in a deep breath and put out his hands, "What do you wanna know?"

"Well..." Dan said, taken aback. Jacob's direct question was unexpected, and left him unsure where to start his enquiry. "Well, how about what you've been doing between Vietnam and now? I don't mean about looking for mum, I mean what else?"

Unsurprisingly, Jacob took out his tobacco tin. He made them a roll up each and began, cautiously, to tell his tale.

"You know, being a 'Nam vet, you got some bad blood when you came back, and I didn't even wear my colours. I felt like I wanted to merge back into society like I'd never been away," he began.

"I stayed with some friends in NYC but they couldn't cope with my moods so they asked me to move out," he said, kicking a stone with his foot. "I had nowhere to go, so I took up with a few ex-hippies who were making a living dealing a bit of dope and sometimes some whizz, although not many people were doing that in those days."

Dan nodded him to continue.

"So...I didn't have much direction I guess you could say, and then I met a guy who said he could change all that."

"Who was he?" asked Dan, frowning.

"An ex-soldier who'd decided to set up a commune for like-minded vets and their partners, or sympathisers with our plight," Jacob paused to cough. "He said I could live there. I didn't have many other options so I did."

"And what was it like there?" Dan asked.

"Madness!" Jacob grinned. "Good madness at first, we grew our own weed and sat around telling stories from the war. There was a good group of girls there and we all kind of..." Jacob looked suddenly sheepish, "got on."

Dan laughed. "You mean..."

"Yeah, that's what I mean," he replied, chuckling at the memory. Dan felt his face colour slightly, but Jacob seemed oblivious.

"Anyway," the older man continued, "it all went along like this, you know, until this guy joined up who had a lot of anger.

We all liked him but he was on the edge, like if you said the wrong thing he'd just explode. But funny, man, he was funny, like you felt kind of honoured if he chose to share a joke with you."

Dan nodded, "Like at school when the cool kid hangs around with you at breaktime?"

"Exactly that, Dan. So he starts talking about 'them' and 'us' as if people who didn't make it to 'Nam were somehow a different breed; like it was their fault we had to go, like somehow we could blame all of the shit on not just the politicians but people living on the next block or people who worked in stores or basically, anybody who wasn't a veteran."

"What about the girls?"

Jacob laughed. "Oh, he tried to keep them on our side of the fence. He actually didn't need to try so hard. He'd have every single one of them and then they'd come back for more. They just hung on his every word."

"Women are weird," Dan said, thinking of Fi and some of her romantic choices.

"They are…anyway this guy, we called him Baggy but his real name was Shaun, he decided we needed to do something about the 'them' and 'us' situation. He organised a protest, which we'd said needed to be peaceful. It was about how vet's were treated like shit and how to make people see we were just ordinary guys who'd done a job, you know, we weren't all mindless killers."

"Let me guess," said Dan, flicking his cigarette onto the floor and stubbing it out with his shoe. "It all went pear-shaped."

"Pear-shaped? Yes, you could say that." Jacob looked out at

the stream and paused a few seconds. "Baggy had taken a knife with him." He shut his eyes, as if revisiting the memory. "Once the cops started to pressure us, he slashed away at a few of them. I was right behind him and so I got arrested too. We were both thrown in the slammer. One of the cops died. When it came to trial, some lady insisted I had a knife too even though they never found one on me. Baggy made out I was the ringleader and no-one came to my defence. The other guys were shitting themselves too much and just wanted to get on with their lives. I didn't have anybody really."

There was a pause and Dan almost ventured a question but then Jacob cleared his throat.

"I got 10 years for manslaughter," he said. He didn't look at Dan, now, but went to grab a bottle of coke from his bag. They sat in silence for a moment letting the dust settle.

"It was partly because of it that I came to find you," he explained. "You see? Too much time wasted."

Dan nodded and leant forward onto his knees, thinking about what he'd been told; processing it. He turned his head askance towards Jacob.

"And you didn't have a knife, did you?"

Jacob looked almost as if he had expected this question and shook his head silently.

"Sorry to ask," said Dan. The old man shrugged.

— — —

They had walked another half an hour, making small talk about the flora and fauna, and Dan recounting times when he was a child and Faith had brought him here. Jacob asked him how his 30th birthday had been, and Dan was surprised that he had remembered; that he even knew. His reply had been suitably evasive, but Jacob had seemed satisfied.

The old rope swing which used to hang from a tree was no longer there, but Dan could remember the spot, and the thrill of hanging off it and swinging over the gushing river. It had started to rain so they headed back along the path. The rain brought out the aroma of the rhododendrons and weighed down their petals so they were almost kissing the ground. The footballers had retreated under a tree, their tops over their heads as if they knew it was just a passing shower. One of them, a girl, ran out into the rain with her arms outstretched towards the heavens. Dan and Jacob laughed at the same time; Dan because he wanted to join in and Jacob because he could no longer remember what that felt like; that freedom of spirit, but he was glad it still existed.

On the bus, Jacob was very quiet and Dan began to think maybe it was best he hadn't known about his dad's spell in prison. Maybe he'd pushed Jacob that bit too far. He let his mind wander to his mum; what the hell would she think of this whole thing? Would she ever forgive him if she found out that he was seeing Jacob behind her back? It made more sense, now that he knew about Jacob's chequered past, that his mum shouldn't know. The whole idea gave him a bubbly panic feeling in his stomach so he shook it out of his head and got his Discman out of his bag. He touched Jacob's arm and said, "Do you mind?" Jacob smiled and shook his head. Dan put his headphones in and let the music permeate his mind and weave in amongst his thoughts. He watched the passing fields as they turned into villages and then more modern semi-detached houses and then into the grey high rises of the city, feeling like he was on a journey through time.

Pulling up at the bus station, the two men trudged down the aisle and out onto the curb. The smell of piss hung on the air and Dan noticed a bit of graffiti on the wall of one of the shelters which said, "Time for a change – fuck the police!" Well, he thought, it made a change from the usual phone number and offers of sex which peppered the rest of the run-down bus station. Fiona used to say one day she'd come down here with an aerosol herself and correct all the grammar. They walked down, past the hippy shop where his mum got her health food products, which nestled right next to a fried chicken shop, and on its other side a massage parlour called 'Bubbles', where it was rumoured you could get a hand job for the right price.

When they reached the lion statue, Jacob turned to Dan and said, "I guess I'll see you next week?"

"Yeah, that'd be great." They shook hands.

Jacob lingered and then said, "I hope you don't think badly of me after today."

"No," Dan replied. "Not at all."

Jacob sighed. "That's good."

Dan reached into his coat pocket. "Look, do you need any money? I know you might be proud about it but, well, we could call it a loan. I don't know how...well, I thought you might not be very...I don't know what your situation is at the moment."

Jacob looked embarrassed and was silent for a second before saying, "You know, that would be great, and of course it's a loan."

"Great, I've got £20 on me, but if you need more we can stop at a cash machine," Dan said, rummaging in his pockets for the £20 note he remembered having from earlier. He thought he'd found it in his back jeans pocket and brought it round to give to his dad before he realised it wasn't money but the flyer someone had passed him earlier that day. He unfolded it to take a quick look. On it was the logo of a sunrise over a cityscape. *The People of the Sun,* it read. *Join us if you want to make a change to your life.* Dan made a short noise of acknowledgement to himself, thinking it sounded interesting. He put it in his coat pocket and then retrieved the note from the front pocket of his jeans where he had stashed it earlier. As he passed it to his father, he looked up and felt suddenly alarmed. Jacob was staring at him, completely motionless, and the colour drained from his face. He didn't even take the money. His eyes, filled with anxiety, darted from Dan's face to his other pocket where he had put the flyer.

"Dad," Dan said, quietly at first, and then more loudly as if Jacob had slipped into some other state of consciousness and needed waking up. Passing shoppers glanced at them. After a moment, his father took the money off him and said almost under his breath, "Thank you. I'll see you next week."

Dan watched him walk away, with his slight limp, and couldn't escape from the sick feeling he had, as if something inevitable had been set in motion which couldn't be stopped, like a runaway rollercoaster taking all its screaming passengers loop the loop over and over until: crash. He shivered and pulled his coat around him, walking towards the fountain in the market square.

— — —

It was a Thursday and Fi had escaped The Blank Page for 20 minutes, desperate as she was for some distraction since she had had only one customer that morning and had tidied the shop to death in the mean time. She had purchased a new top for the weekend, some kind of leopard print affair. It wasn't really her but was in the sale and she'd needed a bit of retail therapy. Leaving the shop, she threw her bag on her shoulder and ventured once more out into the warm air, the streets holding an array of shoppers. Excitable children wove in and out of the throng, their anxious parents shouting after them, afraid to lose sight of their offspring, but perhaps more afraid of losing their precious cargo, plastic bags of all colours holding the unloved toys of tomorrow.

The most enthusiastic Big Issue seller she had ever known was in his usual spot as she approached.

"Hi Paddy, how are you?"

"Hey you, I'm doing well out of this y'know," he smiled, "the sunshine and everything."

She leaned forward to pat Paddy's dog, which lay peacefully by his feet.

"I suppose people are feeling more generous are they, because the sun's making an appearance?" She fished out a £2 coin from her pocket. "Sorry it's not more…are you sleeping here tonight?"

"Nah, I've got a bed at the centre tonight, Fiona, and a meal too." He patted his stomach. "My luck's in."

Fi laughed. "Good news. I'll see you soon, bye Bonnie." She gave the dog an affectionate pat. "Enjoy your night of luxury!"

Paddy laughed as she walked away.

She wanted to laugh too but then suddenly she didn't know

if that was the right thing to do. A metal box, sporting the slogan 'Begging is not the answer', now inhabited Paddy's former spot but she had never felt moved by metal, only by flesh and blood, worn blankets and hungry looking pets, on the streets by association.

She wandered through the crowded city centre and onto Macklin Street, where she opened up the shop and pulled down the post-it on the door which said 'Back in 10 minutes'. Straight away she picked up the familiar scent she so loved, that of old dusty books, musty and plump with wisdom and stories. She wandered into the back and put the kettle on, reaching down into the box of books that Dan had got from a house clearance, which she'd been saving until this afternoon so she could while away some time. She plucked one out at random, opening it about half way through without looking at the title.

His pocket weighted down, the man took the first steps of his long journey into the unknown, his heart heavy with sorrow.

The bell on the shop door rang and she jumped, and pulled the curtain aside slightly to take a peek at the customer. A man stood there in tight jeans, trainers and a scruffy combat jacket, and he was looking right at her.

"Hey there, I didn't mean to give you a shock," he said, smiling. "You dropped your sunglasses outside."

"Oh right, thanks," Fiona came out from behind the curtain, brushing imaginary bits from her trousers in a nervous gesture. "Thank you." She took the glasses off him.

"I'm always dropping them actually...it's amazing, I've had them for years and they always find their way back to me."

He looked somewhat familiar, but her mind could not place him.

"Well, who can blame them, I guess..." he replied with a grin.

"Well...thank you," she replied, with a little giggle, which she immediately wished she could take back.

"No problem."

He turned to go but then hesitated.

"While I'm in here actually, do you have anything on Lenin?" he asked, frowning at her seriously.

Fiona became acutely aware that she didn't know if she'd heard him correctly and that her knowledge may be being tested.

"That's deceased Beatle Lennon?" She ventured cautiously, "or communist-type person Lenin?"

"Lenin." He said, not smiling.

"Well, not exactly, no. I don't know if you have it but we've got Das Kapital by Marx? I suppose it's in the same ball park." She giggled nervously, and then wondered why she had used a silly American expression which had never before this moment passed her lips.

"Hmm," he said, staring at her again. "Got that already."

His eyes wouldn't let her go, so after what seemed like ages but was probably just a few seconds, she looked away, embarrassed. He laughed then, and she felt she had been let off whatever test he was employing. What exactly was going on here? She usually felt so confident around her books but not now. She was tongue-tied, suddenly.

"I could order something for you, if you like?"

"Sure, that would be good. I like to support local businesses."
She smiled at this unexpected offering, and turned to go and
fetch the laptop from the back of the shop. Setting it down on
the counter, she turned it on and waited for it to whirr into life.
It was an old one of Dan's. Phil was a bit tight and refused to
get them a computer while this was still working. Every now
and then, she and Dan considered throwing coffee on it but then
they knew they'd be screwed until Phil got round to sorting it
out.

"Which particular book were you after? I can see if I can get
it for you at the wholesalers or tag it onto our next order."

He arched one eyebrow. "Which would you recommend?"

"Me?" She looked up at him. "Oh well, honestly, I haven't
read much Lenin. I'm afraid – He cut her off with a laugh. "I'm
joking," he said and walked a couple of steps around the counter
so he could see what she was typing. She tried to concentrate.

"Try 'State and Revolution'," he said, leaning in close to her.
"I don't have that one."

Fi kept mucking up the typing. She always did when
someone was sitting beside her; even more so because she could
feel his breath on her neck. Finding it, she added it to the shop's
order list and hurriedly closed the page, moving out of his space
and pushing her hair behind her ear self-consciously.

"Well, that's that then! I'll need to take a number if that's
okay?" She felt her cheeks redden a little.

He got his mobile out of his pocket. "Tell you what, how
about I call you? Then you'll have it to hand."

Her cheeks reddened even more, even though she knew he
was out of order, she couldn't help but go along with it. The

gall of him! She wrote her number on a post-it note and peeled it off the pad on the desk. Just as she was passing it to him, she said "Oh!" and pulled it back, writing 'Fiona' next to the number. She passed it back to him.

He typed the number into his phone and pressed call, looking up at her as he waited for it to ring. It did, in her handbag in the back.

"Now you have my number," he said, grinning at her cheekily. Again, Fi found herself speechless so she simply smiled back. He turned to go, without saying goodbye and she called after him.

"I need your name! Of course…"

He turned his head but carried on walking. "It's Quinn." As he pushed open the shop door and walked out onto the pavement, she saw him crumple up the post-it note and chuck it in the gutter. It made her feel slightly insulted for a moment, but she knew she would call him. She knew she wouldn't be able to help it.

The week dragged by. Dan had been distant since the weekend and Fi had tried all of her usual tactics on him to get him to open up but to no avail. In the end she left him to it. Selfishly, she had also wanted to talk to him about her weird meeting with this guy, Quinn, but she could tell he wasn't in the mood for that sort of stuff. She had wanted to know if Dan thought she should ring him, but secretly she knew she would do. There were several unfinished texts in her Drafts folder, none of which worked on the right level of cool, so she had abandoned them. And he was *cool*, but not in a laid-back surfer dude way but in an aloof, superior and slightly mysterious way that both unnerved and excited her at the same time.

She decided after a glass of wine that evening, she would do it, she would call him, and she immediately began to rehearse what she would say. At least she'd managed to hold off a few days. He wouldn't think she was a nutcase; on the other hand, he might be insulted and not pick up. If, if. *Stop your internal dialogue*, she thought, quoting Bill Hicks to herself, in her head. A few hours later, she had drunk half a glass of wine with the phone pressed to her ear and on the other end, a curt but polite Quinn was agreeing to meet her the following day for a coffee. She hung up and couldn't help but do that ridiculous 'Yes!' shout out loud to no-one at all, as if she'd won a race or conquered some kind of obstacle, which she felt that she had. It hadn't been an easy phone call but, Fi thought, there was nothing like a challenge.

– – –

"So, yeah, I'm helping a friend out behind the bar tonight at Rosie's, do you know it?"

Fiona knew she was babbling, but couldn't seem to stop. She and Quinn sat opposite each other at Vines, having moved on from coffee to cocktails sometime ago.

"I'm supposed to be there in…" she looked down at her watch, only to find that it wasn't there.

"Oh no, where the hell's my watch? Oh God, I don't believe this!"

"You've lost your watch?"

She shot him an irritated look.

"Yes, my watch is gone…did you notice if I had it on when we sat down? I mean…I remember looking at the time when I left home…oh God, it was my Grandmother's and then my mum's, seriously, this is not good!"

He lent forward and touched her arm lightly.

"Hey, no worries, if we retrace our steps, we're bound to find it."

She ran her hands through her hair in bewilderment.

"I'm good at finding things that belong to you, remember?" He grinned as she crumpled back into the wooden chair, in exaggerated fatigue. She nodded. The sunglasses.

"Besides," he continued, "at least now you have an excuse for not making it to work on time."

Considering this thought, Fi found herself smiling. She felt ridiculous. Suddenly the idea of being so upset by the simple loss of a treasured heirloom seemed rather excessive, and she felt strangely light and free of care.

"Oh well, here's to losing things that belong to you," she announced, picking up her glass.

Quinn tapped the edge of his against hers, "And here's to finding them again."

She echoed his words and, nodding, they knocked back the rest of their mojitos.

Then a tray of shots arrived, resulting in great deal of spluttering from Fi, and an array of slurred expletives emanating from their table, much to the amusement of the young man behind the bar, who thoroughly enjoyed seeing two people begin a lengthy drinking session at 3 o'clock in the afternoon.

They discussed life, the universe, politics, although Fiona let him speak more as he seemed so knowledgeable. Things became heated and time was forgotten until Fiona noticed three missed calls from her friend, Tam.

"Oh shit shit shit!" she said, loudly. "I'm going to have to ring her. I can't work behind a bar like this!"

Quinn shrugged and leant back as if put out by her interruption. She wrote a very apologetic text to her friend and promptly turned off her phone. They were quiet for a moment. Fiona felt she had to fill the silence somehow.

"I feel a bit warm, have I...I've got my cardi on still! Sorry, where were we anyway? You were saying about human rights organisations and – oh, what are you doin'?"

Quinn was kneeling down on the floor and looked, from Fi's slightly skewed angle of vision, to be performing some kind of eastern ritual. "Mecca's that way, I'm sure...seriously, what are you doing?!"

He leant back onto his knees and held up his hand, from which dangled a familiar looking timepiece.

"I believe this is yours, pretty lady?"

She looked from his face, to her Grandmother's watch, and then back again.

Quinn began to laugh.

"Bloody hell! You found it..." Fi let out a small giggle, followed by another and another until she and a man whose surname she didn't know were sharing a fit of hilarity, the small metal table between them, wobbling and creaking in sympathetic mirth.

– – –

Several hours later, they staggered to the local park, Quinn supporting Fi with his arm. She took off her heels and walked barefoot, not caring about glass or needles or dirt. Not caring for the moment about a thing. He was telling her what he thought about society and she let his voice wash over her, distracted by his touch.

"We flirt and flounce with words and wit, but what do we really mean? Nothing but a superfluous comment on how we feel about society or what it could be if we decided to play an active part." At this, he pulled her around to face him. They were under a railway bridge. Fiona gave an inner shudder.

"Were you listening?" He squeezed her arm when he said this.

"Yes," she said, a bit shocked. "Yes...so what part do you want to play?"

"All this?" he asked, "all this is meaningless," he said as he spread out his hands in front of him, "but this..."

Fi felt him move closer to her, and his breath mingled with hers.

"This is you and me," he said, "standing on the edge of a precipice, waiting to jump."

She leant towards him, her face and hands tingling, her body electric.

"I want to jump," she whispered, and in answer, he brushed her lips with his. She reached for his face and caressed his jaw line, his cheeks, coaxing him towards her. Quinn took her hands in his and put them onto his heart, then moved them down his body.

"I already have."

Leaving her hands where they were, he grasped her shoulders and pushed her firmly back so she was leaning against the wall. They kissed, feverishly and frantically; he pushed one of his hands up her top and the other went between her legs. She felt nowhere and everywhere. Fumbling with his belt buckle, she pushed her hand inside his jeans to feel him. He moved away, crouching down and pushing up her skirt. Suddenly she felt his mouth and tongue on her, inside her, and she gasped with pleasure. Then he pushed her around, pulling her hands roughly behind her back and grabbing her wrists. He kissed her neck and ear, whispering, she couldn't make out what he said; his breath made her spine tingle and she shuddered. They had sex like that, vivid and feral, against the dank, stone tunnel, the faint glow from a streetlight illuminating the area behind them. The slow trundle of an overland train could be heard approaching. Fi's face was pressed against the cold of the brickwork and dampness of the moss growing there. Once their breath steadied, time was suspended for a few seconds, or moments; Fiona could not tell which.

Slowly, Quinn moved away from her and she flexed her hands and stretched out her fingers before opening her eyes. Fi's forehead felt sore as she pulled away from the curved wall. She realised she had bitten her lip and tasted blood. She turned to face him and he looked at her tenderly, making her feel almost childlike. She half-smiled back. There was nothing she could think of to say, so she just reached for the lapels of his coat and pulled him closely to her, weaving her arm around his back underneath the heavy fabric, her head buzzing and fuzzy with the thrill.

They ambled back towards the dimly lit park entrance, not speaking, but pausing to kiss passionately. A late night dog walker, looking for his wayward spaniel, happened upon them with an embarrassed laugh and rapidly begun his search in another direction, thinking how wonderful it was that two people could be so entwined with each other that they did not care for, or notice, anything else.

— — —

The next morning, Fi was late for work. When she did arrive at 11am, Dan tried to be cross but she looked shattered, so he left her alone for a while in the back of the shop. When she came out, she still looked slightly dishevelled but smiled at him anyway.

"What's to do?" she asked. "Stock taking? Not that I'm guessing we've sold much anyway…"

He laughed, relieved at her almost returning to normal, and handed her the post.

"Maybe you could sort through these for me? Oh, and if you're making a coffee…?"

She nodded, smiled and walked off with the post to the back of the shop, where they'd crammed in an old bureau, in order to encourage customers to 'try before they buy'.

Business wasn't great. Everyone was going on about Amazon, where you could get fairly recent books cheap and second-hand books for next to nothing. Phil, the owner of the shop, popped in from time to time and said it wasn't a threat; that people wanted to look at covers and feel and smell books before they bought them. Dan and Fi weren't so sure. People were starting to make their decisions in a different way, a quick 'yes' or 'no', to fit in with the speed of life.

Just after midday, Dan asked Fi if she minded him taking an early lunch. He could tell she wasn't in the mood for talking so to avoid an awkward lunch break he decided to venture out into the sunshine and find a spot on the grass in the old churchyard around the corner. In the warm sun, Dan sat and ate his sandwich on scruffy but recently mown grass. The church to his right was boarded up and a customer who'd been chatting to him a few days previously had said she thought it was going to be made into an 'all you can eat' Chinese restaurant. He wondered what God would think, if He existed. The church sat between two busy roads and behind it nestled a grey, concrete multi-storey car-park, which actually *spoke* to you when you entered. In his mind he tied the two together, could it be God's voice saying 'Tap in the code, and pull the door open'? Perhaps He just inhabited the land, like the Native Americans believed, in which case He was housed within the car park and the church, and maybe also beneath the ground where Dan sat. Actually, no. That was the *other* one's domain.

God probably didn't think the same way as humans, but still, a bloody restaurant. Having to sit and watch people stuff their faces instead of worshipping His greatness; spring rolls in the font and a pew full of fat folk with noodles down their jumpers.

He lay back on his hands and looked at the sky. The sun caressed his cheeks and the hairs on his bare arms lifted, like new shoots attracted to the warm rays of light. The beeping of the nearby pedestrian crossing and the coffee-smell of exhaust fumes blended into a sweet song of smoky spring, and the voice of God repeated his instruction over and over into the city air. Soon, Dan was asleep.

— — —

The blocking out of the sun woke him. As Dan's vision readjusted into focus, he saw the outline of an unkempt beard. Slowly, the gaps were filled in as if by an invisible pencil, the expression scribbled into a sad face, or perhaps more one of concern. The face was too close to his, and he could smell the cigarettes on the man's breath. For a moment, Dan thought someone was about to attack him, his brain not making the neural connections required of facial recognition.

The man, as if he sensed the invasion, leaned back and Dan sat up quickly.

"Oh," he said, and gave his eyes a rub. "It's you!"

"You left your wallet out on the grass," said Jacob, in a serious tone. "It could have been stolen."

"Oh," Dan said again. "Thanks…"

He stuffed the wallet into his back pocket and looked around him, piecing together the time of day and searching for the memory of what he was doing here. Pushing his fingers through his hair, he reached in his other pocket for his fags and offered one to Jacob.

"What are you doing here?" Dan asked him, taking a deep suck on his cigarette and feeling a little put out at Jacob's reproachful tone.

"I was on my way to the Jobcentre," Jacob replied.

"Really? I thought you had no fixed abode," Dan sniggered and then regretted it. "Sorry…"

Jacob shrugged. "I wanted to see if there was anything I could do, to fix this city up," he continued. "Like gardening the urban spaces, or maybe cleaning graffiti off toilet walls. Something useful, I guess."

"Good idea," Dan softened. "I didn't think you cared about this city, I mean, you don't have any connection to it except…"

"Except you." Jacob said, finishing the sentence for him.

"Exactly," Dan replied, laughing in an attempt to lighten the mood. He'd noticed that sometimes when he saw Jacob, the old man seemed quite light and other times brooding. He was never quite sure what he was going to get, and although he was trying to be friendly, he resented the sudden intrusion.

"So, aren't you supposed to be at work?" Jacob asked, flicking his ash on the ground and stretching out his legs.

Again, Dan felt a prickle of annoyance.

"I'm on my lunch, actually. It's okay, Fi will open up again."

Jacob smiled wryly. "Does she do everything for you?"

Dan took a deep breath. "Not everything, no. For instance, she doesn't give me blow jobs under the counter or do my washing. That sort of thing, do you mean?"

"Whoa, there!" Jacob said, looking shocked. "I didn't mean to upset you."

"Well, why don't you leave me alone then?" Dan said quickly, feeling his anger make a hole in the pit of his stomach.

"Sorry, Dan. I'm sorry." Jacob put his hand on Dan's shoulder.

"No, I'm sorry. I just…I'm still half asleep I guess."

"I don't want to go. Could we just start again?" At this, he got up and without comprehension, Dan watched him walk away until he was no longer visible behind the church steps. For a moment, he thought the whole thing hadn't happened and then he saw Jacob coming towards him again.

"Hey Dan, fancy meeting you here!" Jacob said, in an over-cheery tone.

Dan couldn't help but smile.

"Yeah, what a coincidence, I've just woken up actually. Come and join me."

The old man sat down once more, and they both laughed. The sun warmed their faces.

They talked about music, for a while, and discovered they had similar tastes. They both remembered clearly the first time they'd heard Pink Floyd's 'The Wall', and recalled in horror the days when Stock, Aitken and Waterman had monopolised the charts. Dan got out his disc man and gave his father an earphone to see what he thought of funky house. Jacob said he was too old for that sort of thing nowadays, although he did like the beat.

"I'm afraid this old guy can't dance anymore," he said to Dan, sadly.

Dan didn't know whether it was prudent to ask what had happened to Jacob's leg but he guessed it was an old war wound, so he kept quiet. The conversation turned to the walk they had taken some weeks back. They had only seen each other once since then, and Jacob had gone on and on about how you could change the world as an individual and the butterfly effect. It was a long and arduous conversation and left Dan feeling bewildered. He had only asked his father what he thought he might be able to do to make himself feel a bit more fulfilled, in these days of political apathy. It was afterwards that he had remembered how odd Jacob had been at the end of their walk in the countryside, and he'd gone to find the flyer in his old jeans. It probably reminded him of his younger days, all the protesting against the war and that it had never done any good anyway. He didn't know whether to confront Jacob with this theory or not. Before he could think about doing so now, Jacob did it for him.

"I remember you were talking about joining a group...?" Jacob said this a little too casually, and despite himself, Dan felt his hackles rising slightly. Whenever Jacob tried to act in a 'fatherly' way he found himself repelled, even though he tried not to be.

"Actually, I never said I was joining a group," he said, "but *you* were implying that it was better to be a lone wolf."

"Oh, yes, I was..." Jacob paused to get a rizla out of his tobacco tin and he began to make a roll-up. Dan tried to be patient.

"When I was young, we all thought we could change the world by taking to the streets, yelling in our loudest voices, waving our placards, that kinda thing."

"Traditional protest, that's what the free world is based on, isn't it?" Dan rolled his eyes to himself as he said it. He wasn't in the mood for this.

"Yeah, but what you find is that one sucker always wants to take over; always has his or her own agenda, y' know?"

Dan rubbed his forehead and sighed as if he'd heard all this before.

"You mean like that guy at the commune, the reason you went to prison?"

Jacob nodded. "Yeah, like him. Megalomaniacs, they should come with a big danger sign. They're not always easy to spot."

"But some people genuinely want to change the world. I don't see how you can discourage me from wanting to do something that makes a difference."At this, Dan looked at his watch and realised he'd had an hour and a half lunch break. *Still, it makes up for Fi being late*, he thought.

"Look, I really need to be heading back now. Fiona will be pissed off, it's gone half two. Maybe we can meet in a week or so?"

Jacob slowly got up and Dan followed. He reached his hand out to shake Dan's. He hadn't done this before. In fact, it was only now that Dan realised they hadn't really ever touched; just the odd shoulder squeeze.

"Meet you at our usual place then…soon?" the old man said, hopefully.

Dan felt himself recoil from the note of desperation and again he realised that he was possibly the only thing in Jacob's life.

"Yeah, shall we say a week on Thursday? I'll see you there about 1 o'clock."

They shook hands, and Dan turned away. He strode purposefully, their conversation repeating itself in his head. The more he dwelled on it the more irritated he got.

Jacob stood on the grass for a moment, watching him go. He watched the way his legs moved and looked down at his own. He limped off in the opposite direction.

CHAPTER **FIVE**

"WELL, HOW ABOUT IT, Faith? Come on, my treat!"

Judy sat perched on the edge of Faith's couch with a glass in her hand. She was trying to persuade Faith to join her on a trip to France during her half-term break.

Faith smiled and took a sip of her drink.

"Well, I suppose I'm on vacation…"

"Yeah, exactly, and do you really want to spend it planning bloody lessons?"

"I don't *want* to spend it planning lessons, no, but I do actually have to plan lessons so I know – "

"Oh rubbish, Faith, you've been doing it for years. Come on, say 'yes'!" Judy was leaning forward, her free hand clasping Faith's sleeve, looking pleadingly into her eyes.

Faith giggled.

"Okay! God, you're a pain in the ass sometimes."

"I know, and it's holiday not bloody *vacation*," Judy said, before taking several glugs from her glass.

"You English can't speak properly anyhow," Faith retorted, turning her nose up to the sky and away from Judy in mock snobbery. "It's not like you invented the language or anything."

"Oh sod awf," Judy responded in her poshest voice, holding her glass out for a top-up.

Faith couldn't believe she and Judy had known each other for 30 years now. Although Faith had never told her friend this, Judy had just about saved her sanity. Dan had been a baby when they met, and Faith was living on a bit of money from her aunt until she found a job. She knew she had to move on, and that if she didn't take steps she would shrivel inside. When Daniel was asleep she would sit on the couch thinking, worries revolving around in her head. Things from her past formed a vacuum which sucked at her; she would feel short of breath and sick. She would go over them again and again, knowing that she could never change them. Then she'd think about Jacob and the not-knowing, and she would pace around the house angrily, punching a pile of cushions so she didn't wake the baby. The anxiety had spread into her daily life as she found herself alone in a strange place with her most precious possession. She had started to check the locks of the house frequently, and she would find herself staring at the cooker until the off switch didn't mean anything anymore; just a blur of shapes. It had gotten so she'd found it hard to leave the house. One morning, a leaflet had come through the door for yoga classes in the village hall. Faith had called the number immediately and booked a place.

The following week, Faith had made her way through the village with her newly purchased yoga mat under her arm, feeling disproportionately nervous. She had put Daniel to bed and her ancient neighbour Dorothy had come round to watch TV and be there in case he woke up. Faith had felt reckless doing this, but she knew she would go insane if she didn't. Dorothy had been trying to see inside her house since she moved there, but Faith had somehow managed to keep her out. So there it was; she could have a good nosey around if she wanted. Faith didn't care anymore.

She saw a variety of people approaching the hall and

suddenly felt nauseous; what if everyone knew one another and it all went quiet when she entered the room, like the scene from that werewolf film? Or what if she had to sit right at the front? She scolded herself inwardly and told herself to act her age.

As Faith approached, she spotted a woman who looked a bit older than herself, leaning over a garden fence chatting to someone. It was late spring, so still beautifully light in the early evening. As she got closer, the woman turned and gave her a dry smile. She turned back to her companion, said a few words, and turned back towards Faith.

She stuck out her hand and said, "The American!"

Faith took it shyly, and gave it an awkward shake.

"I'm Judy," the woman said, "and *these* – she indicated the other women making their way to the village hall and lowered her voice, "are the *villagers.*"

Faith couldn't help but laugh. Before she knew what was happening, Judy had taken her arm and was marching her in through the wooden door of the tiny hall, where expectant faces turned to look at her. She'd smiled at them, buoyed up by Judy's attention, and a received a few smiles in return. She'd set her mat down next to Judy's near the back and studied her fellow classmates more closely. A few of the women sat close together, having a hushed conversation between the three of them; their own little club within a club. An exclusive club, thought Faith. They were glamorous, even in yoga gear. Even so, one of them smiled faintly at her.

Aside from that little group, there were two rather overweight ladies, who sat together at the front, then Judy and herself. She stole a sideways glance at her new friend. Judy had this wild auburn hair, which she seemed to constantly be pushing down as if it was a separate entity with its own desires. She was wearing some spotty pants and a rather revealing top, which Faith was sure wouldn't stand up to the more stretchy yoga moves. Judy turned to her and gave her another huge smile. Faith smiled back, and it was from a place of relief and gratitude that this woman, whoever she turned out to be, had given her some hope that she might find a companion in this rather insular community.

She looked at Judy now, her hair somewhat tamer but still wild. Judy and Robert had no children and she had never expressed to Faith that this was something either of them regretted. They had bought the dogs instead, she had once told Faith when questioned; two Irish setters called Jason and Casey. Dan had been a toddler when the puppies had arrived. He had pulled on their ears and climbed on their backs, and not once had either dog curled a lip or snapped or even shaken him off. When the black cat from across the road had shown interest in Dan, Jason would curl his lip then, as if to say 'keep your distance'. It was like they knew he was precious, and needed to be looked after, no matter what.

— — —

Fi had called in sick. Quinn had come over the previous night and she had cooked him a meal. It felt strange letting him into the confines of her private world and she had hidden her old teddy and taken down a few of her more ridiculous photographs. She hated herself for doing this but at the same time he made her feel like she needed to be more, somehow. She just wasn't sure how much to show him, just yet. He might run for the hills. She found men often did when she laid her soul bare. And for that matter, sometimes women did too.

There was a sexual chemistry between them that was almost tangible. It fizzled and sparked in the air. As soon as he'd arrived and their lips had touched, she felt herself crumble and she didn't mind. They'd just about managed the first course without tearing each other's clothes off. Fi rubbed her arm as she remembered this. It was still a bit sore where he had gripped her while they were having sex. She shivered when she thought of it again. It was different with him, more intense.

Afterwards though, Quinn had got dressed and said he had to go. No explanation and a quick peck on the cheek. She was bemused and tried to distract her worried thoughts by tidying up the dinner and washing up. She'd done something, maybe? To put him off. Slept with him too quickly, maybe, but actually when she thought about it, he was the one who had instigated that anyway. In his hasty departure, he had made her feel discarded and a bit dirty; like it was okay to come round and shag her then disappear to his other life.

Fi searched in her bedside drawer for some papers and made herself a joint. She had sent a text to Dan saying she still had a really sore throat and felt terrible; how sorry she was but that she would be in tomorrow. She didn't have the guts to call because she knew she wouldn't be able to carry off the lie over the phone. There was nothing for it but to hibernate all day and watch old DVD's. Her friends were all at work and she felt too guilty to go out. She opted for an old eighties classic; as the opening scenes unfolded, she tried to recapture what life had been like before, when she was a child. Before boys and men and booze and drugs and sex, when you could run and jump and scramble and dance, and then sleep until it all began again.

Dan knocked tentatively, he had procrastinated many times about whether or not to come, but curiosity had won in the end. After a short interval, the door was answered by a tall man in a hoodie, about Dan's age, he thought, with feathery brown hair and piercing eyes. He introduced himself as Quinn, giving Dan a firm handshake and slightly crooked smile.

He could hear music playing in the background, Van Morrison? The room reminded him of a smoky jazz bar, like the one in the Fabulous Baker Boys, the way the tables were laid out. It all smelled a little stale and unclean. A few men and two women sat over two tables in the far right-hand corner, engaged in conversation. Dan's stomach lurched slightly, in shyness more than anything, or perhaps anticipation of becoming a part of something and no longer his own entity within his own, somewhat dull but safe, orbit.

"Come and meet everyone, we're a small group at the moment but we're hoping that will change once word gets out," said Quinn, gently guiding Dan over to the occupied tables.

"Sure, um, is it okay to get a drink?"

"Oh yeah, of course. Follow me," Quinn headed off to the small bar in the corner, went round to the serving side and spread out his hands.

"What can I get you? We've got…"

He turned his head behind him to look.

"Just a shandy, if that's okay, mate?"

"Sure thing, partner," Quinn replied, cocking an invisible

cowboy hat at Dan and calling the bar man over. He was a bit odd, Dan thought, but he liked him. There was something friendly about him but also closed; like it would take a while to get to know him but he'd be an interesting person to know.

They walked over to the others, and Dan sat himself down in one of the chairs. He noticed the conversation soften and then stop altogether when Quinn had settled himself in a chair too. Quinn put his hands together between his knees and moved them up to his face, looking around at everyone; Dan found this gesture really familiar but he couldn't think why.

"Guys…it's wonderful to have you all here. Some old faces, one new one. This is Dan, everybody."

Dan raised his glass in a 'cheers' to the small group, who nodded, grunted or smiled at him in greeting. One of the women ignored him; she was staring somewhere into the middle distance, and twisting a loose thread from her jeans around her finger. The other woman gave him a shy smile.

You are not here to meet women, Daniel's inner voice reminded him. *Focus, man.*

All the same, he felt a thrill at doing something he wouldn't normally do. Here were people who didn't know him from before; he could be whoever he wanted. He could do something that mattered.

As he tuned back into the meeting, he realised the tone of Quinn's voice had become serious and the man next to him leaned forward to rest his head on his hands, looking engrossed and like it was important.

"This world has got to change," said Quinn. "I can't watch any more people trudge through their lives, ignoring each other, bottling up their feelings, talking shit and worshipping at the church of Westfield every Sunday," and he made money signs with his hands, rubbing his fingers together and miming an exchange of goods in mock prayer.

Dan smiled and then, noticing the others' serious expressions, turned his mouth into a more acceptable shape. He was funny though, this guy.

Quinn went on, lowering his voice, "We need waking up, we need a short, sharp shock, we need to realise how lucky we are, we need to thank the sun in the morning for rising and thank it again for setting,"

He looked around at the group.

"*We* need to make a difference."

He smiled, breaking the tension. Dan wondered whether to clap but thought better of it. "I'm really pleased to hand you over, now, to Simon," said Quinn, gently. "He has an idea about something we can do via email to start the process in people's own homes."

Quinn walked over to the man sat on Dan's left, patted him on the back, and Simon walked up to the table and launched straight into a heated tirade about the internet and how 'we' could use email spam to spread the word that the internet was evil. Dan thought that seemed a little contradictory, but he held his tongue. After all, he didn't want to piss anyone off at the first meeting. He chose, instead, to inspect his colleagues of the People of the Sun more closely. They weren't all that sunny, it had to be said.

Simon, at this moment centre-stage, had spiky hair, made so by a huge amount of gel, Dan surmised, and he wore thick black Buddy Holly style glasses. He did that thing that some Shakespearean actors do, when they are delivering a passionate speech; salivate too much sending forth globules of spittle across the stage, like a precious gift to the audience in the front row.

Thread girl was chewing gum now, her knee juddering. She had blonde hair in pigtails, combats on and a small rucksack at her feet. It was as though she had adopted a style at university and had never grown out of it. It did kind of suit her though; she seemed untouchable, like an unexploded bomb.

The other girl was a bit younger and altogether softer. She caught him looking her way and gave him a friendly smile, her slightly gapped teeth gave her an urchin demeanour but she was dressed smartly.

He smiled back and casually looked away. The other two guys appeared engrossed in Simon's speech. One of the guys had a suit on, with the jacket draped over his shoulder. He was Asian and had an impressive beard, which Dan briefly coveted and without realising he was doing it, he rubbed his own chin.

The other man looked slightly uncomfortable in his own skin. He was a little hunched over, and had that shy demeanour which often develops in people who've been bullied as children. He seemed as though he was doing his best to blend into the background.

Dan wondered, if you believed something hard enough, did it actually happen? He remembered Fi telling him about how, as an overweight teenager on her first few nights out with friends, she would say to herself over and over in her head, 'I am beautiful, I am beautiful'. Sometimes she managed to pull at the end of the night, she said. Fi being Fi, she put this down to her self-motivational speeches. Dan couldn't say what he wanted to say about it as he thought she would misunderstand. It made him sad to think of her having clumsy snogs with twatty locals.

Simon's speech seemed to be coming to a close. A few people, Quinn included, nodded emphatically and he ushered Simon back to his seat.

"Guys, if you want to stay and talk politics, world peace, or anything else you feel fired up about, feel free." He started to put his coat on. "I'm really sorry but I have to be somewhere in half an hour, so this time I'll take a rain check if that's okay?"

He looked over to where Dan was sitting. "It was great to meet you, Dan. Stay, have a drink, make merry. I'll see you next time?"

"Yeah...hopefully yeah," he replied, giving a half wave, his mind going over the pro's and con's of joining this eccentric group and whether to order a drink and attempt to infiltrate the closed ranks via the medium of alcohol.

He decided he would. On his way to the bar, he saw that the girl with pigtails was ordering a drink. She did not turn to look at him when he approached so he decided that was normal and stood as nonchalantly as he could. She was drumming her fingers on the bar impatiently. Dan cleared his throat and saw the edge of her eyes flicker but still she showed no sign of acknowledging his presence. Her drink arrived and once she had handed over her money, the exact change, she ducked out of his way and headed off to the small group who had stayed behind. *This is going to be more difficult than I thought,* mused Dan as again he toyed with the idea of going home. He had that funny feeling of panic he remembered having at school when one day he knew he was no longer part of the cool crew. *You're a grown up,* he told himself, and smiled at the absurdity of it all. He ordered a drink and planned a few opening gambits with which to start up a conversation with these strangers in an attempt to find common ground. Recent news stories wound their way through his mind. He felt sure they would be keen to discuss the latest oil spill or the plight of the bumblebees. As he approached, it looked as though the blonde girl had said something funny, although she wasn't smiling. A couple of the men were laughing and one of them patted her leg – she gave him a scowl and moved it. He pulled up a chair.

"Mind if I join you, guys?" He felt stupid, and awkward. *Ride with it, Dan. Don't let them smell your fear.*

The suited man moved his chair around to accommodate him and just like that, Dan was in. He listened attentively to their discussions and smiled politely at their in-jokes, which of course meant nothing to him. He tried to learn their names as they talked about each other. He'd read that you were much more likely to be successful in life if you were good at remembering people's names. He'd noticed politicians doing it in question and answer sessions. To his amusement, the subject of bumblebees actually did come up but he kept quiet. Suddenly, out of the blue, thread girl asked him a question.

"What do you do?" She had a permanently aggressive stance but the others seemed at ease in her presence.

"I er…work in a bookshop, actually."

"Mmm," she nodded. The shy man who hadn't spoken at all and who Dan hadn't paid any attention to, suddenly piped up:

"Do you stock speciality books or just mainstream releases?"

He sounded genuinely interested and waited for Dan's reply.

"Well, " he began, "a bit of both really – our owner has a bit of a thing about factual books but accepts that not everyone does so he's bowed to the market and let us stock a selection of new releases and the usual stuff, you know – "

Another man began talking over Dan. He realised he wasn't being interesting enough to hold the full group's attention and felt slightly rejected. Shy man was still listening, so he leant forward in order that they could carry on their conversation, which they did.

It turned out he was called Jerry and he delivered local papers, freebies, most of which he said went straight into the recycling, which he admitted did not lead to a great level of job satisfaction. He smiled when Dan told him about a recent delivery of trashy novels which he and Fi had tried to market as 'nostalgic romance', and which after several months had been used in the shop as doorstops, table balancers and eventually given to the local old people's home to make room for new stock.

They swapped numbers, although Dan felt slightly weird about doing this, like he was too old for it, for making new friends. *But,* he reminded himself, *this is all about trying something new.* He was meeting Jacob the following week and was wondering what to tell him. He knew he was pretty rubbish at lying, but at the same time, he wasn't up for defending his actions to someone who he barely knew. *Give the man a chance,* he thought, berating himself. He just wished he could talk to Faith about it all, but was thankful for Fi's opinion on the situation. And, he had to admit, she was right in saying that it was probably easier now they were both adults than if Jacob had turned up when he was little or even a teenager; more of a level pegging. All the same, he struggled to see any similarities between them, felt very little common ground. Fi had said she could see a resemblance but Dan himself could not. They both smoked and liked Pink Floyd, after that, he seemed to be drawing a blank. It was strange to suddenly have a father who he didn't know. Would he ever feel anything like love for this man? How does love evolve between parents, when they haven't been around to see you kick your first football, support you through a bad time, patch up your bleeding knee when you've fallen, or offer advice when you like a girl and want to ask her out. Even his mum had managed that, although Dan remembered wanting the ground to swallow him up at the time. And what if, after all this, Jacob turned out to be an imposter? But Dan couldn't understand why anybody would do that and, whatever his faults, the man did seem genuine. Still, not being able to speak to his mum about it bothered him. He felt sure it would come out sometime, by accident. She would be devastated. Dan put the thought out of his mind.

— — —

It was a Saturday, and Fi's 28th birthday. Despite the usual harassment from her friend Kate about it being criminal not to celebrate, she had thus far managed to fend off organised fun. Still, she wanted to do *something*. She lay in bed thinking about how to spend her day. Not really knowing what protocol was in the first place, let alone with a free spirit like Quinn, she had dropped into the conversation last time she saw him that she was going to be 28 soon. Looking back now, she realised it hadn't been that subtle. He had never told her how old he was. He had a chiselled face, decorated with corners and crevices that made his eyes crinkle when he smiled. She suspected he was at least a few years older than her, not that it mattered. She wondered if it was normal not to know things like that after nearly two months. And yet, this was far from normal. She and Quinn didn't do small talk. There was always a reason to have a conversation; you couldn't seem to meander around a topic. Plus, she had noticed, he always expected her to have an opinion. She felt like a slight let down if she said that something didn't really bother her, or that she hadn't given it much thought; as if that disappointed him, somehow.

She decided she had to get up and do something, anything, so she got out of bed and headed to the kitchen to make herself a massive fry up for breakfast. While things were cooking, her phone rang. It was her mother. She took a deep breath before answering.

"Mum! Hi," she said, breathing out during the greeting.

"Darling, happy birthday. Are you out of breath?"

"No," Fi replied. "No, sorry. How are you?"

"Oh fine, you know, the usual. Your father's not here to speak to you because he's playing golf again, honestly, that man..."

Fi held her tongue.

"What did you want then, Mum?"

"To say 'happy birthday' of course," her mother answered, in a clipped tone. "I'm surprised you're even up. Are you doing anything to celebrate?"

"Well, I'm not sure. Kate wants me to go out to see a band

that's playing in one of the local pubs but I don't think I'm in the mood..."

"Kate?" her mother echoed. "Who's she?"

Fi felt the frustration she inevitably felt whilst on the phone to her mother begin to surface.

"Mum, Kate is one of my best friends here. I've mentioned her a million times."

"Oh have you? Not a million, don't exaggerate darling, it's silly."

"Mother – " Fi could feel her temper about to blow, but her mum cut her off.

"Well, whatever you decide, I hope you have a good time. It's a shame you don't have a man to wine and dine you. Oh well..." Her mother's voice trailed off, and Fi was silent for a moment.

"Right, well, bye mum. "

"Oh," her mother said quietly. "You're going? Oh. Well, happy birthday and...I'll call you again soon."

"Okay," Fi said, and hung up. *Don't bother*, she thought bitterly, and without being able to stop herself, she hurled her phone at the wall. The back came off and the battery flew out. She walked over to the breakfast bar and rested her hands on it, making them into fists, letting out a sound of frustration and anger which came from somewhere deep within. After several minutes, she gathered herself together. Walking over to where her phone had landed, she picked up the various parts of it and put them back together. *Nokias*, she thought. *Marvellous things.* It was not the first time she had thrown her phone against the wall, although usually it was because she couldn't get the damn battery out. She switched it on and waited for her Contacts folder to register. Once it had come to life, Fi wrote a text to Kate: *We're on for tonight, what time do you want to meet and where?* She pressed 'send' and then went off in search of her favourite nail polish.

A few hours later, and after several changes of outfit, she opened a bottle of wine and poured herself a glass. Dan had sent her a birthday text and she remembered he had given her the latest Massive Attack CD as an early birthday present at work that Friday. She found it in her handbag and put it on the stereo, took a sip of her wine and lit up a cigarette. At the corner of her mind, something bothered her, but she didn't want to acknowledge it. She shut her eyes and tried to drown herself in the music; distract herself by thinking about the band she was going to see. There it was again, like an itch. Quinn. She had heard nothing from him.

— — —

The sun on her face felt like warm hands holding her cheeks, and Faith shut her eyes and leaned back in the recliner. She was round at Judy's, lounging on her friend's deck. It was a real sun trap. She put her glass down on the floor beside her and stretched out. Judy had gone inside to fix them some snacks and Robert was mowing the lawn at the bottom of their large garden. She heard the lull of the mower, distant enough to merge into other sounds, such as the gentle tinkling of the wind chimes she had bought for Judy on her last trip away, and the trickle of the water feature, which filled in the gaps when Robert emptied the grass out. The brightness of the sun made little dots appear, which she followed with her eyes along her eyelids. *Like chasing little bugs*, she thought, *you could never catch them.*

Her mind went back to her day at school; she had shouted, really shouted, at a boy. He had been pushing and shoving another boy, quiet and withdrawn. She had lost her temper. What had made her so sad afterwards was that this quiet unassuming child had just let the bigger boy push him around, like he was used to it, like he deserved it. She had said to the bigger one, "I've had enough of you!" at the top of her voice. It wasn't the right thing to say to a child. She scolded herself, now, for her loss of control.

Judy came out and her shape cast a shadow in Faith's closed eyes. She opened them and took a few olives from the bowl in front of her. Judy placed them down between them and sat back on her chair, pulling her sunglasses down over her eyes once more. She was looking at Robert and grinning.

"What?" Faith asked her.

"Oh," she said, turning, almost startled, as if she had been doing it unconsciously. "Nothing, really. I was just thinking that I'm…well, lucky. I know I complain about him but really he's a marvel, you know."

Faith laughed. "Don't all wives complain about their husbands and vice versa? I know you guys treasure each other, everyone can tell."

Judy smiled, pleased with Faith's observation.

"The thing is," she continued, popping another olive into her mouth, "when you don't have children, I think you fill that gap with each other." She took the stone out of her mouth and threw it into the hedge nearby. It fell about a foot short.

"Don't let Robert see you do that," Faith said, "it might clog up his lawnmower."

They laughed.

"I've felt lucky to have you too, Faith, and to be able to watch Dan grow up. Rob has too, you know, even thought he'd never say it."

"Actually he did say something to me once, about Dan. I thought it was kind of heartfelt."

Judy lifted up her sunglasses and looked at her friend. "Did he?" she asked.

"Yeah," Faith reached out for her drink. "He said he thought Dan would make a fine man, that he would be proud if he had a son like that." She swilled her drink round to melt the ice a little more. "I was quite touched."

Judy smiled. "I didn't know he said that." She sighed. "What a nice thing to say."

They both leaned back and shut their eyes, in a comfortable silence.

"How is Daniel?" Judy asked.

"He's okay, I think. Happy at the shop. He has a friend called Fiona..."

"Ooh, tell me more," Judy said, turning to look at her again.

"He says she's just a friend," said Faith, laughing. "Jeez, you're as bad as me!"

"What, you think it could be more than that?"

"I don't know. She came round to the house with him for his birthday meal. You know, she reminded me a little of myself when I was younger. I guess we kind of monopolised the conversation, the two of us. To be honest, Dan was pretty quiet."

"Hmm," Judy said, thinking. "Maybe he just found you two women too much. Men do, you know, find us overpowering sometimes when we get together."

Faith giggled. "Sure, maybe it's just that."

She thought about Dan and tried to piece together his mood the last time they had seen each other. Thinking of him now, she realised he didn't give her many details of his life. She had assumed that this was a male thing, but now she began to wonder if he was actually as happy as he claimed to be. *Or did he even claim to be happy? Was he just 'okay'? There's a difference.* She reached out for another olive and put it in her mouth, the bitter waxy salt taste coating her tongue. She would try and talk to him soon, about his life, about everything or whatever he wanted to talk about.

"Do you ever think about his father?" Judy said dreamily, as if she was half asleep.

"Mmm," Faith said, and then did not elaborate. After a moment, she shut her eyes. "I do think about Jacob," she said. "I wonder what he would think of me."

Judy didn't respond, and Faith turned and saw that her friend's mouth was slightly open and her breathing had slowed. She sat up and crossed her legs in front of her. Looking down at her hands she wondered where the time went. How did Dan get to be an adult? It had happened so quickly. When did she become middle-aged? She twirled her serpent ring around her finger and noticed her knuckle was swollen. Her mother had had this thing called a ganglion, like a lump on your finger. She had said you had to bang it with a bible and that would cure it. *Crazy,* thought Faith, smiling at the idea. At the bottom of the garden, she noticed Robert had switched off the mower and was putting it away in the shed. The lawn looked striped, the different greens laying there together side by side, in perfect symbiosis.

CHAPTER **SIX**

FAITH OPENED THE SHUTTERS of the small chambre d'hôte where she and Dan were staying. As she did so, she breathed in a faint smell of tobacco wafting up from the old men seated below, which mingled with the smell of freshly baked baguettes. Only in France did bread seem to smell like this, and she wondered why that was so.

They had driven from Calais the previous day. On the ferry, Dan had seemed withdrawn and Faith had wondered just how much fun this trip would actually be. He didn't seem to want to communicate with her anymore, and she had run out of strategies to bridge the distance he seemed to have built up between them. She felt like they needed to talk, *really* talk, and she wanted to know what his life was like. She wondered if he still did drugs or if he'd moved on from that, but she knew if she broached the subject he would deny it.

The atmosphere had been strained in the car on the way here, when she'd put on her Joni Mitchell CD and started to sing, expecting him to join in. She had had that feeling of escape and freedom that she hadn't felt in a long time. It hinted at times past with Jacob, when they used to hop on the bus out of town and stay on it until they got kicked off, sometimes late at night. They would either find a place to make camp or get a cheap motel room, giddy with the not knowing, drunk on the spirit of adventure.

It was a long time ago, Faith reminded herself. She tried

to blanket the anxiety which began to form at the pit of her stomach before it sparked, taking a deep breath of the French air and revelling in the warm sun on her cheeks. Dan had driven along the main highway from Calais while she looked at her travel guide and worked out where might be interesting to visit. Dan had said he was exhausted so they'd decided to stop somewhere after three hours, if not before. She'd read a little bit about Peronne and so decided they should head there.

A few doors down, Dan was lying awake in bed, thinking. He wasn't entirely sure, now, why he had agreed on this trip with his mum. He wondered if she was trying to find out about his life and was thinking of how he could avoid questions when they were at such close proximity. It wasn't that they didn't share things, but it was all kept to a level, like there were things hidden and not to be discussed. At the same time, he felt like shit about the Jacob situation. Jacob had expressly forbidden Dan to discuss their meetings with his mother, saying it would 'hurt her too much'. His mum had always been tight-lipped when he'd asked about his dad. Having said that, Jacob wasn't one for giving details himself. Faith had said he was a good man, and before he'd turned up in the bookshop that day, Dan already knew he had been drafted to Vietnam and obviously hadn't come home. Once, when he was little, he'd found some photographs in a box under her bed. He'd looked through, excited that he might find something of his father in there; there were a few of him as a little boy, and one of his mum, about 6 or 7 years old, holding hands with a middle aged lady with curly hair, who wore one of those housecoats he remembered his grandma having. There was another photo he particularly remembered;

of his mother, about 19 or 20, laughing and semi-collapsed on another girl's lap. In the background there was a guy standing at the record player, with an LP in his hand. You couldn't see his face properly, but Dan had always wondered if that was him – Jacob. His mum had looked so young, and so care-free. Faith had gone mad when she'd found him there, with these pictures spread out on his lap. He hadn't understood and was so scared that he hid under the bed until she reassured him enough that she wasn't cross anymore.

Dan sat up in bed and reached for his tobacco tin, wondering where he could get hold of 'un café' without having to walk too far. He had slept in his clothes after finishing a bottle of wine by himself. His heart felt heavy, and he felt a surge of resentment towards his mother for bringing him here. She hadn't pressured him, so to speak, but her friend Judy had to drop out at the last minute and they had two ferry tickets booked. He knew he was being an arsehole but still he couldn't shake the feeling. At that moment, there was a quiet knock at the door and he heard his mum's voice say, "Are you awake, hun?" He glanced at his wristwatch and saw it was just after nine, and he decided to say nothing.

Outside the door, Faith sighed and held her hand up to knock again but changed her mind at the last minute. *He might be asleep,* she thought, although she'd heard him moving about. Whatever he was going through, she guessed he needed to do it on his own. She checked she had her French phrasebook in her bag and decided to venture out to find breakfast. *He's an adult,* she told herself as she pushed open the small door at the bottom of the stairs and walked into the little courtyard that led onto the street outside. She had put her headscarf on and her big Audrey Hepburn sunglasses and she pretended, as she opened the gate, that she was a different woman, a French woman, who didn't care what people thought, who had poise and who lived for the moment. Yes, that's what she would be today. She walked with a spring in her step, saying a light and breezy 'Bonjour' to the two old men, who mumbled a gruff greeting back.

The morning had turned from misty to hazy and the sun began to penetrate through the half-open shutters so that Dan took off his hoodie and shut his eyes, letting the growing warmth stroke his skin. His thoughts drifted aimlessly from past to present to future and back again, choosing not to rest on one particular point. He thought about Fi and wondered how she was getting on at the shop; what would she be doing just that moment – drinking a coffee maybe. That made him remember he was going to find one for himself.

He pushed the covers off and set the ashtray down on the bedside table. Everything in this room was small, petite, so that he nearly knocked off the remnants of his glass of wine from the previous night. There was a doll dressed in lace, sitting in a chair in the corner of the room, looking at him. He resolved to put it in the dresser. Everything was very French, and he chastised himself for being so ungrateful about the holiday. *Make the most of it,* he told himself, *you miserable arse.* Thinking it would shake him out of his mood, he had a shave in the dinted mirror in the tiny bathroom. He had to bend down to see what he was doing. He felt sure that Judy wouldn't have approved of this place. Judy liked the finer things in life. Dan remembered that, whenever he was round at her house when he was little, she would treat him to a Tizer from her soda stream. He remembered being so impressed but also thinking that he would prefer it if she had one of those Mr Frosty slushy makers instead. He'd mentioned it to his mum and she had laughed and said sorry they couldn't afford those types of things, but maybe don't say that to Judy or she might think he was an ungrateful kid. There was that word again. *Come on, Dan, snap out of it.* He grinned at himself in the mirror. Fi would've said to him: *Life's just a reflection of how you feel.* He didn't know where she got all these pearls, as she laughingly called them, but they had the tendency to pop into his head and make him smile. He had a shower and scrubbed off his lethargy, determined now to make the best of this time away. He went down the hall to her room and knocked but no-one answered. Peronne seemed like a small place so he decided he would probably find her if he headed into the town centre on the hunt for caffeine.

The true warmth of the weather hit him when he left the little chambre d'hote and walked across the courtyard towards the centre-ville. Immediately, he felt his mood lift with the sensation of sun on skin. He walked past some unremarkable modern houses and realised he didn't know much about where they were staying or if there was anything worth a look. As he approached the centre, the road suddenly opened out into a neat square, encircled with shops, one restaurant and two tabacs. He tried to follow his mum's train of thought and spotted a boulangerie. That's where she would be, and they might even do coffee too. There was a woman seated outside with huge sunglasses on and as he approached, he realised it was Faith, and that she was smoking. As she saw him, she hastily stubbed the cigarette out and took off her glasses.

"Hey, sleepy, so you found me!" Faith said, looking a little flustered. Dan pulled out the chair and peeked into the shop to check on the drinks situation.

"I'm liking the new look, mum. I didn't think you fagged it anymore, though?"

Faith frowned. "I don't…well, I guess I do when I'm on vacation. It makes me feel like I'm – " She paused, searching for the right word.

"Relaxing?" Dan offered.

"Well, I think I was going to say young again but relaxing sounds better."

Dan grinned and took out his rolling tin. "So, you won't mind if I…?"

Faith shrugged: "No, no, go ahead."

Dan made a roll up and Faith went in and ordered them both a coffee and a croissant each. He could hear her trying her best at French but it was like her American accent came out even more when she attempted a foreign language. Dan wondered if French spoken with an English or even a US accent sounded as attractive as English with a French lilt and then decided actually it was highly unlikely.

They sat and ate their breakfast in peaceful silence. Around them the town was slowly waking up. An older couple sat outside one of the tabacs, sipping some purple liquid, some local drink, Dan supposed. He passed a croissant to his mum and they ate, ripping the soft pastry and smearing it with butter.

A dog tied to a post across the square began a furious barking session, upon which a frumpy looking lady came out from the building behind it, scolded it in angry French and picked it up by the legs, swinging it over her shoulder like a bag. Faith and Dan looked at each other with raised eyebrows.

"I guess they don't have the same attitude to dogs over here," Faith said quietly.

"I dunno," Dan replied, swallowing his mouthful. "We're not in China, they don't eat them."

"They eat horse," his mum replied, not looking at him. He waited for her to laugh but she didn't.

"Snails too," he offered, after a moment. Faith screwed up her face, and waved her remaining croissant at him as if to say, *not now*.

"What's the weirdest thing you've eaten?" Dan asked.

"Really?" She put down her breakfast. "What a totally bizarre question," Faith said, but she began to ponder it.

"I ate octopus once, maybe that's not so weird, but the suckers got stuck on your tongue. It was kind of chewy but nice. And you?"

Dan could only think of kangaroo burger, but then his mum reminded him of when he tried to eat a crab alive.

"It was so pissed at you, it kept pinching the inside of your cheek until finally you spat it out," Faith burst out laughing now. "You just didn't get it; I had to wash your mouth out with antiseptic mouthwash for a week!"

"God, what was the matter with me?" Dan asked, frowning. "What an idiot child."

"No hun, no, you just liked putting things in your mouth. Don't worry angel, you were a clever little boy." Faith grabbed his cheeks and squeezed them and he backed away in mock disgust.

"Urgh, get off mum!"

They both laughed and then sat quietly again, Dan wolfing down the last bite of his food and then taking a sip of his coffee.

A couple of hours later, once they had gone back to their rooms to get sun cream for Dan, on his mother's insistence, they found themselves wandering past the boulangerie once more, and Faith spotted a fort-like building with a big billboard outside. As they got closer, they saw that it showed an advertisement for a World War I exhibition dedicated to the British soldiers who fought in the Battle of the Somme. The room they entered was large but unassuming, and there was no-one there to direct you to this or that exhibit. Faith was pleased. She liked to wander these sorts of spaces at will. They split off in opposite directions. At an interval of a metre or so was a glass cabinet, and inside each, a photograph of a different young man. Underneath, on red velvet and preserved as precious as jewels, were objects; a letter, a lucky key chain or ribbon, a photograph of a sweetheart or sometimes a mother, serious-faced, as if the picture had been taken after she had lost her son and not before; as if she had known what was to come. *So many sons lost, lives wasted,* thought Faith, as she looked. The letters were usually light-hearted; talking of friends and camaraderie, and how they'd given 'Fritz' a good beating as if it was one big bully they'd met on the playground, and some of the men not being much older than school-leaving age, it made Dan wonder if that was how they coped with it all. And always at the end a glimpse of sadness and of hope that they would see their loved ones again, like there was just a smattering of sentimentality allowed; and yet, as an observer, the knowledge that none of these men ever did make it home.

At a point, Dan felt saturated with a feeling of heaviness, a pall which dragged him down; a wave of hopelessness at what had taken place on this soil underneath his feet. His knowledge of France was limited; he hadn't realised they were so near to the infamous battleground. He wondered if his mum had known and remembered her reading her guidebook before suggesting they visit this seemingly insignificant little town.

He glanced around for Faith but could not see her amidst the glass cases so he looked around a little more. She wasn't in the room anymore, and this shouldn't have made him feel anxious but for some reason it did. It was like a pins and needles feeling in his chest, as if he'd imagined her being there, and as if he too was suddenly standing at the front of a battle, facing its horrors alone. He walked briskly out and looked around; it seemed strange to be out again, transported as he had been, back to into the memories of these young men, long gone. Now he found himself back in the clean, light and airy foyer, returned from a trip through time. Then he spotted Faith just outside. She had sparked up a cigarette and was leaning against the outer wall. She was holding a hankie in her other hand. As he came through the door, she turned quickly and smiled at him, but he could tell it was with effort.

"Maybe it wasn't such a good idea to come here?" he ventured, feeling awkward and unsure whether to give her a hug or gloss over her tears to save her from embarrassment. He put his arm around her shoulders. "That was really moving, wasn't it?"

She nodded. He knew what he wanted to ask, but wasn't sure if he should. After a moment, he said, "Did it remind you of…my dad?"

She didn't respond for a few seconds, and then she nodded again.

"It's just so god damn pointless isn't it? War. I get it, that sometimes powerful people have an idea they can take over the world and persecute people who are different. They need to be stopped. But you know, in the end, the scars it leaves. They can't ever heal, can they?"

"What happened to him?" Dan had never asked her so directly and he immediately regretted it. Her face became closed, defensive.

Staring into the middle distance, she said "I told you, he never came home. He was Missing in Action." He waited for her to continue although inside he felt the frustration towards her build. Why wouldn't she just be honest? Did he dare ask her about afterwards? He tried to form his words carefully.

"Did you ever think he was…alive? That he might, you know, come and find us?"

Her face screwed up as if she was about to break into tears and Dan felt panic as he realised he couldn't handle his mother properly breaking down in front of him. She was always so together. He almost cringed inside, repelled by her uncharacteristic show of weakness.

She pulled it together although her voice wobbled when she replied.

"They knew he'd been badly injured. There was…evidence. Plus they looked for him. I'm sorry, Dan."

"What for?"

"Just the way things turned out. I've done my best."

He felt a sudden surge of empathy. "Yeah, I know." He reached out to squeeze her arm. "It's not your fault, anyway."

She was quiet, and turned away to put her handkerchief back in her handbag. She took a breath, as if to begin again.

"Let's go find some lunch," she said decisively, taking his arm. They wandered back to the centre ville, saying nothing, their thoughts, unbeknownst to each other, mingling with surprising similarity and yet tinged with secrets held close and embedded within the walls of their different hearts.

— — —

They only stayed in Peronne for two more days. There was not so much to see after the exhibition. Although they planned to visit the sight of the Battle of the Somme, Faith backed out at the last minute, so they pin pointed a couple of places they could just about manage to squeeze in over the week before they headed home from Calais.

In Epernay, Dan bought a postcard for Fiona and filled it with subverted clichés about France, which he hoped would make her laugh. She hadn't texted him so he assumed the shop was okay and that she didn't have any other exciting news. He bought some champagne to take back, and some obligatory local cheese. His mum entertained herself at the artisan market, practicing her French and haggling over a scarf or bag. They wound their way across and up the country, calling at Carnac so Faith could wander about the standing stones, soaking up their energy, she said. They had almost reached something, a point of no return at the museum in Peronne, but since then, it was as though both had retreated into what they knew best: the silence of history, that strange human desire to keep our essence concealed, even sometimes from those we love the most.

A few weeks later, Dan received a text from an unknown number asking if he was going to meet that night. He wracked his brains until he finally realised it must be Jerry from the People of the Sun group. They had swapped numbers, but Dan mustn't have saved it in his phone. He hoped he was right and sent a message back saying, *Hi Jerry, yes I'll be there, same time same place?* Jerry replied in the affirmative. It felt funny having a new 'friend'.

Fi's moods had been somewhat unpredictable since he'd returned from France. He asked her about it; if it was some idiot guy messing her around or even problems with her parents but she just avoided his questions, blaming hormones, the weather, even the phase of the moon, until he'd given up asking. He had told her about his trip but had found that, when she had said something like, "I bet you and your mum managed to talk loads," it had made him feel irrationally annoyed, so he'd stopped. When Fi talked about his mum, it was as if they shared something, a connection, which he could only observe. When she had gone with him to Faith's for dinner some months ago, they had suddenly become as thick as thieves. It was like that thing that girls do, when they really like each other and are a bit pissed, they just…giggle and whisper and seemingly revert back to primary school behaviour. He had never seen his mother like that, even with Judy. Dan hadn't taken much notice at the time but now, when he considered it, he had felt a little bit like the court jester. The two women had laughed at old photographs of him, and a couple of times when Dan had gone into the kitchen to fetch more wine, he had walked in on them sharing what he thought were relationship stories, their voices fading upon his entering the room.

Did Fi know more about his mum's past then even *he* did? He knew that they had texted one another every so often since, but up until now had presumed it was just about shared interests. Were they sharing more than that? Had Faith told Fiona her version of their trip to France, and if so, what was to tell? She wasn't even his bloody girlfriend!

He left work that day with the beginnings of a headache. To make it worse, the weather had turned cold and the first drops of a massive downpour fell when he was still about half a mile from the Fu Bar, which was where the group had their fortnightly meeting. He arrived soaked, and feeling sorry for himself. He was debating whether to just duck into the bar next door, text Tipper and write the evening off in a haze of alcohol when a familiar voice said from behind him, "Hey man, you came back, glad to see you," Quinn put his arm around Dan's shoulders in the manner of an old friend. He was weird, but somehow Dan couldn't help but like him.

As Dan entered, a few faces turned towards him and he recognised some from the first meeting. He waved by way of greeting, then sought out Jerry, who was standing at the bar. When Dan approached Jerry asked him quietly what he wanted and ordered him a drink too. They leaned against the bar, not talking, until Dan felt the need to fill the silence.

"So, what have I missed?" he asked Jerry.

"Since you last came? Well, let me think." He paused. Dan liked the way Jerry didn't rush what he was going to say. He thought that an admirable trait. He knew he was guilty himself of talking shit just to fill the gaps.

"We had an interesting talk last time, from Mo, the chap sitting over in the corner?" Dan recognised the Asian guy he'd seen at the first meeting.

"He was talking about discrimination in business, hidden pay caps, demeaning language, that sort of thing. Then I think the time before it was a good old-fashioned rant from Ella."

Dan looked blank, so Jerry indicated by lifting his glass in the direction of the waif-like girl with blonde pigtails. She was of indeterminate age, and today was wearing some rather fetching laddered stockings, doc martens and a paisley dress.

"She's a proper anarchist," Jerry said. Dan started to laugh, thinking he was joking but when he glanced at the Jerry's face he saw he wasn't. He caught the laughter in his throat before any more escaped.

"Anyhow," Jerry continued, "You've chosen the right meeting to come to. Quinn's talking tonight."

Quinn was standing centrally and setting up a mike. There hadn't been any microphone at the first meeting Dan had attended but then, he noticed, there were about three times as many more people this evening and a different kind of buzz around the room.

He and Jerry went over to grab a seat. There weren't two together and Dan found himself sitting next to Ella. He wondered if anarchism was a natural turn-off for most men but, as he caught a glimpse of her thigh, found perhaps it was not for him. She wasn't exactly pretty, but there was something edgy about her which he found attractive. He wondered if she and Quinn had ever shagged, and suspected that they had. Maybe they were even together. *Best not go there,* he thought.

Quinn cleared his throat and the room went quiet.

"People! It's great to see you." A few of the audience clapped, which made Dan cringe slightly. He felt like he was in an AA meeting in America. Why clap someone just for saying hello?

"Oh no, please," said Quinn. "Wait until I've said something you like – then feel free to applaud!" Some people chuckled at this. "I'll get straight to it, guys. Before I do though, I'm glad to see some new faces tonight and to welcome back some old ones too. Dan," he nodded, and Dan raised his glass, slightly embarrassed, "glad you could join us."

Dan was aware suddenly of Ella scowling at him though the corner of his eye but he didn't meet her gaze.

Quinn's talk was about political action. It was interesting, and he was a born public speaker. Dan thought he must've watched videos on how to gesticulate to make a point; when to smile, that sort of thing, only unlike Tony Blair, when Quinn smiled you actually believed it.

He talked about Gandhi and the power of non-action, but that he believed that this no longer fitted with the pace of society and that a different approach was needed; an aggressive one. He believed in effective protest and the power of shouting the loudest, emphasising the importance of a clear and unified message. He mentioned, briefly, acts of protest which involved breaking the law and said this was sometimes the only way.

His speech was radical, and yet Dan felt excited by it. Quinn was right – why should we follow the rules set for us by those privileged few? He said that vandalism was just art from the heart. He was full of sound bites like that, but they stuck in your head. He took questions at the end, and several hands were raised.

"How do you feel about violence in protest?" asked one newcomer, a woman, who Dan had seen standing with what looked like her partner before the meeting began. He was now sat next to her.

"To me," Quinn said in a measured way, "violence is another way of expressing your anger. If you feel something, do it, within reason of course." He winked. "Hey, when things get violent or out of control on a march, it guarantees news coverage. Doesn't that mean it helps your cause?"

"But what about people getting hurt?" the woman continued. "Surely you don't condone that? Doesn't it give you a bad press, as a protestor?"

Quinn smiled at her. "Kathy, right?"

She blushed slightly and her expression softened as she nodded.

"There is only one thing in life worse than being talked about, and that is not being talked about. Oscar Wilde. It's what I live by but hey, no need to agree if you don't want to. I won't force you. Unless you want me to." He winked at her again and held her gaze for a few seconds. She looked away, embarrassed, and Dan noticed her partner reach out and put his hand on her back. She looked around at him and he removed it. There was a hush in the room for a moment, and Dan looked around hoping to catch someone's eye to share his surprise, but no-one looked.

After a couple more questions, Quinn dispensed with formalities and headed over to get himself a drink. He was followed by several people. He left in his wake, an air of authority. Jerry looked at Dan as they left their seats to get another beer themselves, and shrugged.

"He says what he thinks," Jerry said, a note of admiration in his voice. Dan didn't reply. He was thinking about the exchange between Quinn and the woman. He looked around to see where they were and noticed just as he did so that she and her partner were leaving through the side door; he walked ahead and she trailed behind, shooting a glance behind her, over at the bar, before she left. Quinn's back was turned.

– – –

Jacob was playing solitaire. His seven rows of cards were neat. He imagined there was someone sitting across from him, watching. He took the top card from the waste and placed it onto the Hearts pile, one step closer to completing the game. He found it satisfying. In prison, quite early on, he had come across an incomplete deck of cards in the games room, and surreptitiously smuggled it back to his cell. He had made himself replacement cards from any cardboard he could come across. He would flatten out the inside of an old loo roll, or sometimes his neighbour two cells down gave him cigarette packets. His drawings were meticulous. He had not known he could draw until prison. He based his figures on the guards or other inmates. It gave him a source of entertainment; the enjoyment was heightened when he fantasised about the scenarios between the characters, doling out his own form of justice. Unfortunately, the pack had been confiscated and, for the so-called 'violation of cell rules' he had spent a week in solitary. *Oh, the irony,* he thought as he recalled the occasion.

Right now, as he neared the completion of one of his foundation piles, a wave of restlessness engulfed him suddenly. He looked down at the cards and across the room out of the window. He could hear the same sounds he always heard; the odd beep of a horn, the ebb and flow of engines at the nearby traffic lights, the click of his electricity meter in the corner of the room. He thought about Dan and their last conversation. He knew he had been too forceful; no, not forceful, perhaps parental would be a better word. He had tried to sway Dan's opinions about the group he wanted to join by telling him a story about when he himself had been young. Disaster. The young never listen to the old, not really. They cannot look at an old, wrinkled face and picture it long ago, no matter if they say they can, or if they want to. *They don't really believe that we might know best,* Jacob thought. He looked at his watch. Five minutes past five. He had an idea. Leaving the cards as they were on the table, he grabbed his coat and stuffed his tobacco pouch into the pocket, along with a box of matches. He walked down the staircase with a purpose, buoyed along by an idea. It was Thursday. He had been handed a free programme for a local film festival and Hitchcock's 'Young and Innocent' was playing. He had not seen a film at the cinema in many years, and he felt he deserved a bit of a break. He took the longer route around Monk Corner and then approached The Blank Page. Just as he did so, and as he had hoped he would, he saw

Dan's colleague, Fiona, locking the front door. Realising she may not recognise him and not wanting to give her a shock, he said "Hi," before he had reached her. She turned and looked at him blankly for a few seconds. He was just about to say "Dan's dad…" when her face lit up with recognition and she smiled and said,

"Jacob, fancy meeting you here!"

He was touched that she had remembered him, and he could feel himself blush slightly.

"I just live round the corner," he said, adopting a casual tone. "Had a good day at the shop?"

"Okay, yeah. Quiet really. Boring when it's like that. Dan's… he's got the day off today. Still," she continued, shrugging. "I got a bit of paperwork done."

"Oh, good. Well, I'm walking into town if you're going that way?"

"Yeah, I am as it happens. I was going to see if I could get to Way Ahead, you know, the music shop? They have old DVD's there in the bargain bucket. I fancied something weepy to watch later on."

Jacob swallowed, his nerves about to get the better of him, before he reminded himself that he was old enough to be her father and therefore not a threat.

"I'm heading to the film festival…" He paused, finding the right choice of words. "If you want to join me…? I thought I'd catch 'Young and Innocent'. It's early Hitchcock though, may not be your kinda thing."

To his surprise, she did not say 'no' straightaway.

"I like Hitchcock. I've never seen it."

"Neither have I, " he said, as they walked past a takeaway. The smell of kebab curled up his nostrils.

"Well," she said, putting her hands in her pockets. "It's probably better to watch something like that than some crappy Hollywood romance. I guess I shouldn't indulge my bad mood."

He nearly asked her what was wrong but held back. She didn't know him so well. They were approaching the turning down Green Lane where the independent cinema was. He wondered what she would say. He slowed his pace a little.

"So, I'm this way."

She stopped and looked at her watch.

"Oh screw it, yeah. I'll come with you."

She linked arms with him, and he felt a comfort that he had forgotten existed. They walked together down the narrow road, Fiona reducing her pace to accommodate his limp, and turned into the wooden doorway of the small old church, and into the warm light of the cinema foyer.

Two hours later, the closing credits showing on the screen, the lights were slowly raised and Jacob blinked into the brightness. Many people had left the cinema, but he turned and saw Fiona was still there next to him, although she had placed her handbag on her knee and was ready to go. For a moment he felt strange; it was a shared experience, almost intimate, and it had been a long time since he had shared anything with anybody, especially a woman. She looked at him and gave him a warm smile.

"Thank you, I really enjoyed that," she said, touching his arm. "It was so clever of him to use the song like that at the end!"

"Did you guess? I didn't. He was a clever guy, Hitchcock."

Jacob got up and realised embarrassingly that his leg had stiffened up. He tried to hide it, but he couldn't seem to manoeuvre himself around the top of the aisle and down the top step. Fi reached out to steady him.

"Want to sit for a minute? I don't think they'll chuck us out just yet."

He nodded and they sat back down, Jacob stretching his leg out and rubbing it self-consciously to get the circulation flowing again.

"If you don't mind me asking…" Fi said, hesitantly.

"How did it happen?" Jacob replied, finishing her sentence.

"Sorry, we hardly know each other. You don't have to tell me, it's fine."

Jacob shook his head and waved off her anxieties. He began to form the words in his mind. *A war wound. It was a wound I picked up in 'Nam.* Somehow, he couldn't get the words to come out of his mouth.

She started to say something but he just said, "It's a long story. It's…I'm not proud of it."

"Honestly, please. It's fine," Fi said, and they sat for a moment. He saw out of the corner of his eye she had got out her phone. Unaware he was watching, she read what he guessed must be a text message and he noticed her face change. A darkness passed over it and she put her phone away and didn't turn in his direction for a moment. He felt suddenly protective, but knew this was not really an appropriate response. To stop himself from saying anything wrong, he tried standing up and found his leg was less rigid now. He waited for Fiona to stand, and rather absent-mindedly she took his arm again and they went slowly down the steps of the auditorium.

Fiona was quiet, and Jacob felt he had to fill the silence.

"So, you liked the movie then?"

"Yeah, I really did. I've seen 'Psycho', like everyone, and I watched some of 'Rear Window'. Not that I didn't enjoy it, I think something else was going on at the time so I was a bit distracted." She paused. "It's a clever twist. I wonder where he got his ideas…"

"Well, real life can be pretty weird," Jacob replied. "I guess he was a genius, although not that much of a nice guy by all accounts."

"Yeah, so I heard."

They walked on until they reached St Peters Church and she slowed at the small wine bar on the corner. For a moment, Jacob thought she was going to ask him if he wanted to join her for a drink. Looking down at himself and briefly at the bar's exterior, he knew he would have to refuse.

But she didn't.

"I'm sorry Jacob; it's been lovely and I'm so grateful in bumping into you, but I'm meeting a friend here so…"

"Hey, no problem at all," he said, breaking off the link with her arm and standing to face her. "Great to see you again, Fiona."

"You too," she said. As she leant forward to give him a peck on the cheek, he noticed a man seated at the window inside get up and head for the door. He was tall and he was looking at Fiona with an air of possession. She turned and half-waved at him.

"Well, bye." Jacob said, and she said, "Thank you" one more time and was gone. She walked past the man in the doorway but he held Jacob's gaze for a few seconds, unsmiling, before following her back into the bar. Jacob continued to look after them, and then he turned away, his quickened heartbeat echoing a dull and persistent thud in his ears.

CHAPTER **SEVEN**

FAITH SAT IN HER bucket chair, a relic of her former life which she had had shipped over with the rest of her belongings, mainly records and books, when she had moved to England. Her friends in New York had bought it for her and Jacob when they had moved into their apartment, affectionately christening it the Chair of Enlightenment. It was old and moulded to her shape, and it had seen better days in a lot of ways. She remembered, now, sitting here with Daniel lying across her as a baby; how she dared not move for fear of waking him; the exhaustion and the elation she experienced in equal measure; the worry of doing something wrong and the sense of achievement when they had gotten through his first year, and then the next and then the next; it had been a band aid over her grief, and the necessity of motherhood had pushed her onwards.

At the school where she still worked part-time, she had built up a good relationship with most of the children. There was a knowing she felt, in that she could tell when there was something bothering them, or when they hadn't had any breakfast, or if something unpleasant had gone on at home. She would say, "What's eating you?" and that would cheer them up. On the last day of the autumn semester, the children had all made paper snowflakes. When she'd taken them down from the window, she found herself guessing which child had made each one before she looked at the name on the back, and mostly she'd guessed right. There would be something about the way they had cut their patterns; Helen so meticulous, Frank so minimalist. Is this what washed-up mothers do? Fill the space of their children with other people's? Dan hadn't come round since they'd returned from France. She felt as though he was avoiding her. She knew she'd made mistakes as a mother, but she didn't know how to undo them now.

Some days the kids at school drove her crazy. When she told them off, they would say she sounded 'Englisher', and she would correct them. She wished she could talk to Dan about it; she thought it might make him laugh. They came out with such bizarre things.

She was taking another sip of her coffee when she heard a knock on the door. As she approached, she saw a man's shape fill the glass and felt disappointment spread across her stomach when she realised it wasn't Dan's. She toyed with the idea of ignoring it; she had her afternoon planned out and didn't feel willing to budge on it. *Probably just a delivery or something,* she thought, then checked her hair in the hall mirror and went to open up.

A man about her age was standing there, only he had turned to look down the street as if he was thinking of abandoning his visit altogether. He jumped slightly at the opening of the door and turned to look at Faith. She saw a face of kindness, more creased and wrinkled and weather-beaten than she remembered, and now sporting tortoiseshell glasses, but still familiar after all these years. Despite a twist of nerves, she felt a broad grin spread across her face and as it did so, one formed across his, filled with relief.

"Christopher! Oh my god…" She put her arms out to hug

him and they embraced on the front porch, without a care about peeping neighbours or the way things ought to be. They both stepped back with hands clasped together.

"Faith, you look fantastic."

"Don't be silly," she laughed. "We both know that's a big fat lie!"

She welcomed him in, remembering the mess in the front room, but it was too late to do anything about it now.

"Oh my god, how are you?" Faith asked him, feeling suddenly self-conscious that they were still holding hands.

"I'm...I'm well. Wow, Faith, it's been so long since I heard from you. I wasn't even sure you'd still be at this address."

"Oh gee, well, I would've told you if I'd moved, of course I would," she dropped his hands gently. "I guess life has just gotten in the way..."

He nodded and waved away what he'd said, as if to dismiss all the time that had passed between them. "Sure, sure," he said, not unkindly. "I'll be honest; it's the same for me too." They looked at each other, for one of those moments where you feel like one of you is telling the truth and the other is not and you know it.

"Sorry about the mess, it's usually tidy, I know this makes me sound so English but would you like a cup of tea?"

"Oi'd lav a cuppa!" Christopher put on a mock English accent.

"That's terrible!" Faith replied over her shoulder, laughing as she left him in the hall.

"My best Dick Van Dyke," he said, taking his coat off and hanging it on the bottom of the banister. Faith found she didn't mind the familiar gesture, and was surprised.

In the kitchen however, she felt her heart going crazy, and had to tap her fingers on the work surface. She felt physically sick and it took a minute to recognise the feeling as nervous excitement, so long had it been since she'd felt it. It took her right back to her early twenties, before Dan, when anything could happen, and who knew what was around the corner. Her head whirred with ideas of what she might say when she went back in the room but she kept drawing a blank. She stirred the tea and remembered Christopher took sugar; it was strange, she thought, how the memory retained useless facts like that and yet sometimes discarded the really important stuff.

She walked into the living room and realised there was a heap of photo's on the carpet which she hadn't yet looked through. Christopher had one in his hand and was studying it. He looked up at her and smiled.

"Good days, Faith, huh?"

"They sure were," replied Faith, searching for something to add and failing, instead sipping her cup of tea to fill the gap.

"Well…I hope you don't mind me just turning up at your door like this," Christopher said. "It was a bit of a whim, I kinda acted on impulse, you might say…" He laughed nervously, and pushed his glasses up onto his nose like Clark Kent.

Faith smiled and said, "I know all about that."

Christopher cleared his throat, put the cup of tea down and turned to her.

"So, really, how come you haven't dropped a dime or sent me a letter in so long?"

Faith couldn't help but giggle at this gorgeously familiar phrase, which she hadn't heard in such a long time.

"Sorry Chris, for laughing I mean, it's just…yeah, I'm so sorry I never called. You know after I started working full-time and Dan started school it was like life was, I don't know, mapped out and it just carried on. I guess I lost track of things, of people…"

"And how is …Daniel?"

She leant forward and put her cup down on the floor, taking a breath.

"Chris…," she couldn't look him in the eye. "I guess it just never felt like the right moment and I didn't know what you were doing, or where your life was headed, y'know?"

Christopher sighed gently, and got up, walking over to the window.

"Uh huh," he replied.

The impending silence was not uncomfortable, for the moment anyhow, and neither of them tried to fill it. Faith became strangely aware of the noises outside her cottage. Since she had moved there, a new housing estate had been built around her, and she was now overlooked on two sides. They were building yet more houses so that the village was merging with the next one into a mass of red brick 'little boxes'. She could hear some kind of construction truck going past, a mother shouting at her child, number 34's dog barking, high-pitched, more like yelping. It was dark outside, and the newly installed street lamps shed unwanted light directly into the room; the winter months having crept up again without her even noticing. She closed the curtains. Finally she spoke.

"He never did come back, did he? Jacob?"

It was more of a statement. Faith already knew the answer.

Chris turned to her with a sad smile and shook his head.

"You never accepted it, did you?" He asked. "You never moved on?"

"Yes, I did," she replied, feeling a flash of anger. "I moved here, I got a job and brought up my son," At this, she shot a glance up at him then looked down at her hands. She fiddled with the end of her sleeves. "I have a good life here, friends and interests. Actually, I know how this sounds but...I'm relieved."

He walked over towards her, wearing an unreadable expression and she almost felt herself shrink back into the chair. Before he could speak, she shot up and went into the kitchen, hearing him exhale as she did so. She took a bottle of red wine from the rack on top of the fridge and fiddled with the corkscrew, her fingers stumbling over the twisted metal and her breath quickening. Annoyed at the tears which sprung in the corner of her eyes, she muttered quietly to herself: *It's okay, there are no rules for life.* She stomped back to the living room holding the bottle in one hand and two glasses in the other.

Christopher's expression relaxed and he opened his hands before him and said, "Hell, why not?"

"Exactly," replied Faith. "It's past five thirty."

She poured them both a glass.

— — —

A few hours later, they were sat on the floor cross legged recovering from a bout of hysterical laughter. Faith was holding a photo of herself, Christopher and their friend Moll, all sporting bellbottom flares and ridiculous hats.

"You know, we thought we were just the grooviest! Didn't

THE **HEART LADDER**

we?" asked Faith, giggling.

"We *were* pretty cool though," Christopher said, pretending to be serious. "We could get into any nightclub on the east side, especially when you wore your lucky purple hat…"

"That hat…Jesus, I might still have it somewhere!" she replied, as she took another sip of her wine. She went to top Christopher up but he put his hand over his glass.

"I can't, Faith, I gotta get back to my hotel," he explained. "Besides, I can't keep up like I used to."

He got up slowly, and stretched, rubbing the small of his back.

"How did we get old?" Faith asked to no-one in particular, as she went up onto her knees. He held out his hand to help her up and she took it. They looked at each other for a moment, and then she went into the hall to get his coat. Christopher hovered there, as if he wanted to say something but couldn't find the right words. She held out his coat to him and was just about to tell him how great it had been when there was a knock at the door.

"Oh!" Faith said, with a start.

"You got friends coming round?"

She laughed at the very idea. Judy was away and she wasn't in the habit of having gatherings, although she missed the days when she had.

She opened the door and saw Dan standing before her. He looked odd and she thought from his half-shut eyes that he must have been drinking.

"Hey mum! Mind me popping over?" He gave her an awkward hug. "Oh, have you got…someone here?" Dan shook his head as if this idea was too much to take in.

"Well, mmm hmm, this here is Chris, an old friend from NYC."

The two men shook hands and Christopher walked away looking behind him as Faith mouthed *Sorry*. He waved his hands at her as if to say *no problem*, looked at her for a moment and then Dan, and then he was gone.

"You okay Ma?" Dan had already gone into the kitchen and had found the corkscrew on the side. "Got any booze?"

She was about to say something like she thought he'd had enough already but held her tongue. He hadn't called her 'ma' in years. Dan had grabbed a wine glass and was heading for the living room. He didn't seem to notice the mess and slumped down on Faith's bucket chair. *What is it about men,* she thought, *that they think they can just treat your house like they own it?*

Despite this, she poured Dan half a glass of wine from the bottle and picked up her own. They clinked, and she sat back down on the floor and gathered up the photo's. Dan's foot was tapping.

"Where have you been?" Faith tried to sound nonchalant.

"I met up with Tipper and his mate Dave, and we were supposed to go to a club but it got cancelled and then they pissed me off so, I dunno, I decided to come here. Stupid!"

He wasn't drunk, she could tell, but his eyes were all over the place. He was talking fast and it seemed like a part of his brain was somewhere else.

"It's kinda strange for you to come here, I mean, to your mom's, on a weekend too. I didn't expect it."

Dan laughed, "No! You had a date, ha!"

Faith scowled at him despite herself. "I told you, an old friend. Not, I repeat, *not* a date. I'm too old for dates."

He took out a cigarette and was just about to spark it up. Faith took it out of his hand and said, "Uh uh, you know the rules in this house."

He shook his head and stood up, steadying himself on the door frame and venturing into the kitchen and towards the back door. She heard him fiddling with the lock, and felt a surge of irritation, of anger at this man who she couldn't for the moment identify as her son. She walked to stand in the doorway.

"What the hell are you doing?"

He was fumbling with the key.

"Dan, what are you on?" Faith asked, and then shaking her head, she said, "Forget it, I don't want to know."

She opened the back door for him and held back from her mothering instincts to sit with him, to make sure he didn't injure himself or set fire to a shrub. Walking back into the living room, she picked up the last couple of photographs from the floor, and, looking at the moments they captured, tried to transport herself back there. Was it really as care-free as she remembered it? Was she really that happy? Or was it just a snapped illusion, resting there forever on the plastic emulsion, etched in by clever light and the gradual erosion of her memory?

Later, they had had a fight. What she understood was that some guy had been impersonating Jacob and that Dan had been taken in. In a short space of time, Dan had nearly finished a bottle of wine and couldn't seem to focus on her anymore. She had managed to get him upstairs to his old bedroom and watched him drift off into an intoxicated slumber, until soon he was snoring. She'd grabbed the Indian throw off her own bed and draped it over him, and then gone back down to the kitchen and poured what was left in the bottle out for herself, taking the washing up bowl out of the sink on her way back and placing it on the stairs to take up for him, just in case. Now, she sat back down and sipped her drink slowly. *What a day,* she thought. *The universe is up to something.* She let herself relax and tried not to think about how she would break it to Dan in the morning. Why would somebody pretend to be Jacob, and how did this man know all about their situation? It made her stomach turn over. Taking another large gulp, she got up again and poured the rest of the wine down the sink and went upstairs to bed.

The next morning she woke up with a sore head, but a certainty about what she must do. She made a mental note that she was too old for impromptu drinking sessions, but excused herself immediately afterwards because it had been a highly unusual situation; one that had certainly called for alcohol. She got up to open the curtains and then climbed back in bed, sitting up and bathing in the unexpected winter sunshine. She shut her eyes. Sometimes, on mornings like these, she imagined there was somebody lying next to her. Often it was Jacob she pictured there, but that was too hard and she felt too old now. He was still a young man in her head; it didn't seem quite right, somehow. Even when she tried to remember what she had been like, what she had felt then, it never worked. Other times, it was just a man she had conjured up, with features she had borrowed from other people. Today, she imagined it was Chris. It surprised her that she didn't feel repulsed by that thought. *Perhaps when you get older,* she pondered, *the person you want lying next to you doesn't have to be so much an object of desire. Perhaps a friend is better.* Faith remembered what desire felt like, but had not acted upon it in a long time. When Dan had first left home, she had struck up a relationship – more of a fling – with a man who lived a few streets away. They had met one night in the local pub, when Faith and Judy had ventured out for what Judy had called a 'celebratory' drink, but Faith had considered more of a patch on the sudden aloneness caused by Dan moving out. She had seen Carl before at one of Judy's barbecues but had never really given him a second glance. He came to join them and bought them each a couple of drinks. He had been easy to talk to, and interested in her life. It had been a long time since Faith had reminisced without feeling an overwhelming sadness, but with Carl she'd found she could talk about New York and her younger days with enthusiasm. In turn, she found him quite fascinating. He was a potter by trade, selling his wares at local markets. He had worked on the stock market but after his divorce, had given it all up to live in the countryside and make pots. Judy had insisted on nudging her throughout, like a naughty teenager, and Faith had enjoyed the attention. It had been the first time in ages she had let down her guard. They had swapped numbers at the end of the night and had begun a relationship which had lasted several months. On their third date, they had slept together. It had been wonderful, and new, and different. When Faith had chastised herself in front of him for being 'too easy' he had simply said, "It's just love, two people giving each other some love; what's wrong with that?" It had made perfect sense. For a while she'd walked with a spring in her step, and felt that her 42 years of age was nothing. Judy had commented on how much happier she seemed, and Faith had actually started to believe that they might have some kind of future together. Carl shared things about his past with her, and she felt she could share some of her secrets too. After a month or so, he had begun to talk about his ex-wife more. Faith noticed she came up in conversation quite frequently, in fact. Whilst she believed in the sharing of experiences and in honesty, it had begun to annoy her. Eventually, she had sat down with Carl and asked him outright, did he still love Jackie? She knew what answer she had hoped for but she didn't get it. Carl had realised he still had strong feelings for his ex-wife and that he wanted to 'reunite' with her, as he put it. Faith had pointed out that it would have been better, and braver, for him to tell her himself rather than let her draw her own conclusions, but hey, she'd thought, that was men for you. She had been angry and then later, hurt; devastated, in fact. Once she had picked herself up and dusted herself off, she'd put an invisible yet impenetrable guard around her heart so no-one could get in. She couldn't escape the feeling that she didn't deserve to find a man to share her life with so, from then on, she kept herself romantically hidden. Now she imagined Carl was next to her and it made her upset. *Enough goofing around, Faith.*

She suddenly remembered through her hangover fog that Dan had stayed the night. Getting out of her bed reluctantly, she grabbed her robe and quietly opened the bedroom door. Across the hallway, Dan's old bedroom door was slightly open. She looked in and saw the top of his head sticking out from under the quilt. Standing there for a few moments, she could imagine he was a young boy again. She used to watch him just like this, or sometimes she'd sit next to the bed and drink her coffee before she woke him up for school. *To watch your baby sleeping is a joy you can't describe to people who don't have kids,* she remembered thinking at the time. What was he doing to himself these days? How long had he been hanging around with this stranger, this imposter? It hurt to think of him taking drugs, although god knows, Faith had experimented herself. This was different somehow; like he was looking for something in all the wrong places. She believed he himself was aware of this, but knowing Dan if she had pointed it out he would just kick back at her and tell her to mind her own business. Why was it so damn hard being a parent, and yet so important too? She leant forward and touched Dan's head. His hair had been blonde as a baby; now it was a sort of sandy brown. She shut her eyes and took herself back to another time, when he had filled all the gaps in her life, and then some. Now who was she? And where was her little boy? And if this feeling she had in her gut was anything to be heeded; if it meant that trouble was ahead, where would she be without him? The thought was too much to contemplate. Suddenly he stirred and she shot her hand away, got up quietly and left the room.

She had a long, hot shower and took two painkillers to sort her head out. God knows, she needed as clear a head as possible to face today. She threw on some clothes and noticed as she walked past his room that Dan's bed was empty. She paced down the stairs, expecting to see Dan sitting in the living room watching TV, like he used to do when he'd lived with her. She planned to make him a strong coffee, bacon and eggs and then sit down and tell him the whole goddamn story. She couldn't keep it from him anymore. She knew she'd been wrong to in the first place. As she rounded the hall and stepped into the room she saw that he was neither in the armchair nor sat on the couch. She called his name but there was no answer. She hadn't heard him leave. Still grasping onto a shred of hope, Faith went into the kitchen. Empty. She sighed a long breath out, and her mind began to race. When had he left and where would he go? She cast her eyes around for a note but quickly dismissed the idea. Most likely he'd gone home to lick his wounds. She picked up her mobile phone from the mantelpiece and turned it on, waiting impatiently for it to come to life. No messages. She wrote, *Hun, I hope you're okay, don't worry about last night but you need to know − I think someone's taking you for a ride. I'm so sorry. Call me so we can talk, I mean properly talk, love Mum x*

She pressed 'send' before she could change her mind.

− − −

"So tell me about this mystery man. Finn, is it? You've hardly said anything, and hasn't it been, like, months or something?"

Fiona's friend, Sian, had a slightly sceptical look on her face, and this was what Fi had dreaded. Although she had prepared an answer which she hoped would put an end to any further enquiries.

"I've hardly seen you," she said, turning it back on her friend, "and it's Quinn. He's very intellectual, into the issues of the day, you know, interesting!" Fi took a sip of her red wine. They were in a bar in town. It was early evening, but the beginnings of the Saturday night razzle dazzle were filtering through; girls with very little on, men sporting checked shirts. They were like a tribe, Fi thought. A townie tribe. Sticking close together so they could take on anyone who wanted to threaten their enjoyment of their night out.

"Ooh," Sian interest was piqued. Fi wasn't sure if this meant her plan had backfired. "What kind of issues?"

Fi put her glass down. "Well, um, the environment, partly. And the plight of humanity, I suppose. How technology is taking over our lives and we're becoming less and less, well, *human*."

"Mm hmm," her friend replied, looking thoughtful. "Sounds like he's converted you already!"

"Not converted. I thought about these things already," Fiona said defensively. "But he puts them so well, we have some really interesting discussions."

Sian began to smile and she leant forward, giving her friend a wink. "And…?"

"And what?" replied Fiona, knowing exactly what.

"Is he…sexy? Have you slept with him?"

Fi laughed in spite of herself. "What do you think?" They both giggled. "He's…well, more than sexy. He's…"

"Hot!" Sian said, and raised her glass.

"Hot is an understatement, but yeah, for now, that'll do."

The girls clinked glasses and the conversation turned to Sian's job and what a wanker her boss was. Fi was relieved. She didn't want to say that things hadn't exactly been going how she'd wanted them to with Quinn. It wasn't that he didn't make her insides turn over when he looked at her, but maybe it was best that her friends didn't know too much about Quinn. Every time she saw him now she felt like maybe there was something not quite right. At first his mystique had attracted her and she had felt at the beginning of an adventure; like this person could open her life up to new possibilities. It was dangerous and thrilling. It had been six months now and, much as she didn't want to lapse into so-called 'normal' behaviour, she knew she *was* doing, and Quinn berated her for it. The fact was they had only actually seen each other maybe 12 or 13 times. She just didn't understand why he couldn't send her a quick text if he wasn't going to come round, or make one of their dates. It was just common courtesy, surely, she told herself, aware that if she pushed him too far, she could be deemed a 'psycho'. She felt utterly trapped between her expectations and what was considered acceptable behaviour. Many evenings, experiencing his prolonged absence, she had drafted text after text, and picked up the phone to call him countless times, but in the end had held back, stewing over her dissatisfaction.

The worst thing was that he had such power over her. She ached for his physical presence like she needed her morning cigarette. The yearning took over and even worse was that she suspected he knew this. If she could let her mind rule, maybe she could convince herself that the pain in her heart wasn't real and just get on with normal life again. She had done it before. Was it time to end it? The thought made her shudder. But often, she just felt like she was on the sidelines of his life. She knew he was heavily involved with his pressure group, as he called it, but he didn't seem to want to discuss this with her. She had guessed it was the same group that Dan had mentioned, although she hadn't mentioned Dan to Quinn. She didn't know why. Maybe she wanted to keep something for herself. Sometimes it felt like he wanted to suck the life out of her, and all her secrets, and part of her wanted to give in completely. He, on the other hand, kept his revelations clipped and controlled. She thought he was probably a good orator, and sometimes she felt like she was just another audience for him. The sad thing was she could listen to him for hours, if he would only stay with her that long. Even now, he hadn't stayed the whole night. She ached for him when he'd gone, and hated herself for it. Whenever she had asked him to stay, he had become angry so she had given up. He didn't want to be tied down. She was scared of trying too hard and of him one day recoiling. *How dare I want more?* Fi thought, wryly.

Sian had to leave at 10 because she worked for an events company, who were sending her off to Berlin the following morning on a conference. Sometimes Fi looked at her friends and wondered what they thought of her life. Did they think she was pathetic, somehow? Why would they think that, they were her friends? But she couldn't escape the suspicion that people wanted to change her. She wished she could just be how she was and that would be that. She'd texted Quinn on the off chance he was around and he had said he would come over later, but not given her a time. Walking through the market place, she thought about the previous weekend, when her parents had come over for the day. She had spent the whole day trying to prove herself; that her life was worthy. She hadn't wanted them to come to the flat, so she'd agreed to meet them in an upmarket cafe. She'd taken ages to decide on her outfit and eventually found something that didn't have holes in, and wasn't particularly 'hippy'. Even so, her mother had given her the usual look up and down and made some comment about her own outfit and where she'd bought it from. Fi had replied that that particular shop was for older ladies, which had not pleased her mother one bit. Her dad, as usual, sat and ate noisily and interjected only minimally, although had a rather embarrassing choking fit at one point. She felt like screaming at them, "What's the fucking point? Why are you even here?" but instead she clenched her fists under the table. After an excruciating hour-long lunch, she excused herself only to be persuaded to stay because they had something 'important' to tell her. The important thing was that her father had been diagnosed with a neurological condition. Now, she tried the words out on her tongue. Her dad had explained that it was some kind of illness that attacked the body, but Fi wasn't sure what that meant. Her mum, for once, had been quiet and let him talk. Her father hadn't seemed upset, so she thought maybe it wasn't too big a deal, until she had got up to go and her mother had reached out to her and hugged her, close. So close, Fi had felt her bony frame for the first time in years and been taken back to childhood, when she had craved affection from her and found very little. Now she froze slightly in her mother's embrace and felt her mother's necklace digging into her chest. She noticed the smell of her hair, which was like heather. Now, it made her shiver to think of it, and she felt a tear like a pinprick in the corner of her eye. She rubbed it swiftly away and walked on, towards her flat and warmed herself up at the thought of Quinn coming over to see her, however short-lived the pleasure may turn out to be.

There were some late night skateboarders trying their talents in a nearby office car park, and as she walked she nearly tripped over a couple snogging in a doorway. The sounds of town gradually faded and the noise of the black cabs and the odd group of late-night party goers took over. Fi settled into a steady pace, as she tended to do when walking home alone at night. *Always look like you know where you're going, and show no fear,* was her motto. A week ago one of her male friends had been 'happy slapped' just around the corner from her place; some stupid craze. Fi herself had never felt intimidated or threatened around this neighbourhood though. She turned the corner at the top of Drew Lane and walked up the short distance of Roebuck Street and into the small courtyard where her flat was. She put her key in the door. Suddenly a shape lurched out of the shadows to the right of her, where the residents parked their cars. The security light hadn't worked in weeks but Fi hadn't been worried as she felt safe where she lived. She started to scream but the sound was caught in her mouth by a gloved hand, and she could feel loose threads in her mouth and on her lips. Instinctively she reached round to grab something, anything on her attacker's person that might hurt him but he grabbed one of her arms and pushed it up her back until she screamed in pain. She tried to shove backwards against him but it was like all her strength had gone, suddenly. Still behind her, he turned the key and shoved the door open, pushing her up the stairs. She kept stumbling but he pushed her onwards. Her right knee was stinging when they reached the top and rounded the corner towards her flat door. Her mind was working overtime, in survival mode, and she tried to kick her neighbour's door but was wrenched away. He put the keys in her hand and growled 'Open it'. She did, thinking maybe she could grab something, anything, inside her flat or at least lock herself in the bathroom and call the police, if only she could get away from him. Her heartbeat drummed inside her head and nothing looked real. Things took on a shimmering quality as he pushed her through her sitting room door and face down onto the couch. She couldn't breathe properly. She tasted vomit in her mouth and tried to scream again but it came out as a sob. A voice whispered, in her left ear, "You want this, Fi, don't you?" while she felt her jeans being undone and pulled down. She couldn't compute that this person had just said her name. He knew her. She knew him. Was it...? She felt a hand in her knickers and another on her back. Her voice free, she shouted amidst tears "What the FUCK are you doing to me?! Who are you?" The man removed his hand from between her legs and pulled her hair gently away from her ear.

"It's me, baby. Surprise."

"Quinn?" she spat and reeled round with a fist, catching him on the jaw. His hand reached up to his face, which was covered with a scarf and she lurched towards him, now free and not held down, scratching his face as she did so.

"YOU FUCKING PSYCHOPATH, you...you RAPIST!" Fiona was screaming at him and crying at the same time.

"Hey, hey, hey," he said, reaching out to her flailing arms but she screamed again.

"Don't you TOUCH me! Don't come near me! Never again!"

Quinn put his hands out as if to say 'calm down', but he didn't say anything. He leaned against the breakfast bar, getting his breath.

Fi had collapsed on the floor by the side of the sofa, and she couldn't get her breath. She seethed in her panic, her face felt aflame and, suddenly ashamed, she realised her jeans were still out of place and she fumbled with them, pulling them up and doing the zip up as far as she could, but her hands wouldn't stop shaking. Exhausted, she crumbled into a heap. She did not know how long she sat there. It was the smell of cigarette smoke that roused her. Then she was aware of Quinn by her side and crouching down. He reached to touch her hair and she flinched.

"Baby, I thought you'd find it...sexy. I thought you were open to this sort of thing."

She couldn't get her words out so she remained silent for a moment. Then all she managed was, "You hurt me." Her voice came out in a croak.

"No more than any other time, though, hey?" he said, coldly. "I thought you liked it rough."

She felt him lean in towards her and she turned away.

"You need to go now," she said shakily.

He stayed for a short while, kneeling there, resting his elbows on his bent knees, looking at her, but he didn't try to touch her again. And finally, she was aware out of the corner of her eye that he had stood up. Fiona shut her eyes and waited until she heard the door slam. Opening her eyes, she saw the keys there, on her breakfast bar, and a still-burning cigarette in her ashtray. Stunned she stayed there, only reaching onto the sofa for a cushion to rest her head on. Her body and mind shut down and she fell into a strange sleep. She woke up like that in the morning, and everything was the same, but of course, nothing was the same too.

Fi spent the next few weeks in a blur, but slowly and surely she felt that she was managing to put that night behind her. Thankfully, Quinn had not been in touch. She felt, now, an incredible rage towards him for creating that memory she now had; one filled with fear. She had decided not to go home for Christmas, despite her mum guilt-tripping her about her father's illness. She couldn't face the hypocrisy of it all; the fake smiles, her parents' vacuous neighbours and all the skipping on the surface of meaningful conversation. There would, of course, be the inevitable questioning about her love life, and then the equally inevitable retreat on Fiona's part, up to her old room (now the 'spare') to watch Christmas specials and have a sneaky joint out of the window.

It made things worse that Dan had been missing work recently. So far, she had managed to cover for him, but she knew it was only a matter of time before Phil discovered his absence. Plus there were things he usually did that she now found herself doing and making a mess of. Finally, she had texted him pleading for him to come in before Christmas and help her with the orders. On Christmas Eve, she was dusting the final few shelves of the shop before they closed. Dan had made it in to work, much to Fi's relief, and was finishing off sorting out the desk in the office. They had had lots of orders to pack for Christmas but not nearly as many as the previous year. In fact, the shop takings had not been reaching a healthy balance for a while. They both knew that things were changing. Even the Waterstones in town, their fiercest competition, was struggling, according to Dan's friend who helped do their books occasionally. The previous week, Phil had come in and delivered a rather cryptic speech about hard times; Fi had felt sure he had plagiarised some of it from a Dickens novel. She'd told Phil that Dan was sick.

Neither of them had talked about the possibility of working elsewhere, but packing books quietly off to Edinburgh, Leeds, Cornwall, even Italy, it seemed like every little action had greater significance. Dan wouldn't explain to Fi what he had been doing, and she didn't want to pry. A shadow had attached itself to their friendship and they had both felt it; as if something lay between them. A chasm, no, perhaps that was too extreme – but certainly a gap that hadn't been there before.

When Dan had put in an appearance, he had tried to talk to Fi about the group and Quinn, but she always changed the subject. So it had seemed to Dan as though she didn't really want to know about his life anymore, and he felt bitter about it, *especially after all the time I've listened to her ridiculous accounts of flawed men and ill-fated love affairs*, he thought. At the last meeting, Quinn had asked him to help with a 'recruitment campaign' he was running for the People of the Sun; Dan didn't mind doing the donkey work, and he needed to feel like he was filling his days with something worthwhile. He knew Fiona would cover for him – Christ knows, she owed him for all the times she'd been late or called in 'sick'. Mainly, his job was to call people up who had registered their interest at various political forums Quinn had attended over the past six months. He was surprised to find that most of them were still interested and his instructions were then to take an email or postal address so he could send them the group's official leaflet. It excited him to be involved with the development of the group; but at the same time, he felt slightly removed from it; looking at the other members, it was as if he wasn't quite *like* them. They had well-formed views, where he felt somewhat on the outside, wishy washy. The worst thing was he actually cared what Quinn thought of him and so he held back in discussions.

He set the phone to voicemail and listened out for Fiona. They had been such good friends once. He started to feel guilty and chastised himself for what he'd just thought. Just then, she came through to the office and he smiled at her; she smiled straight back and held his gaze.

"What?" Fi asked him.

"Oh, nothing," he replied. "I was just thinking it's been ages since we talked properly." He couldn't meet her eye. She pulled the stool from under desk and sat down on it.

"Yeah, it really has. I didn't know if you wanted to talk to me anymore. You seem so…busy."

Her eyes looked slightly moist and Dan wondered if it was the beginnings of actual tears. As if she could read his mind, she said,

"Oh, it's the polish. Makes my eyes water a bit." She rubbed them on the back of her hand and smiled again. "Well, what shall we do about it?"

"What?" Dan asked, momentarily confused.

"Us. Not talking much anymore. I've always thought that a decent quantity of alcohol and perhaps some loud music works a treat in breaking down barriers. There's a cover band playing at the Carriage tonight. What say we celebrate our last day at work in 2004?"

Dan laughed. "What cover band? Don't tell me, the Love Cats aka the Cure, or what's that other one…Take This? I have my standards."

"You? Standards? You mean if it's not house music it's

rubbish," she said, jabbing him in the side affectionately. "I agree, it may be a bit shit. But squint a little and you could be in the presence of greatness. Add several tequilas into the mix and you'll be transported back to the 70's, I can virtually guarantee it." She grabbed her coat from the corner.

"Tell me who it is," Dan said. "The fake Beatles? An Elvis impersonator?"

He made sure the fax machine and computer were switched off and followed Fi across the shop floor and towards the door.

"Mate," she said in a faux dramatic tone. "It's only the Strolling Stones."

"Oh man, I can't wait to see their version of Mick Jagger," Dan said, sweeping his eyes round for a final check of the lights.

"Snake hips, oh yeah," Fi said, chuckling. "Could be interesting, very interesting!"

"Pervert," Dan said, as Fi locked the door and checked it.

"'Bye shop," she said, and patted the door frame. See you next year."

They began to walk down Macklin Street in the direction of town. As they walked, Dan noticed a few flakes of snow appear before his eyes until there was a steady fall. They walked in silence; after 10 or so metres Fi took hold of his arm. He turned to her discreetly and saw a few snowflakes nestling on her woolly hat like confetti, and on the strands of hair which fell out from under it, and on the tip of her nose. She didn't turn to look at him, but he was sure she had squeezed his arm a little bit. Their footsteps became softer as a layer of white appeared gently before them. In front of them, and over the tops of the lower buildings, the tip of the city Christmas tree in the market square was just visible, a gold star nestling in its top branches. Other people trudged in their various directions, each with their own important things to be getting on with; each with their own stories to tell. Right now, this was trivial, irrelevant, thought Dan. Somehow he felt that there was nowhere else he should be.

Two hours later, they were standing at the back of a sweat-filled room. The clientèle was definitely what you might call a mixed bag. There were the usual 'locals', bikers and mid-life crisis-ers, all over 45 at least, peppered with some young folk; a few punks, Goths, and normal looking people. Dan was aware that he and Fi fell into the last category, which he felt sad to conclude made them seem a bit boring. He noticed that Fi was also looking around her at their fellow drinkers.

"We're boring!" he said loudly down her ear. She frowned at him and shook her head.

"It'll get better!" she replied, shouting so the reverb hurt his ear drums.

This time, he shook his head and grinned.

"Not the music – us!" He pointed towards himself and then to her. She screwed her face up at him, not understanding. He shook his head and shrugged in the universal gesture of 'never mind'. Mick's doppelganger (and he did look quite a bit like the real thing) was wailing along to 'Angie'. Fi joined in every now and then but she didn't know all the words, having professed herself not to be a 'proper' Stones fan. When she didn't, she and Dan would slot in their own random lyrics. The song ended and everyone cheered. Say what you like about cover bands, thought Dan, but as Fiona had pointed out, have enough to drink and you did kind of believe that you were in the presence of real rock stars. The guitarist began to twang repeatedly on one note alongside a solitary drum beat. You could tell something good was coming. At the same time, he and Fi and the rest of the small but enthusiastic crowd recognised the first echoing notes from 'Gimme Shelter'. The mood in the room changed and everyone woke up. Even the more decrepit locals started to tap along with a foot or a tobacco-stained finger on the side of a pint glass. The lead guitarist broke into the famous riff and Fi and Dan sang along with the crowd to the melody. A few of the Goths decided that this was a good point at which to start moshing, and threw their long black hair into the air and into the pints of the people standing behind them. This led to the flicking of beer on the audience nearby each time a head was swung, but no-one seemed to mind. Dan and Fi were punching the air and singing their own version with great enthusiasm, while fake Mick gyrated on stage and flicked his fringe in that unmistakeable way.

A couple of hours later, they spilled out onto the street with the other revellers, and Fi went to hail a cab. They both got in, not realising they hadn't decided where they were going. The taxi driver started getting impatient with them until Dan gave him the name of a club out of town, where he thought he might be able to score. On the way, Fi lay down with her head on his lap. Again, the taxi driver started getting twitchy so Dan spoke to him in as sober a way as he possibly could, having consumed a disgusting amount of shots; at just £1.50 a pop, who could say 'no'? He was slightly concerned Fi might puke on him. Absent-mindedly he stroked her hair, and now and then he asked her if she was okay. Every time she nodded in response, it caused him to feel slightly aroused. He tried to think of other things, like his grandparents or Nigel Lawson naked; that usually worked.

They pulled up at the club and the hard house vibrations could just be heard from the inside, resonating outwards into the night air. Dan had texted Tipper but had no reply, although he felt he could almost guarantee his presence here. If not, there was sure to be someone else he could get pills from. He shook Fi awake and paid the taxi driver. It had been a good idea to go out together, and he didn't want the evening to end just yet.

Fi started shaking her head, but she was smiling.

"I don't think so," she said, laughing. "I don't even know how to dance to this stuff."

"No-one does!" Dan said, pushing her forward so she reached the door before him. "Besides, I'll get something that'll help us dance!"

She shook her head again but smiled at the bouncer as he ushered them through. The volume of the music suddenly reached out to them and filled their ear-drums. Fi turned around to look at Dan and stuck her fingers in her ears, but he laughed and pulled them out. He took her arm and led her to the bar where he bought them two vodka and red bulls.

"This'll perk you up!" he shouted down her ear, and she said something he couldn't hear, but took a big glug from her glass and looked around her. Dry ice covered the feet of the dancers, and it got into the back of your throat, the smell curling around your nostrils like tendrils. There was a whiff of poppers in the air, and dotted around on loungers, clubbers sat in varying states of fucked-ness: some with their heads in their hands, feet still tapping along with the beat; others running their fingers through their mates' hair and generally being off their heads. Men caressed men, but not in a gay way. Women swapped pills on each others' tongues, and everyone loved each other, for this moment, for this tune, for this night, until the sun came up and they all came down.

Dan looked around for Tipper and eventually spotted him on the dance floor right up next to the DJ booth. He was jumping up and down and pointing with great enthusiasm. Dan mouthed to Fi to 'stay here' and pointed in Tipper's direction. She shrugged and started fumbling in her handbag for her tobacco tin. She pointed to a nearby sofa that was free and they parted. On his way across the dance floor, Dan was jostled good-naturedly and nodded at by way of apology several times by grinning faces that couldn't focus. *That's where I want to be,* he thought. He tapped Tipper on the shoulder and his friend turned and embraced him enthusiastically. Dan rubbed his fingers together in their own gesture for drugs and Tipper fished around in his pocket. He passed a bundle of cling film discreetly into Dan's hand and Dan found two pills and took them out, putting the bag back in Tipper's pocket. He felt in his jeans for his wallet but Tipper waved him away, giving him a sloppy kiss on the cheek. Dan went off to find Fi and Tipper got back to jumping, not noticing the change in tune, or not caring; the beat was always the same anyway.

Fi was skinning up on a flyer, and had been joined by an older moustachioed man who Dan felt immediately Fi would not be attracted to. He smiled politely at the man, but he felt sure he was one of those clubbers who sought out the weed smokers so they could have a cheeky toke and move on. Fi didn't seem too bothered, but Dan shuffled himself in politely between them. Moustache man didn't really react but neither did he move. Turning his body towards Fi, Dan took her hand and she looked at him confused. Then she opened her palm and saw what he'd put in it and pulled a sceptical face.

"Just this once!" he said. "I'll look after you." To his surprise, she shrugged her shoulders and put the pill in her mouth, immediately pulling a face. He grabbed her drink from the floor where she'd deposited it and put it to her lips and she took several gulps. She gave her head a shake and then grinned at Dan mischievously.

"You'd better!" She said, and tore a roach for her newly completed spliff out of the rizla packet. Dan was aware of movement then, and was relieved to see that their unwelcome companion must've got the message and had got up to go.

After sharing her joint with Dan, Fi had lain down on the couch in the club. Her head was spinning. Sometime after, she was unsure how long it was, she sat up. For some reason, she couldn't seem to see, or get any words out. She started to freak out but thankfully Dan was there and held her hand as she staggered off to find the loo. She knelt over the toilet bowl and stuck her fingers down her throat. It was like her body needed to purge itself of alcohol before she could embrace this new sensation.

Now, Fi found herself sauntering across the dance floor. As she passed people, she danced, joining in with them. No-one seemed to care; they smiled at her, grabbed her hand and twirled her around. She made her way across like this, almost floating and searched Dan out with her flickering eyes. She walked up to him and he looked at her, giving her a big grin. Grabbing his hands, she pulled him up and hugged him, then led him off to dance. She didn't know what she was doing but however she moved, she seemed to be in sync with the music. Every now and then, the higher synth sounds gave her little shivers up and down her spine and her neck. Dan pulled her towards him and they danced like that for a moment. She didn't know how long they were there, but Dan gave her water when she was thirsty and she didn't seem to want for anything else, except to move, to not stop moving.

CHAPTER **EIGHT**

FAITH SAT STARING OUT of the window. For the first time since he'd left home, Dan had chosen not to spend Christmas with her. She tried to think rationally, but her heart wrenched with an invisible tourniquet, tightening and suffocating her until she had to go and do something to take her mind off it. She had talked to Judy about it at length; her friend, always pragmatic, had said she must've expected the time would come eventually, but Faith had only ever anticipated it happening when Dan had his own family. He hadn't been in touch with her. She had started a letter to him, but she had wanted to read it out in person. Walking over to the old desk in the corner, she opened one of the compartments, and retrieved it now, unfolding it and starting at the beginning:

To my son,

I don't really know how to start. I guess I've never offered you much advice and I've kind of let you go your own way. Now I can tell you one thing I've learned, that nobody warns you about life. One day you think you've got it made, and all of a sudden the blanket is whipped away from you and you're out in the cold. Mine and Jacob's life had been full of promise and smiles and blissful ignorance. In the background of everyone's lives there though; the war in Vietnam. Sat around in our apartment in the evening smoking reefers and listening to Bob Dylan, me and J and our friends set the world to rights.

We shouldn't have been out there, the U.S., and the stories we heard about the madness of it all sent chills up our spines. What was it we were fighting for anyway? Why were we so afraid of communists? It wasn't the same as fascism, what sort of a threat was it anyway? And all those innocent people dying. The world was changing. We felt at the same time free as we did lost.

"Let's make a baby," whispered J one night, when we had felt full of energy and life. There was madness in the darkness and excitement drifting across the city streets, protest and passion permeated the air.

A couple of months later, J received the letter, drafting him to 'Nam. One of the very last drafts as it turned out. Nixon was proposing an all-volunteer army but Congress had granted an extension. What were the odds, we asked ourselves? We tried to get along with life but I felt like he was shutting off from me, bit by bit. So we argued, hell, we fought like we never had before. You have to remember we were so young, younger than you are now. What do you do when you find yourself a pawn in a bigger game? When suddenly the life you thought you had is no longer your own? We saw sides to each other we didn't know were there.

Still, on his last night we had a party. All my friends from the university and J's family and friends from his old neighbourhood came; we enjoyed and endured every minute. All we wanted to do was be alone together but at the same time it was the last thing we wanted to do. Then we'd have to face it; then it became real. And the cracks had set in on what we had, already, in anticipation of what was to come and the injustice of it.

I kept asking myself, how would I remember his touch and his features? How he laughed from his eyes and how he looked at me when he wanted me? He kept saying that he probably wouldn't be out there long; that the war for the U.S. was ending, but I just had a bad feeling about it all. We played 'Forever Young' and all sang *together; with the windows open wide onto the possibilities of a New York night.*

I didn't say a proper goodbye, more like a see you soon. We held each other and then clasped hands and tried to freeze-frame our life together – to mould and gel it all close so we could never be separated, even though it was inevitable. I prayed for some miracle to happen; I planned how I could alter our futures, but I no longer felt of any use. We were powerless. Like all the other families whose lives had been caught up in all the other wars. Bit parts in the production; expendable extras. After he'd gone, I went through all of his things. I put away his old leather gloves to wear when winter came, to keep him with me. Their creases reflecting the crevices of his precious hands; where he had folded his skin into them. It was May 1973. For a few weeks I heard nothing from J. As each day went by, my thoughts grew darker and I started to entertain the possibility that something had happened to him. I was drinking a lot. I didn't know what I was doing. I couldn't face reality and all the harsh words we'd said to each other those past weeks. I saw a lot of Christopher, the guy you met last night. He was kind to me.

Then out of the blue I had a short letter; it was kind of scribbled and his handwriting was loose, like he'd been distracted. It said so little, really, but I held it to my heart and tried to go back in time to how we were. In it was a picture of J with his uniform on, flanked by two other guys. It was so weird seeing him with his arms around people I didn't know; our lives having been wound together like a tapestry, dotted with friends and people from our neighbourhoods. I tried to imagine what they talked about, what their days were like, what he dreamed of at night.

The following Wednesday I was at work. I felt so nauseous I had to go out the back and leave a customer just standing at the counter.

It happened again the next morning and, as I threw up over the toilet I prayed it was just some stomach bug. After waiting weeks for that letter, now I was waiting for my period to come. I pretended it was nothing but I knew, deep inside, like everyone says you do. After three months I sat down one day in front of the big window that looked out on the skyline, lit a candle, had my last smoke and said to God and life, "Bring it on, I'm ready."

I wrote to J telling him everything, and then ripped up the letter. I wrote another and folded it into an envelope, putting it under my pillow that night. I put on the old gloves and held my cheeks as if it was him, I imagined his kiss. I put my hands on my belly and tried to channel his love and his forgiveness. I curled up, ready to emerge a stronger creature in the morning.

I sent the letter but I heard nothing back. Maybe I never really expected I would. I saw my friends a lot that September, and tried to pretend like everything was okay. They came and helped me sort out the nursery, which was really a box room but we made it special. We stuck up old album covers from the sixties with oversized flowers cut out with multi-coloured card. We painted old bottle tops and hung them from cotton, so they caught the light and made patterns on the walls.

Somebody's sister had a cot she wasn't using anymore and a neighbour donated a stroller. I went on marches with friends and work buddies; we held our placards and shouted our slogans. The politicians seemed to be listening, unless they just thought they wanted us to shut up so started to say what we wanted to hear. The damage in Vietnam had been horrific; to all concerned. I sometimes, in my darker moments, wondered if I could face J coming back carrying some of that damage with him. What would we say to each other? Even though he'd gone out when the combat was coming to an end, it didn't mean he wouldn't see the effects of war – all those damaged folk. Life would never be the same for him. And then I cursed myself for thinking such thoughts.

The months drifted by and I still hadn't heard anything back from J. I drifted from one thing to another while my baby grew inside me. I felt I was having a boy, and longed for you to come; longed to feel that unconditional love and to wake up my frozen heart. I filled my days with work at the jewellery store, mending watches and rethreading beads for hippy customers and go-getting businessmen, whoever drifted in and then out again. Did you know it's called horology, the mending of watches and making of clocks? The human race hasn't always been so concerned with time passing; if the sun was on our faces, we'd be up, and when night fell, we'd sleep. I tried to live my life that way so I felt more connected to the planet, so I felt more connected with J and wherever he was.

One day I came in from a protest which had gotten kind of heated. We were all for a peaceful expression of wishes but impatience was growing, and there was a taste of menace in the air from the street cops who seemed to surround us and herd us backwards. A few folk got angry and the crowd started pushing. I was nearly six months pregnant and I couldn't risk being in the middle of a ruckus. I put my head down, and pushed the opposite way. My heart was going like a drum in my ears and suddenly I realised the weight of my responsibility and felt overwhelmed. Tears started to form and I let out a great sob; good thing I did as it caught a few folk's attention and they formed a circle around me and got me to the other side of the street. I took some deep breaths and tried to focus.

I walked away from the crowd and caught a cab back to the apartment, the cab driver kept asking if I was okay and did I need some air, I didn't want to talk about it. I let myself into the apartment and that's when

I saw the telegram, official-looking, lying as if abandoned, on the floor. I leant on the back of the door and slid down, clutched my belly and moaned. I shut my eyes for a long time and when I opened them again, I opened the envelope too and read the words 'missing in action'.

Jeanie and Moll and Chris, between them, got me sorted out and back on my feet, in some kind of way. Moll said she'd come with me to birth classes, and every week we faked contractions, she rubbed my back and I even managed a few laughs sometimes. When I looked at my soul, though, I wondered if I'd wished it to happen. Don't judge me, please. But I wanted to punish myself for what I'd done.

Also, what I couldn't escape from at night were the words in the telegram that told me what had happened to J. Actually it just sounded like they didn't really know; it was political guff, a lot of it, but there were some small details. There had been a freak storm, J was with eight other men and they had gone out on a reconnaissance mission. Trees were blown over and in the chaos the men got separated. When it died down and they reconvened, there was no sign of him. But they found something awful; I can hardly think of it. They found his hand, just there, where he'd been. Even now, I screw up my eyes tight and banish that image from my mind. I can't think of him in those woods, part of a war he didn't even believe in and no reason even for him to be there in the first place. When the contents of the letter sunk in, I tried not to imagine what had happened to him during that storm, or what state he might be in now. There was no talk in the letter of rescue or reassurance; there was no mention of a funeral. In my dreams, he lay broken and in bits or captured by the Viet Cong. I wondered who the other men were; how I could find out, what they could tell me about what it was like for J out there, whether he had gotten my letter. I wondered if he even knew about the baby, and then I hoped he didn't.

I was due on February 20th, my mother's birthday. I had no birthday to speak of myself, although Chris knocked with a bottle of fizz that evening and we shared a glass. I think he was hoping for more. I felt numb inside and bitter, and like nothing could ever mend me. After he'd gone, I watched reruns of 'I Love Lucy' and wondered if life could ever be like that; lived on the surface, jokey and light. I remember the day I got the letter, a week before Thanksgiving. I'd gone for a walk (more like a waddle) around Central Park. The hobo's were in their usual spot, bedraggled and dirty. One of them had made a fire and it reminded me of some weird tribe. They all sat round drinking their liquor or staring at the sky. It was unusually warm that day though, and I remember I took off my winter coat and rolled it up on the grass so I could prop myself up in some kind of comfortable position and feel a bit of warmth from the winter sun on my face. Something inside me lifted a bit, shifted until a glimmer, just a hint of hope pushed its way through. I thought I knew what I had to do and I asked the universe for a sign. God knows, I needed it. On the walk back, you were kicking like mad; it made me giggle and I got some funny looks from a few passers-by. When I opened up the metal door to get into my building I saw an official looking envelope lying there. My heart just leapt into my throat and I had to steady myself against the wall. I crouched down and reached awkwardly for it and pushed it inside my coat. I felt faint and had to lean against the door for a few moments until I could make the stairs. Each step up felt heavy and leaden.

An hour later, I reached inside the coat and took a deep breath. As I went to open it, I saw the postmark was from England, which just didn't make sense. As I read, the words washed over me like warm milk, such a comfort in what they were not, and I began to feel that I might have found a path for myself again, for us. It was typed in caps and in that clipped English way, precise and clear and polite. It said that my Aunt Denise had died and I was the only person mentioned in her will. Despite seeing her at mom's funeral some years before that, I always remembered her as she had been when I was a child, making fairy cakes and with her cool hair, like a beehive I think it was. She'd always worn a checked apron and she wasn't really my aunt, but my mom's best friend from college. We'd visited her on the few times we'd made it back there during my summer vacation. My dad would go off and explore the country side and mom and I would sit in Auntie Denise's little garden drinking her homemade lemonade. Mom always changed when she was with her; like she was lifted. She wasn't as strict with me, and used to let me climb the old oak which was down the lane from the house, standing there on its own. (You even played there when you were little, but you may not remember.) It must have been hundreds of years old. My imagination would run wild with the ideas of what the tree had seen. Maybe lovers, hiding in its massive roots, highwaymen lying in wait in its shadows. James, the boy from the nearby farm, even said someone might have been hanged there. I remember not thinking that was true; it didn't feel like an angry place. Plus it's not a tree's fault if the humans around it use it for ill.

So Denise had come to mom's funeral but I couldn't face speaking to her for long; she looked how I felt, broken with it all and with an aching heart that she hadn't been there at the end. I think she felt so guilty it never let her be. The letter told me she had left me her house and all its contents; that if I decided to accept, I should make a trip to their offices in England by November 30th so that they could sign over the deed to me and give me the keys. There was even a check enclosed for the cost of the flight. Denise had thought of everything. I leaned back in my chair and let my eyes drift to the ceiling; I followed the familiar crack that started at the light fitting and went across towards the kitchen; when J and I had moved in, we'd stuck some glow stars up on the ceiling and they were still there, but dusty. I could just make out the Big Dipper, but it was covered in cobwebs. I breathed out a long sigh. Maybe this was Denise's way of feeling like it had been worth something; their friendship. Her life, even. She hadn't had any children and it only then crossed my mind that she must've felt that bond with me, although at the time I guess I never realised, being young. I felt suddenly so sad that she'd gone, and it was a feeling compounded by my own guilt. I couldn't go there right now, not to that dark place in my heart, but what I could do was make a new start. Thanks to Denise, I could leave that place behind and we could start anew. 'We', I thought and rolled it around my head; we, a family, my family, my baby.

I still had some savings J and I had put aside for our future. I hadn't touched the money since he'd gone but now I withdrew it all and changed it to pound sterling. In the bank, I cashed the check, hopped on a bus and went to the travel agents downtown, even though there was one just around the corner from my apartment. I came home buzzing, like I'd had too many coffees, with the airline ticket burning a hole in my pocket.

I made a decision to be bright and breezy and get on with life; I told Moll what I was doing but asked for her to give an abridged version to anyone else who asked, and say that I'd gone to visit relatives abroad and she didn't know when I'd be back. I talked to you as I packed. I could feel myself cutting the ties, each one, as I left object after object that reminded me of J. I did take some old photo's and his gloves though, and as many LP's as I could fit in my case, wrapped in items of clothing.

We escaped, you and I, in a yellow cab, weaving our way through the streets of the Big Apple. Breathing in the familiar smells I said farewell to the past. Later, as the plane took off, I closed my eyes and pushed away the darkness until it was like it never existed, and my head and heart were in the clouds.

When I pulled up outside the cottage in my rental, I felt a shudder of excitement. The little door was the same, and outside on the front step was the old watering can I remembered, with some kind of stick poking out of it. Frost had decorated the laburnum bush near the small green gate, and iced the edges of the lawn. Near the garage were a few wooden sticks still standing and just about holding on to some shrivelled up old beans which no one had picked. I felt a lump in my throat as I spotted, hanging from the small crab apple tree, a mobile that I'd made for Denise so many years ago. Made of tin foil and coke bottle tops, it caught the sun all of a sudden and reflected a small rainbow onto a patch of the road where the ice had melted into a puddle. I couldn't believe it was still there, but I guess these things just become part of the furniture over time, so you don't even notice.

I opened the gate and walked up the path to the front door. As I turned the key and opened up, the familiar smells of childhood drifted out and danced around me, making me heady with nostalgia for days that had gone; days of innocence and simple pleasures, or problems that could be fixed in a moment.

I had brought some of the things from the nursery with me and the first thing I did was go upstairs to what had always been 'my' room. At that time, Aunt D had no central heating so the room was always cold. She would tuck me in herself, under the old-fashioned blankets and eiderdown. I couldn't move properly but it was like being cocooned; I would wait sleepily for my own body heat to permeate the bedclothes and envelop me for the night. I sat on the single bed, running my fingers over the old white bedspread. It was right, this. I almost believed I *could forget my life in America. It was me and you, darling, against the world. That day, I decided to call you Daniel. It means 'God is my judge'.*

Faith paused and looked at the clock. She knew what she needed to say, but not how to say it. Checking her phone, as she had been doing periodically for weeks, she saw, yet again, she had no messages. She reached for a pen from the mug that Dan had made at school, an ugly mug, she thought it had been called. She pulled a face at it, and made herself smile. She nibbled the top of her pen. *Come on Faith, grow some balls,* she thought, and began to write.

— — —

It was pouring with rain when Fi opened her curtains, which felt like a bad omen for the day ahead. *Typical spring,* she thought. She crunched on her slightly burned toast and tried to shake the feeling of gloom. She'd snoozed her alarm too many times because it was cold and dark outside the confines of her bed. As she was pulling on her boots, a song popped into her head, an inane ditty from the 80's; she couldn't quite remember the name. She wondered what made your brain do that, just throw random things up like that. Could there be some reason, or was it just to distract you from darker thoughts? *Maybe it's your mind showing you who's boss when your heart and soul threaten to take over.*

Phil had been in touch in the New Year, explaining that the shop was overstaffed and asking her to cut down her hours. He said he could no longer justify keeping both her and Dan on simultaneously, but suggested they do alternate days. Fi had no choice – she couldn't be without a job, but at the same time it wouldn't give her enough money to pay the rent. She had been putting the word out that she was available for bar work but so far to no avail. It meant that she and Dan didn't see each other much; their days only crossing over once every few weeks when it was time to place an order or get stock ready for a book fair. She had, in fact, only seen him twice since they had reopened. The first time, he had been distinctly cool, blaming a hangover. Fiona had not been entirely convinced. That night, at the Carriage on Christmas Eve, she had felt they had restored something which had been on the verge of breaking. And later, they had gone to a club. Her memories were hazy but she knew that they had danced, and had fun, and later talked, although she couldn't remember exactly what about. They had gone back to Dan's. She remembered being sat on his carpet next to him; that it had felt like the right place to be. And that morning it was Christmas, and she had experienced a rush of joy at being, for once, herself. He had fallen asleep and she had got a taxi home at about 8.30am. There was nobody on the streets, and fresh snow fall coated the city, bringing with it a sense of clarity, a crisp and untainted world of possibility and chance. Fi had felt on the verge of something, on the cusp of something new. Later that day, she had texted Dan but she had not heard back. As the hours had passed and she'd opened her presents from her family and the few from her friends, her heart began to sink. She realised, in her heart, she had hoped that they would spend the day together, but as the hours ticked on it became obvious that wasn't going to happen.

The second time their paths had crossed, she had reached

a conclusion that somehow she had fucked up, although she couldn't fathom how. What had they talked about that night? What had she said? Racking her brains, she remembered that the conversation had turned to Jacob at one point. Did she tell him she had gone to the cinema with him that time? Would that really upset him so much? She had wanted to make conversation, and asked him about how it was going with Jacob in the hope he might shed some light on how he was acting towards her. He had merely shrugged and said, "It's not," but when pressed hadn't offered her an explanation. Fi felt like something somehow had been damaged; like the night out that was supposed to renew their friendship had somehow gone tits up, and she now found herself an outsider to his world.

She grabbed her coat and her handbag, making sure the shop keys were in her pocket. There were CD's all over the floor near her stereo and half a bottle of wine on the side. *Detritus,* thought Fi, as she unlocked her flat door and walked out into the hallway.

When Fi arrived at work, to her surprise Dan was there. He was talking on the phone – he raised his eyebrows at her and she shrugged, doing the sign of a text. She listened to his side of the conversation as she put the kettle on and opened up the two letters on the side addressed to the Shop Manager.

"It's not in print anymore, I'm afraid, so there's nothing we can do for you," Dan said, a note of barely disguised exasperation in his voice. A pause. "Well, perhaps you should do that then, Madam, goodbye." He slammed the phone down. Fiona grimaced to herself. *I should have texted him, but how was I to know he'd be here?*

"Fi, we need to talk," said Dan gravely, pulling up a stool for her, so she was sitting and he was standing.

She couldn't help it but something in her heart rose up, like a bubble floating to the surface of water, a glimmer of hope. She smiled back at him, her stomach suddenly twisting up.

"It's just not good enough, Fi, you coming in late like this all the time."

She pushed his leg with hers in a playful gesture and giggled. "Not all the time! Besides I didn't know you'd be here. That customer sounded shitty, let me make you a – "

He cut her off in a firm voice. "No."

She was startled and nearly dropped her coffee cup.

"I've had enough," he continued. "I'm here doing all the fucking books and trying to keep the shop afloat while you just swan in whenever you feel like it,"

Fiona gulped. "But why didn't you say something? They've always been up to date when I've come in. I didn't think you'd want me to do them, that you'd think I was trying to take over..." her voice trailed off.

"No, I wouldn't have. Maybe I should have said something, but now I am." He looked at her in a way that made her shrink, like some kind of shot-down Alice.

"I'm sorry," she said, in her small voice, trying to hold back tears. "I thought, with all the time off you had before Christmas...I covered for you then." He was looking at her coldly. "It's just a misunderstanding," she continued. "That's all, isn't it?"

"Well, you need to sort yourself out, Fiona!" Dan virtually spat this at her. "I don't know who the fuck you're shagging this time but he clearly doesn't work a 9 to 5 job."

She felt like shouting at him, *I'm not shagging anyone. He turned out to be a psycho. And you think the sun shines out of his arse!*

Instead she said, "Have you been checking up on me? Maybe I am late sometimes, but I always try and work hard once I'm here." She knew she sounded pathetic, like she was talking to a headmaster. Why was he making her feel like that?

"Phil's been calling in. He told me."

Fiona was silent. Dan looked at the floor and then back at her, and his eyes briefly implored her to speak but then just as quickly he realised she couldn't and he walked out of the little office.

The world took on a hazy quality as things Fi thought she knew wobbled into a different type of focus. Looking down, she saw that her hands were shaking, and she noticed a mark on her trousers, which she hadn't noticed this morning. She licked her thumb and rubbed at the mark, which just seemed to look worse. What was it? Milk? Wine? She didn't know. Through the grey window, rain was still falling. *Pathetic fallacy,* she remembered it was called, when nature reflected your own feelings. Inside she felt empty and yet she knew she had to function. Dan was still her boss, he had given her a warning, that was all it was. Why couldn't Phil have done it himself? Whatever the reason, she knew she needed to rise above it and move on. She knew she shouldn't have been coming in late. Reaching into her pocket she pulled out a screwed up tissue, opened it out to a bit that she could use, and blew her nose quietly. Checking herself briefly in the toilet mirror, she took a deep breath and pushed her way through the wooden beads and into the shop.

Dan was holding a clipboard with orders attached to it, and his eyes were fixed on the shelves in front of him.

"Would you like me to do that?" she asked.

"No, no..." he said. "Maybe you could tidy up the library corner and check that new delivery," he said not turning around. "Please," he added, inclining his head slightly in her direction but unable to look at her directly.

"Of course," she replied, lingering a brief moment, and then turning towards the other side of the shop. She felt as though he was looking at her back as she walked, yet knowing this wasn't enough to make her turn around.

— — —

It was 11am but the cafe was nearly empty, save from a few students who looked like they hadn't been home yet from the night before. Cobbers was this little, hidden place down a side street. Dan had discovered it years before on a quest for an all day breakfast cob, at Fiona's request, when they were having a particularly dire day at the shop. When Quinn had asked to meet, he'd felt instantly that it needed to be somewhere he was comfortable, and he'd also felt slightly paranoid about being overheard. Quinn had hinted at the significance of what was to be discussed, but not the content; in his words, "something big". Upon relaying this to Ella, Dan had tapped his nose in compliance, before he realised that wasn't quite the right gesture, although he couldn't quite remember what was. Ella had encouraged him to go, saying it would be good for him. He hadn't been home in days and had been rejecting calls from Fi all of yesterday morning. She had left a few angry messages but in the last one she had just said, "Call me". He hadn't had much sleep and days and nights had merged into one. He and Ella had been shagging, eating, drinking and then doing it all over again, and Dan felt himself in a weird fog of weariness and newness which wasn't altogether pleasant, but was at least different. Ella had told him he was wasted at the bookshop; she had known Quinn for a while and she really believed he could change the world. She said that Quinn had gone 'on and on' about Dan when they'd met, because he could see something in him; potential. Dan had wanted to go home yesterday but she hadn't let him, or rather, had used her powers of persuasion to get him to stay. She was sexy in a weird, slightly unhinged way and Dan felt teetering on the edge of things while in her company. Ella had only let him leave that morning because it was Quinn who'd called on him. Dan hadn't heard from Fi again and he felt like he might have got away with it for now, and after all, she knew she'd been taking the piss coming in late every day.

It was a Saturday and town was crawling with the lichen of the night before, a smell permeated the air, of stale beer and yet peppered with a strange, opaque undertone, which Dan could only associate with early spring. This time of year always seemed to smell the same. He ordered a cappuccino and a bacon sandwich. The young man behind the counter was new and had taken ages to notice Dan, despite several loud coughs. He was at that moment trying to create a swirl in the foam of Dan's drink. In the end he gave up, shrugged and looked at Dan apologetically, opening his hands out in front of his heart. This was when Dan realised he was actually deaf. Dan smiled back and put his thumb up to say it was okay. He took his order and found a table in the corner. It was a bit wobbly, so he rolled up a drinks mat and stuck it under one of the feet. He felt sure that Quinn wouldn't like a wobbly table.

As Dan waited, his mind drifted once more to Fiona and the last time he had seen her. She had come in late, and Dan had pulled her up on it, simple as that. She had taken it so personally though, and then barely spoken to him the rest of the morning. Instead of letting it go, he had pursued it and what started as bickering had quickly developed into an outright row. She had asked him why he thought he could interfere in her life, and he had pointed out that this was work, and he was her supervisor. She'd burst into tears and slammed a pile of books down on the counter. When he followed her into the back, he lost his temper and said some stuff to her that he thought she needed to hear, and then he'd walked out.

About two minutes away from his house he'd literally walked into Ella; he'd been storming along and she had stopped to rummage in her bag and they'd collided. He'd invited her in and she'd told him she only lived around the corner and asked him to come to hers. On the way, she'd talked about the group and told him he'd been missed. He'd felt secretly pleased to hear this.

He was going over this chance meeting again in his head, when the annoying buzz of the door went off, and the entrance of Quinn interrupted him from his train of thought. Pulling off his cap as he entered, Quinn shot a quick glance around the room and Dan caught his eye and waved. He mock-saluted and went over to the counter to order. One of the students, a girl with dredlocks, started giggling, and her friend turned around to look at Quinn. It was bizarre, really, the effect he had on people, especially females, it seemed. Quinn casually ordered his drink and, nodding a 'thank you' to the guy behind the counter, he sauntered over to where Dan sat. He gave the student a look on his way over and Dan could see from here that she was blushing. Dan couldn't help grinning at him when he sat down, but Quinn looked serious and didn't even acknowledge what had just happened, which made Dan feel a little childish.

"How you doing?" he asked, taking a sip of his coffee, and pulling out one of the white plastic chairs.

"Alright mate, yeah. I've been a bit busy but…hey, well, it's good to see you!" Dan felt he was gushing slightly and tried to pull himself together. Quinn gave him a dry look which Dan didn't know how to take.

"Look dude, I'll get straight to the point. I wanted to meet you today because I need to know, firstly, if you're totally committed to the People of the Sun and what we believe in,"

Dan hadn't been ready for the sudden seriousness and was taken off guard. He suddenly had to abandon all of his prepared small talk and he didn't know what to replace it with. Quinn started to drum the fingers of his free hand on the table, which made Dan realise he was taking too long to answer.

"Yes, I am, like I said I've been a bit busy and I'm sorry I didn't come to the last meeting but – "

"Hey," he touched Dan's arm. "I know you've got stuff going on, fuck the shop, more power to the little man, y'know?"

Dan wondered exactly what stuff Quinn was referring to and

how he knew about the shop. Had he been talking to Ella?

"So to cut to the chase, this is your chance to change the world." He paused.

"Are you in or out Daniel? Enquiring minds want to know..." At this, Quinn gave him a crooked smile and reached forward to squeeze his arm again.

Dan took a deep breath. *Fuck the shop*, he thought. *Fuck my normal life, fuck Fiona, fuck...*

"In," Dan replied, and the collar of his shirt began to feel a bit too tight. "Definitely in." He took a gulp of his cappuccino as Quinn's face relaxed.

"Excellent! I knew it," he shook Dan's hand enthusiastically. "You can tell those who are committed and those who just come along to ride the wave, you know? They make me sick those fucking hangers on, looking for a bit of excitement, jumping on to one cause and then the next like some political orang-utan or something!"

Dan laughed nervously, and was relieved when Quinn laughed too. The atmosphere lightened up. He felt like they were having a normal conversation now, that he was just a part of an everyday scene, and that was fine.

"I like that analogy, that's brilliant," Dan said confidently. "I'm not one of those, although it sounds like fun."

"Yeah man, whatever..." There was the awkwardness again. Dan thought maybe the best thing would be to shut up and listen. "If you aren't one of those, or some other limp-wristed gobshite, which I know you're not, then I want to discuss my plans in more detail. You up for that man?"

Dan nodded and took a sip of his cappuccino, which burned

his mouth but he tried not to let this show. Quinn lowered his voice in a conspiratorial manner.

"As you know, we need to take action, and we need some of our key people to play an important role, namely you and just a handful of others," Quinn paused dramatically.

"Hey, what can I say? I trust you mate."

Dan nodded again. He was a 'key person' now.

"So a lot of this has to be on the down low dude, but logistically speaking, you need to get yourself down to London in four months time...can you do that for me?"

"Well, um, in theory, yeah, I'd have to sort it with work, but I'm sure Fi...I'm sure we could sort it out," Dan replied. Fiona felt very far away, almost like a lost cause, and he pushed her easily out of his mind.

"Well," Quinn said, giving him a wry smile. "I guess a few more days wouldn't hurt, hey?" Dan didn't really get his meaning but smiled back and then watched as Quinn finished his drink and artfully chucked it into the waste bin near the door.

"Meanwhile, we've got the protest coming up in a few weeks. Ella said you guys would give me a hand flyering and drumming up interest. I presume that's cool with you?"

Dan was surprised Ella had included him in the decision; she hadn't struck him as the couply type. At the same time, he didn't feel a refusal was an option.

"Of course, let me know how I can help," he replied.

"Great stuff, have to run now Dan, it was nice seeing you," Quinn said, as he got up to go.

"Oh, of course, you probably have a lot of...lots to do," Dan replied, stumbling over his words a bit and feeling slightly foolish.

"I'll be in touch," Quinn said as he was walking out. "Say 'hi' to Ella..." he added, with a wink.

– – –

Dan walked through the centre of town, going over Quinn's words in his head. Town was busy with young mothers and kids who should be at school but were skiving because it was only a day or so before Easter break, hiding in doorways with their hoods up and sneaking cigarettes. The kids not the mothers – they just stood talking while their babies cried or licked ice lollies, dropping them on the floor and crying again. He saw the man on the corner next to BHS shouting 'good news' and telling them of their ultimate salvation, while in the background a Peruvian band played the pan pipes. It was a tune he recognised from childhood – something his mum used to play. He knew he was being an arsehole but he still hadn't got in touch with her.

His mind returned to the conversation with Quinn: what was this 'something big'? As if in answer, his phone vibrated in his pocket. He picked it up. Quinn: *Couldn't talk properly in there but wanted to see you face to face.* Dan typed in *I'm 100% up for it, any details?*

A moment passed and Dan thought he had overstepped the mark by being so direct. Quinn wasn't the sort of person you questioned – he gave you the information when he was ready. A message: *A big statement, some danger, but serious recognition! Delete this text and call me from a payphone this evening. Q.*

What the fuck? thought Dan. *Some danger...* He slowed his walking pace and thought about what to do. Although he knew he needed his life to have some meaning, now the opportunity had presented itself, he didn't know if he had the balls to do it. And what was *it*, exactly? Of course, they *were* activists. If they wanted to make an impact they had to take drastic action. He wondered if he could talk to Ella about it. He realised he was heading that way without thinking, and stopped. He knew what she would say. He suddenly became aware of how little he knew her. Looking one way, he saw Macklin Street and felt himself turning towards it. Tentatively, he made his way up the shallow incline, past the bizarre hairdressers cum model railway shop and the closed down laundrette. The Blank Page's sign was blowing slightly in the breeze. As he approached the front door he noticed the small post-it note saying 'Out to Lunch'. It was not Fiona's handwriting, although it looked vaguely familiar. He turned away, puzzled, and then saw a familiar figure making its way towards him. Phil, the owner. *Shit.* Dan looked down at the floor and turned to walk the other way. He didn't want to see him. He hunched up his shoulders and put his hands in his pockets. He walked far enough that he felt safe and turned. No-one there, Phil had obviously let himself back into the shop and Dan had got away unnoticed. He rummaged around in his pocket for his fags and lit one, taking a deep inhalation which gave him a head rush. He kept walking, more slowly now, and found himself heading out of town, past the funeral directors and homeless shelter, towards Grant Street, where he knew Fiona lived.

At the off licence on the way, he picked up a bottle of red wine, in the hope that it would build a small bridge and that maybe they could share a glass while he talked to her about his predicament; if she even wanted to speak to him. She must have the day off, he thought; she might not even be home. He didn't know what he would do if she wasn't, but it would probably involve heading to the local park and drinking wine out of a paper bag like on the old American films his mum liked. His phone rang; it was Ella. He rejected her call. His mind drifted as he paced forward.

Approaching Fiona's street, he caught the sweet smell of honeysuckle from a small patch of hedge which bordered the pavement for a few feet, and a bird scuffled about, startled by his passing. It seemed so quiet up here, compared with the city centre where he had been just moments ago. Walking into the courtyard where Fiona lived in her little flat, he felt lighter and at the same time, more purposeful in his intent. He didn't look up at her window, but noted in the corner of his eye that it was open. The bedroom curtains were closed, but he thought he could hear some music. It sounded like Radiohead, or Jeff Buckley, a mournful male voice, haunting the air. He pressed her doorbell and waited. A moment later, she put her head through the window and, seeing it was him, she let out a small yelp of surprise.

"Hi," he said, shading the sun from his eyes as he looked at the outline of her. "I brought wine..." He couldn't tell if she was smiling or not – he thought not – and she disappeared.

He gulped, the light feeling he'd had wavered a little, and then a bunch of keys landed at his feet, giving him a shock. He looked up again but she wasn't there. After trying two keys, he found the right one and let himself in, feeling a weird bubbly anticipation which he couldn't account for.

As he rounded the landing, Fi opened the door of her flat. Her hair was tied back and she looked as though she was in her pyjamas. She didn't smile and she didn't let Dan in straight away. The bubbly feeling dissipated and he felt suddenly that he didn't know what he should say.

"So…" she said, smiling weakly with her hand on the edge of the door as if to form a barrier.

"So…" he said in response, searching for the right words and finding them. "I'm sorry for my behaviour at work…I had some stuff to sort out, in my head. I didn't need to be such a shit about it."

"Mmm," she nodded, "Alright." But he knew it wasn't. He looked at her brightly painted fingernails, scuffed and gripping the door. She noticed him looking and loosened her hold, then turned away and gestured for him to follow her.

Over her shoulder she said, "Sorry, it's a bit of a mess."

The flat smelled of weed and some kind of incense or scented candle, and the sunlight made patterns on the living room wall that looked like the branches of the trees which leaned over the courtyard, almost like a reflection. There was an old maroon sofa, which looked as though it had once been grand but now had a permanent imprint of its owner on one side, and a notebook and some CD's on the other. There were cushions everywhere, and an old record player in the corner. Dan wondered if it still worked and then saw the answer in the pile of LP's strewn by its side. The music was on softly now, which made Dan think that Fiona had planned to let him in all along. This made him feel a bit better. She sat down on the sofa and he looked around for another chair, but there wasn't one, so he plumped for the biggest cushion and sank down on it. Wordlessly, she picked up a silver tobacco tin and started to make a roll-up, which she then handed to him.

"Thanks Fi," he said. She shrugged. The little gesture did something to his insides, plucked at something and he suddenly felt very sad.

"I'm sorry for being an arsehole," he said, in a long out breath. "I've not been feeling myself lately."

He knew this sounded pathetic. She looked at him squarely in the eyes.

"Really? I hadn't noticed."

He started to explain and then realised she was being sarcastic. They smiled at each other, and the icy atmosphere between them began, on the edges, to show the first signs of a thaw.

She leaned over and lit his cigarette and then her own. He looked around again and said,

"I really like your flat. It's very…you."

This made her laugh. "People always say that when they don't like your taste, have you noticed that?"

"No! I love it, it's…hippy and retro." He took a drag on his roll up.

"Well, thanks. I take that as a compliment."

They were quiet for a moment.

"Glass of wine?" He proffered the bottle of Bordeaux and she looked up at the clock. It was just after 2pm.

"Umm," she said, but that moment of indecision was all he needed and he got up and walked to the small kitchenette.

Fiona laughed. "Top right hand cupboard over the sink," she told him. "A *small* one for me, please."

Over a glass of wine, they talked about what they'd been doing, each leaving certain parts out for fear of exposing themselves too much, because things hadn't been right and now they needed fixing. When Fi reached over to the bottle and topped up their glasses, Dan felt some relief. He wasn't going to be kicked out just yet. He felt he didn't want to go anywhere else. He turned around to look at the pile of records and picked up one by Muddy Waters.

"Mind if we put this on?"

A smooth, deep voice broke out, peppered by crackles from the scratches on the record. Dan grabbed another cushion and sank down with his hands behind his head.

'I want you to rock me like my back ain't got no bone', the man sang.

"Good choice," said Fi. He saw her take three rizlas out of her tin and stick them together. Dan shut his eyes.

'Throw your arms around me like a circle round the sun. I want you to call me daddy, let me lay down in your arms.'

His mind drifted back to the conversation with Quinn and something began to gnaw at his stomach, but he told himself he hadn't agreed to anything yet. He could still back out. He knew he wanted to talk to Fi about it but wasn't sure how to start. This music was taking him back in time somewhere.

A nudge on his leg stirred him from his daydreams about smoky jazz clubs, and he opened his eyes. Fi held out the joint for him. He took a long drag and put it down in the ashtray beside him.

"I do need to talk to you about something," he said to Fi, as he felt his head lighten.

"Oh, sounds serious," she said, pushing her hair out of her eyes and pulling a cushion off the couch so she could sit facing him on the floor.

"I'm all yours," she said.

"It *is* serious, Fi," he said, then giggled.

"Obviously!" she replied, laughing and then pulling the corners of her mouth into a frown. "No, seriously, I am listening. Ignore the expression on my face…"

He sat up and clasped his hands in front of him on his lap. The joint had gone to his head but he wanted to be able to think clearly.

"What would you do if someone asked you to do something that you knew would change your life, but was dangerous?"

Fi's expression darkened. He took a swig of his wine to steady himself.

"Oh…I wasn't expecting that," Fi said, reaching for her drink. "Do you mean something…" She lowered her voice, "Something *sexual?*"

Dan nearly spat out his wine. "No!" he spluttered. "Trust you to think that!"

They both laughed and then found that they couldn't stop, each feeding off the other's amusement. After a couple of moments, Dan pulled himself together enough to say, "Something that might change the world."

Fi stretched her legs out so they were touching Dan's and she leant back on her elbows.

She stopped laughing but maintained her smile.

"Well," she said, looking him directly in the eye, "do you mean change it for the better?"

He leant forward again and picked up the joint, taking a drag as he spoke.

"I think so."

The record was stuck. Muddy kept saying *'Rock me, rock me'*, over and over again. Fi pulled her legs under her and leaned across Dan to reach behind him and give the stylus a nudge.

Her shoulder was right by him, nearly touching his chest. Her long necklace brushed against him. He noticed she had a mole on the right side of her neck which he'd never seen before. He felt as though he should pull back, as though she was too close but something was pulling them together. As she moved back, things seemed to slow and he watched his hand touch her head. She stopped and looked at him. He pushed his hand into the strands of her hair and felt them run between his fingertips. Something was happening here. Her eyes were slightly red and her expression almost reproachful, and yet at the same time, he knew at that moment that he could not stop what he was doing; that it was somehow inevitable. That whatever had led them to this moment would not let it pass by unnoticed. She reached out and put her hand on his cheek and her fingers were soft. He pulled her towards him gently and for a brief moment they paused, lips almost touching, as if that line didn't have to be crossed, as if it *wouldn't* be. Then they began to kiss. Cold fingers running up his spine, tingles and pinpoints of light in his head. Their bodies drew together so that their top halves were pressed against each other's. Dan's arms around her, fighting a surge of emotion the like of which he had never known before. Lost in time and frozen in a moment of pleasure, there they were like a painting, the two of them…

Until Fi pulled away.

For a brief moment, he felt her hand rest on the back of his neck and then she removed it, and the skin underneath felt cold again.

"Sorry, I…" She looked down at the floor and moved away, back to her cushion. Dan found himself staring at her, dumbly.

"Sorry," she said again. "It's just I…."

He sighed. "I know, I thought – "

"How do you know? I didn't tell you." She sounded a bit hurt. "You never asked me about it…"

"I thought you'd tell me if you wanted to," he said. They settled back in their seats, apart from each other. Fi put her head in her hands.

"Can I have one of your roll ups?" Dan asked, quietly. A sour feeling like a grey mass arched its fingers and readied itself to take hold of him. He swallowed.

"I didn't think you wanted to know," Fi replied, a note of bitterness in her voice. She got up and went over to the window. It had stopped raining and a large puddle had formed in the courtyard, reflecting the clouds above it. Fighting against it, she felt tears forming and knew that she couldn't turn round. The song that was playing faded out and the new silence that formed was not comfortable.

"Maybe I should go," Dan said. Fi nodded, knowing that she couldn't speak without betraying her distress. She heard him leave and moments later, watched him walk across the courtyard. Of all the men she thought would leave her like this,

Dan had not been one of them. Something in her insides ached at the sight of him walking away, his back unturned and his departure so swift that she reeled from the shock of a day that could have gone one way and now could only go the other. She pushed the curtain over and shut it out.

– – –

It was Monday and Dan was back in work. Fiona had called in sick, and this time Dan hadn't challenged her, but he hadn't dared talk to her about the weekend. Shortly after leaving her flat the previous Saturday, Ella had called and he had answered. He had felt as though he suddenly had nowhere to go, so he'd headed to Ella's house. As he walked, his disappointment at how the afternoon had panned out had started to morph into anger. Fi should have told him she had a boyfriend before they'd kissed. He assumed because she hadn't, that it was nothing serious. Why had she kissed him back if it was? When he remembered the afternoon, he thought about the way she had leaned over him; how she had got him stoned. She must have known something might happen. The more he mulled it over, the closer to a decision he came – that Fi couldn't help herself. She threw herself at men and now he was the latest on her list. He thought back to the way she talked about some of her conquests and suddenly felt pity for those hapless males. He shook his head, and quickened his pace.

When he'd reached Ella's house, she opened the door wearing a man's dressing gown. He'd pushed his hands inside and felt her nakedness. He had shoved her on to the bed and let his hands and body do whatever he wanted to do to her, because that was what she wanted. It had been real and flesh and hard and life. Afterwards, he had walked out to the payphone across the road and called Quinn.

And now he was standing on the third step of the step ladder in the shop, when he heard the bell go. He replaced the book he was examining and climbed down to greet the customer. The man whose back was turned, now faced him with a big grin.

"Dan! How's it going, man? I never knew you worked at *this* shop, how about that…"

Quinn walked over with an outstretched hand.

Shocked, Dan climbed down from the ladder and shook it.

"Quinn…good to see you again, have you got a day off from the – "

He paused awkwardly, wanting to say 'cult' as a bit of a joke but suddenly knowing Quinn wouldn't take it too well and swallowing it – "…office, so to speak?"

Quinn grinned mischievously and tapped his nose. "Enquiring minds…!"

His face became serious and he leaned in closer to Dan.

"You still in, Dan? We're counting on you."

Dan nodded and said quietly, "Did you get my message?"

Quinn winked. "Sure did, I was waiting for the right moment to call. You free later on?"

"Yeah, of course," Dan replied, still trying to work out how Quinn had known where to find him.

"Well, shall I….leave you to it or…can I help with anything?" He said, shakily.

Quinn put the book back on the shelf that he had been holding and looked at Dan.

"Well, actually, I was kind of looking for someone."

Dan felt a twinge of something unpleasant around his consciousness.

"Oh? Someone who works here…or perhaps you know Phil, the owner? He's into – "

"Fiona, dude, is she in today?"

Dan felt slightly sick and tried not to let it show.

"She's not, actually, no. She's off today." He knew he sounded prickly but couldn't help it. He felt a flash of anger but didn't really know why.

"Hey, no worries! Maybe I'll swing by again tomorrow. "

Another shoulder squeeze hand shake combo and Quinn was gone. Dan stood silently for a second, and then had a quick glance around to see if anyone was lurking in the shop. When he found no-one, he walked into the back and sat down on the tall stool and breathed again. *What the fuck*…he thought. *What just happened?* He ran his fingers through his hair and took a deep breath while his mind tried to piece things together.

Why was he so freaked out that Quinn now knew where he worked? Was it more because he felt like he had agreed to something he couldn't un-join? Quinn and Fi…was Quinn her *boyfriend*? She hadn't even told him who she was seeing, which was unusual for her, but he'd suspected it. So she thought he knew it was Quinn; that's what she had meant last time he'd seen her.

Before now, she had always told Dan about her various sexual misdemeanours and ill-fated lovers. At the beginning he'd secretly felt that it would be okay, just some arsehole who she'd picked up and it would all end in tears, and at the time he had felt bad for thinking that way. But now he thought about Saturday night and felt slightly queasy as the memory of their kiss came back to him; the feel of her skin under his fingertips. She had seduced Quinn? How long had it been going on? His insides span as he tracked back in his memory to their conversation. Had he said anything about Quinn's plan? Some parts of it were blurry. He had kissed her, he had kissed Quinn's girlfriend. *Shit.* He sank down onto the second step of the ladder and bit his thumbnail, the panic rising to his chest.

He took out his mobile and wondered who he could call. He scrolled through his phonebook, past Fiona, past Jacob, and phoned his mum.

"Hello, Faith?"

He loved the way she answered with her own name. He hadn't even realised it was a quirk until he was old enough to ring people and realised not everyone did this.

"Mum, it's me. How are you?"

"I'm fine," Dan could tell she was smiling. "My god, Dan, you haven't called. I've been real worried. I thought you...Is everything okay? Aren't you at work?"

"I am but it's really quiet," He didn't know how to continue.

"So are you, quieter than usual. What's up?"

"Mum can I come over next week? Sorry I haven't seen you or even called for ages. It's just..."

"Please come over, Dan. We really need to talk to each other, to catch up. I've missed you sweetheart."

"How about next Thursday?"

"I shall put it in my diary," he imagined she said this with a wink, since she kept herself to herself. She'd always called herself a bit of a hermit. She didn't press him about his silence, which he was glad of because he didn't really know what to say.

As he sat there, he looked around at the shop. He could be anywhere. Who knew where he was? Who even cared about him, right at that moment? *What's the point in me?* Dan thought, bitterly. He thought about Jacob and how he had let his father down; how he hadn't been who he was meant to be. And now Fi. She had lied to him. She had treated him like everybody else. She was the same as all the rest.

He felt a sudden and fierce anger surge through him like the tide, and he took a book from the shelves and hurled it across the shop with a guttural noise which sounded almost alien to him despite it coming from his own body. He grabbed at more books and threw them with all his might, all the while roaring at the world, swearing and cursing until the shelf was empty and then he stamped on them, sweating with rage and yet cold inside. When finally his madness was spent, he slumped onto the floor. He knew what he had to do.

CHAPTER NINE

"WAKE UP HUMANITY!" sang the crowd in a dirge. "ONLY WE CAN SAVE OURSELVES!" And repeat. Dan stood with a placard and thrust it into the air in time with the shouting. Ella was ahead of him, awakened as she was by the public spectacle and probably the sniff of speed she'd had before they'd left the house. Dan hadn't partaken, but Quinn and Ella had shared a line. They seemed really familiar, physically; Quinn touched her often, Dan noticed – partly because he didn't have the same ease with her. Even *he* found Quinn attractive in a weird way; one of those, if you *had* to be gay for a night, who would you choose, that sort of thing. Then he thought maybe it was supposed to be someone famous, not someone you were currently standing next to in a crowd of people, whose sweat you could almost smell, whose arm was pressing against your own. *Stop with the gay thoughts,* he told himself, and thrust his placard up again for another go.

There were at least two hundred people here, Dan guessed; not bad for a couple of nights of elicit postering and a bit of daytime flyering in the city centre and suburbs. It confirmed to Dan that Quinn really had tapped into something; not that he himself was ever in any doubt. The protesters moved like some kind of swarm up the narrow street and past the posh shops. People came out to see what the commotion was. There was a police presence ("always a sign of success" Quinn had said when they'd arrived that morning to see barricades already up.)

Ella detached herself from the crowd, going up to two smartly dressed women standing in a shop doorway and getting right in their faces with her placard. They recoiled. Dan did inwardly, but then saw Quinn turn to him and laugh, throwing his head back, so Dan laughed too. Ella returned, fired up and eyes wild. Two other protesters broke out behind and did the same. The police began to look at each other, and there was some pressure around them, almost invisible, like a small tightening of a knot on a limb, that you could hardly notice but it was there. They spilled out onto the market square, where they were promptly directed by the police down Friargate and past the greasy spoon where Dan and Jacob had first talked.

He hadn't seen his father for weeks. Embroiled in his affair with Ella, he had spent most evenings talking with Ella and Quinn about the future of mankind and how we'd all taken the wrong path. He'd quit his job at the bookshop, much to his mum's dismay. He'd told her he was pursuing something more meaningful and that he had paid his taxes all this time, so why shouldn't he get the dole for a while? She had insisted on giving her a letter she had written, the one she'd mentioned before. He had only stayed for a half hour. The letter still sat unopened in his house on the coffee table, where he had thrown it when he'd gone to pick up some more clothes.

He hadn't heard from Fi since that night, and he didn't want to. It was like a veil had been lifted and he could see here for what she was. Plus she was sleeping with Quinn. It was simpler to break ties. Once he'd decided to do these things, life seemed easier, simpler. There were fewer decisions to make but he felt more alive than ever. He looked at people around him and wondered when they would all wake up. Quinn's philosophy was that in the western world we needed a massive shake up. We needed a near apocalyptic disaster to remind us of our priorities. Too long had we been munching at the trough of capitalism side by side and yet separate. We needed to join together and take action. He said something was in the pipeline, and this 'gathering' and others like it would pave the way for people's awakening (Quinn didn't like the word protest). Ella would join in enthusiastically with these discussions, except she would lean more towards the animal rights side of things. She believed animals would rise up and take over, and that one day we would all live as one, with equal rights. Dan knew that 18 months ago, he would have laughed at such talk, but now his mind had been opened. He was no longer tied to his 9 to 5, shackled by old friends and habits. He could do what the fuck he wanted. The one thing he did feel bad about was not seeing Jacob for all this time, and he couldn't imagine what he was doing. He hated to admit it, but he didn't want to lose the old man again; or rather for Jacob to lose him again, since that was more the way of things.

As for his mum, he had felt weird seeing her. He had confronted her about the time he had turned up on her doorstep that night. She wouldn't speak to him but kept thrusting that stupid letter into his hand, so he had lost his temper and walked out. Dan thought back to the man who'd been visiting her that time. He wondered whether there'd been some romance but quickly put the thought out of his head. He'd only gone round on a whim. There had been things he needed to tell her and things she'd needed to know.

He couldn't remember at what point he had blurted it out, only that he had…

"Right, I need to tell you something, something big. The reason I didn't before now is 'cos he told me not to say, because he still cares that much about you, god knows why."

He swigged at the bottle of wine in his hand, watching, in his dazed and severed consciousness, Faith's expression change.

"What are you talking about exactly? Sit down, please." She had an unusually stern tone, but it had only served to make him even angrier.

Dan stayed standing. He leant forward for effect and felt himself nearly stumble on drunken limbs. "My dad!!" He laughed wildly. "Back from the dead, ha ha! Who'd have thought it, and a nice guy too!"

Faith turned very pale. She felt a sick feeling envelope her heart, slowly placing its cooling, strangling fingers on her insides.

"Are you saying that Jacob has found you?"

"Yes, for god's sake! Jacob!" Dan shot back at her. "He says he looked for you, but you'd disappeared. He told me what happened in Vietnam, and how you'd just gone, when he got back, he looked for you," Dan was waving his bottle around so at each gesture of emphasis it spilled on the floor. His mother did not react.

"Aren't you going to say anything?"

Faith opened her mouth and then closed it again.

"So it's true!" Dan spat. Faith stood up and finally found her voice.

"You don't come into my house mouthing off without giving me the chance to explain," She said this quietly, but she stood up and walked a few steps towards him.

"Then explain!" he shouted back at her.

"Not until you sit the fuck down," she replied through her teeth. The unexpected swear word was like a slap and momentarily sobered Dan up enough to look for the nearest chair. He slumped down, his head spinning from the adrenalin and the alcohol.

"You said the 'f' word..." he mumbled, with his eyes shut.

"I did." Faith answered. "Now why don't you tell me what this man is like, the one telling you all these things. Where did he come from? How did he find you?"

Dan rubbed his eyes. "He came to the bookshop, he's a nice guy."

"So you said, Dan" Faith said, her voice wavering slightly. "And how did he find you?"

"I dunno, he tracked me down, you can do that these days, with the internet and everything. You can find out anything,"

"That makes me feel a whole lot better," Faith said, maintaining a cool exterior despite her insides briar-twisted like a thorn bush. Dan sat forward and rubbed his forehead. It occurred to him now, that Jacob didn't seem like the kind of guy to use the internet. He didn't even have a phone. Maybe he'd got someone else to do it for him? But how did he even know Dan's name? Hadn't he gone missing before he was born?

"Mum – " he began, looking up at her swaying form. He thought he might pass out in a minute.

"Describe him to me," Faith demanded, firmly. "What is he like?"

"You should know, you – "

"Cut the bull, Dan," she said, cutting him off. "What does he look like?"

"Old!" Dan giggled despite himself. "Older than you, haggard-looking, a limp, looks like me."

Faith remained silent. She clasped her hands in front of her, on her *lap and twisted her serpent ring, around and around her finger. She couldn't look at her son at this moment.*

"Don't you want to know more? He has a grey beard. He looks like a tramp!" He snorted. "Got a tattoo on his arm but it's like numbers not a picture."

"Anything else? Distinguishing features?" Faith said, settling back into her chair slightly and putting her hands over her mouth as if to brush away something she wanted to say.

"No mum, he's just an old man. Lonely, old man. A bit weird! Funny sometimes…" Dan's voice was trailing. He had closed his eyes and sleep was calling, beckoning, and it was a relief to let go of the fury and the hold of the booze and the arguing and the fact that nothing would ever change.

— — —

Dan was being jostled and he shoved back. Someone had started a new chant, "Fuck the police!" and a small group of the protesters took it on. There was a new air of aggression as they rounded the corner of Surgeon Street, near the church where the Chinese restaurant had opened its doors, and the smell of noodles and soy wafted out. Suddenly, Dan heard a window smash and turned, half expecting it to be Ella. A man had pulled himself halfway up a lamppost and was shaking his bloody hand in the air, shouting, yawping in to the crowd, his eyes crazed. The building was a disused office, still bearing the name of the publishing company that had been housed there. Now, another man climbed up and joined in the roar. Some of the crowd broke off, now directly pushing in the direction of the police at the side of the crowd. Quinn had commented that there seemed to be too many police officers and Dan noticed now that it seemed disproportionate to the size of the protest. The noise grew and he noticed a few of the officers getting out riot shields. No-one had expected this.

He turned to look for Ella, but she had disappeared. Quinn was still close behind him, grinning. He grasped Dan's shoulders and said something which Dan couldn't hear. Dan began to feel crushed. Quinn still had hold of his shoulders, and people around him were becoming unsteady on their feet. Pushing, pushing with suddenly nowhere to go. His breath quickened and he pushed his placard down and into the people at the side of him. He created a small gap, crouched slightly down and pushed his way through as best he could. Using the placard as a kind of prodding stick, he eventually surfaced at one side of the chaos and found himself at the corner of Junction Road. Jacob's flat was just 200 metres away. He cut through the walkway behind the tyre shop and began a swift pace towards his father's place. As he walked, he realised he wasn't worried about Ella. Was that because Ella was her own person, he wondered, or because he didn't care enough about her. There was something dirty about her, in a sexual way, but also like she was somehow *unclean.* Unhinged, for certain. That was what had attracted him to her, partly, in the beginning. He reached the red door of the old terraced house where Jacob lived. The paint was peeling off and the edge of the door was slightly battered, as if someone had tried to force it at one time. He'd never been inside before, once picking Jacob up from here but waiting outside at the old man's instruction.

Dan went to ring the bell and then noticed that the door

was slightly ajar so he pushed it gently and walked in. The tiles on the floor felt dusty under his feet. There was a smell of old washing, left to rot, and then by contrast some kind of cleaning product. It was dark, there being no windows and no glass in the door. He found a timer light and pushed it, but it wasn't much lighter. Jacob was number three. He walked along a narrow corridor, spotting two doors, one with a number one on it and one with nothing on it at all. He surmised that Jacob's flat must be on the floor above and made his way up the creaking stairs. It was the kind of place you wondered what went on behind the doors; Dan wondered if you could rent a room by the hour. Did Jacob care? Or was it just that he didn't have a choice? They had never discussed money in any depth, although Dan had happily paid for drinks and bus fares when they had spent time together. As they'd got to know one another more, he had formed the impression that Jacob was somehow comfortable in his poverty. Either that or he had some money stashed away somewhere and chose to live like this for some unknown, possibly masochistic, reason. To punish himself, maybe.

The door at the top of the stairs said number 3. Dan knocked and waited. No reply. When he knocked a second time, the door moved slightly and he realised that this one too had been left open. He started to feel nervous. What would he find? Had something happened to his dad? It had been weeks since they had seen each other, and as far as he knew, he was the only person who gave a shit about Jacob. He suddenly felt awash with guilt, and pushed open the door, half expecting to find his father lying dead on the floor from a heart attack, or some such fate. The room was virtually empty. There was an ashtray, half full, on the small coffee table and the curtains were half closed, although a large bay window let quite a bit of light in. Smoke and dust filled the air, and it smelled stale, like an old cupboard. A single bed lay in the corner, half-made, and Dan wondered briefly if anything was ever finished in this place. He hoped to God when he was Jacob's age, he wouldn't be living like this.

He called his father's name but there was no reply. *Should I just wait?* He thought. *What if he doesn't come back?* But it was a welcome relief to be out of the madness of the protest. He couldn't even hear it here; perhaps they'd moved on or it had dispersed. He remembered his mum telling him about the marches she used to go on about the Vietnam War in the 60's and, despite himself, felt a flash of admiration for who she used to be. *But that was before all the lies.*

Dan sat down in the solitary armchair, which faced the window, and let the rays of sun, refracted, touch his face. He suddenly thought of how he hadn't laughed in a long time; why was that? The stupidity of other people; that life was too serious to be flippant about; that he was no longer who he used to be – someone who didn't care enough. Someone who joked about issues and who, day to day, only concerned himself with the goings-on of his own, sad little life, and that of Fiona's. He screwed up his eyes and pushed his fingers through his hair hard, as if to remind himself of where he was; to check in with the present. It was when he opened them that he noticed a small notebook on the coffee table. It was old and battered, with some kind of creature on the front, a dragon perhaps? Or another kind of winged myth from a fairytale, etched into the dark red leather. There were scraps of paper and the edges of photo's sticking out. Instantly, Dan knew what he should *not* do at this moment. *Don't look inside.* And yet, there were decades of his father's life that he knew nothing about yet; some of which Jacob was decidedly cagey about and Dan couldn't help but resent him for that. Why go to such lengths to find your son, after all this time, and then keep stuff from him? Why not just lay it all on the line? He could feel himself making excuses for what he was about to do before he'd even done it.

He got up and walked the few steps to the table and quickly opened the front cover. There was an inscription there, written in some calligraphic style. "Lo, that the doors will be opened; Unto a future that washes away the darkness of the past with truth and light; may that time be yours..." Dan wondered if it was biblical, but he was pretty sure that Jacob was a man without faith. He suddenly realised what he'd just thought and the irony of it. Under the inscription was simply the letter 'F'. *So it was a gift from Mum, it must have been.* Jacob had kept it all this time. Perhaps she gave it to him before he went to Vietnam, to give him hope? *And look how that ended.* Dan sighed.

He knew he shouldn't continue with this invasion, but before he could tear himself away he had pulled at the corner of one of the photographs. It was torn around the edges so he expected it to be one of his father and Faith or some other image from that time, but when he looked it took him a moment to focus and process what he was seeing. That was him, wasn't it? And Fiona, taken from the outside of the shop. Dan was closer to the lens, with an open book in his hand, and Fi was perched on a step behind him. He felt puzzled and then slightly on edge. When had Jacob taken this? There was nothing to indicate this in the picture itself. He had never seen his dad carry a camera. His curiosity awakened, he pulled another photograph out, despite feeling nerves lick at the edge of his stomach, hinting at something he shouldn't know. Here was Dan alone, outside his own house. It looked as though he was just leaving to go out. It had been taken in the dark with a flash, which lit up Dan's face in a weird glow, in contrast to the darkness around him. Now he felt sick. Jacob had been following him? Watching him? Another thought picked at the edges of his mind, unformulated yet, but it didn't make sense so he didn't follow it, not yet. Something said *stop* and yet he carried on; this time opening the book somewhere in the middle. There were some bullet points here, with notes written freehand, messily scribbled and difficult to decipher. Something about 'the flyer', 'Fiona' and other things he couldn't read. He turned the page and found a neater passage. As he read it, his blood turned cold. It said, *Tell him I joined a cult or something, a charismatic leader. It all went wrong. Why in jail? Firearm/weapon? Some kind of violence but I was a scapegoat. He needs to believe me. Might stop it all from happening, might change everything.*

Dan put the book down and felt a tinge of vomit in his throat. So Jacob had made that up? Why? What else had he lied about? He flicked backwards with a sick and unstoppable sense of curiosity. He saw, on another page, *Vietnam? I had an accident and then looked for Faith – no forwarding address. Found him how? Internet? Through friends? Might not ask. Need to build trust or it won't work.*

Things began to add up, and the more they did, the more they fell apart. The lies, the lies the man had told, and for what purpose? How could he have been so stupid? And how could this now happen, after everyone else had lied, or turned out not to be who he had thought. The biggest one of all had been the last for him to discover.

At that moment, Dan heard some footsteps on the stairs. He turned towards the door, ready to unleash the full force of his anger. As if in slow motion, the door opened and there stood Jacob, with a pint of milk in his hand. He stood motionless with one hand resting on the door frame. He smiled at first, for an instant, and then his smile disappeared. Dan found that he could not speak, so he picked up the notebook and walked over to Jacob, shoving it in his face.

"What the fuck is this, old man?" he spat. Jacob looked at the pages and back at Dan, his face blank.

"Just my diary, that's all. How come you're here? I wasn't expecting – "

"Your diary?" Dan interrupted, his voice quaking with emotion. "I'm particularly interested in the part where you plan what lies you're going to tell me, do you know the bits I mean?" His voice had grown to a shout. Jacob grabbed the book off him.

"You shouldn't have been reading it." He turned away, putting the book back on the table. "They're not lies. I just needed to plan how…how I was going to approach you, in case you thought I wasn't for real."

Dan stormed up to Jacob until he was right in his face.

"BULLSHIT! Admit it, you're not my father, you're some fucking weirdo who decided they want to live out some fantasy and fuck up someone else's life in the process. How long were you following me? I've seen the photos!"

Jacob was quiet. He walked over to the couch and put his head in his hands. Dan followed him.

"So you're not denying it?"Dan asked, laughing maniacally. Jacob looked up at him, his mouth open but no words forming. "Answer me!" he demanded, banging his hand on the glass coffee table. A crack formed.

"It's not what you think, Dan. I want to…to help."

"YOU want to help ME? It's you that needs help you crazy fuck, I tell you what – you can help me by staying out of my life. For good. Don't contact me again, I mean it." Dan turned abruptly to go.

"Just let me explain!" Jacob shouted after him but he was too late. He heard the bottom door slam and sighed; a long, defeated sigh, an out-breath in which was held all the sorrows of time. Had he failed? It couldn't be so. There must be another way.

– – –

Faith was covering the Year 3 science class for her colleague, and the children were over-excited.

"Mrs Anderson, what are we doing?" asked Ben, rocking on his chair.

"It's Miss Anderson, and you'll find out in a moment," she replied, tapping her nose and trying to set up the newly-installed projector so it would work.

Without looking behind her, she shouted "Back in your seat, Miss Lizzy!"

Lizzy did a comedy freeze as Faith turned around, and some of the other children giggled wildly.

"She's frozen!!"

"Calm down guys, please."

"But how did you know, Miss?" asked Will and Emily in the corner. "How did you know Lizzy was being naughty when you weren't looking?"

"Teachers know everything," Faith said, in her most mysterious-sounding voice. Her lesson was about plants and she passed around some big sheets of paper for each table.

"Write down everything you know about plants – let's see which group can come up with the most interesting facts." The kids scrabbled over pencils and there were the obligatory why's about being able to sit with so and so or use the computer. Tim sat staring out of the window.

"Tim won't join in Miss," said a little girl whose name she couldn't remember.

"I can see that, you make a start and I'll see what I can do," she replied, smiling. She crouched down next to Tim, who had his head in his hands. "Hey Tim, I think the group need your help, how about it?" He shrugged, and gave her a look.

"You want to talk about what's eating you?" This got a smile. "Is it something with big sharp teeth, or is it just having a little nibble?" He shook his head and tried not to laugh. "Which one?" Faith asked. "Can we scare it away?" He nodded.

"I've heard that these kinds of monsters get really scared of little children when they laugh a lot, haven't you?" she continued. Tim nodded again.

"Right everyone, pencils down." Faith stood in the middle of the classroom. "We need to make Tim laugh – who wants first go?" Lizzy leapt up and down with excitement. "Lizzy –

what a surprise! What can you do for us?"

"I can run in slow motion, Miss!" The kids laughed, and someone said "Oh yes!"

"Come on then, let's see it."

There was some cheering, which Faith shushed down. Lizzy stood up slowly, and began her robotic manoeuvre around the classroom, pausing for fake collisions and pretend falls while the other children put things in her way or tried to put her off. Before long everyone, including Tim, was laughing and he came and sat with the rest of his group. Faith laughed too, and suddenly felt a wave of emotion, unexpected, like a shadow. Her eyes filled with tears. She quickly turned back to the board.

With pen poised she asked, "Okay then gang, what have you all come up with? Ben, let's start with you." Discreetly, she rubbed her eyes with the back of her hand. You had to be careful – children noticed everything.

Faith turned the key in the ignition once but the car did nothing. She tried again and the car sputtered into life briefly, then faded once more. She'd been meaning to take the damn thing to the garage but kept putting it off. It wasn't dark quite yet, but she knew that most of her colleagues had gone home while she'd stayed to get her lessons prepared for the next day. Not only that, but they had an inspection that week and she'd gotten behind with her paperwork.

She turned it again, mentally crossing her fingers; nothing this time. She got out her mobile, a cast-off from a friend's daughter. Dan always laughed at it. She found his name in her phonebook. They hadn't spoken since she'd given him the letter and she didn't know if he'd read it. She couldn't face the thought that she might have yet again pushed the most treasured person out of her life for good. *Stupid, stupid woman,* she called herself. And yet, she knew she had to be honest. What did life mean if you weren't? Faith had spent days agonising over what to do when she realised that he was a 30 year old man, and she had no power anymore.. She felt obsolete, and all of a sudden, sat in her malfunctioning car, completely alone. Despite her misgivings, she pressed 'call'. As predicted, it went through to voicemail.

She popped open the hood and got out to take a look. She was proud to know her way around a car engine a little, but in this situation she only knew to check the battery was connected okay and that was as far as it went. She hated to admit it but it was at times like these that life would be easier if she had a man around; although, that in itself was no guarantee of help. She surmised that, in another situation, she could call Judy's husband Rob, but he was useless at mechanical stuff. Faith fished out her breakdown card from her purse and called the 0800 number. The man on the other end of the line reassured her that someone would be out to her as soon as possible. *Shit,* she thought, starving and rummaging in her hand bag for sustenance. She discovered a Snickers bar and got back in her car to eat it.

Faith was not usually one for feeling vulnerable, but as the light crept away and shadows took over, she found herself thinking about her current situation in more detail. She hadn't left a message for Dan, so he didn't know what had happened. The school where she worked was a nice school in itself but in a bit of a crummy area of the city. She guessed she might've looked kind of obvious sat there in the car park with her in-car light on. She could switch it off, but then how would the RAC man see where she was? Well, hers was the only car in the car park so they wouldn't miss her, surely. She turned it off so she was sat in darkness. Getting her phone out again, she began a text to Dan, but she was struggling to see the keys properly. Finally, she sent a brief message explaining that she was okay but waiting to be picked up from school on account of car trouble. She'd try and call him tomorrow, and hoped he was okay.

As she placed the phone on the seat beside her, she became aware of movement outside the car park. Her heart gave a flutter as she saw two, no, three boys shimmy over the gate one after the other. *They're just teenagers*, she thought, and she tried to say to herself that they wouldn't be interested in her. Which she was sure would be true, but still she felt a surge of anxiety in her chest. *Like a sitting duck,* she thought before she could put the expression out of her mind. Had they seen her before? They were probably just down here to smoke fags or weed or just vandalise the playground walls. God knows, she'd had enough of trying to scrub the graffiti off with the Year 6's on detention. It always came back a few days later.

She continued to watch as the boys made their loping walk across towards the old school hall, about 20 metres or so from where Faith sat. When was it that teenagers became so...well, so unusual, Faith wondered. They even moved in a different way these days; like they were dragging the other half of their body reluctantly along with them. Their sideways glances – designed to unnerve, or borne of insecurity? And so many more mental health issues these days, or maybe they were always there, just unrecognisable amidst adolescent angst and hormone swings. The tallest of them had gotten out a can of spray paint, and was beginning to make his mark on the stone bricks, while another boy sparked up a cigarette or joint and passed it onto his friend after a couple of drags. What was it that made your friends, at this age, so hugely important – vital to your well-being, and why that inherent desire to push your parents away?

She remembered Dan going through a death metal phase; Faith would be downstairs, listening to the scream of Napalm Death or the slightly more tuneful Mötley Crüe. She would turn up her music to combat the dirge, but she knew if she asked Dan to turn down his, it would go right back up again after a moment or two. He had grown his hair long and he wore those black, tight jeans. Faith never knew how he even got them on in the morning. There was a goth-girl he hung out with. She had, or at least thought she had, lots of attitude. Faith had gotten the feeling she had a troubled home life, and once she thought she had spotted some cigarette burns on the girl's forearm, on a rare occasion when she had let some of her flesh see daylight. She was only in her late thirties herself, at the time. It was so strange to think that Dan was 31 now. Where did that time go? What would they be doing 10 years from now? She felt a sudden sense of loneliness, a premonition of the years to come; of a separation from her son.

She hadn't noticed until that moment that two of the boys were walking towards the car. Her heart thumping, she tied to rearrange her expression to one of casual indifference. *Don't show them you're frightened.* She wound down the window as they approached.

"Alright sweetheart," one of them said. Faith couldn't help but smile inside at the absurdity of this pubescent boy of about 14 calling her 'sweetheart'.

"Fine, thank you," she replied. "Are you boys having fun? I see you're decorating the school walls again. It's a shame; it takes a long time to clean off."

The other boy looked embarrassed and looked down at his feet. The first one said,

"What's it to you?"

"Oh nothing," Faith said. "It's a pity there's nowhere else for you kids to go these days, that's all."

The boy looked at her as if he'd expected a different kind of response. Then he kissed his teeth at her and said,

"Yeah, whatever lady, laters." He banged on the side of the car, which made Faith jump, but she was relieved to see that he had already turned away so hadn't noticed. The second boy looked to his friend and back to Faith.

"Sorry about the graffiti," he mumbled, and sloped off after his friend.

She watched as they talked to each other, the boy who'd banged her car relaying the conversation to the older one with the spray paint; the quieter boy kicking an invisible stone around on the concrete. Some lights appeared then at the gate, and the boys turned around, startled, then quickly ran off towards the playing field. Now that she could – now that the imagined danger had passed, Faith smiled. *Just boys,* she thought. Fifteen minutes later she was sat in the tow truck next to a bearded RAC man, who was telling her about his day. She tried to listen but found herself switching off, her eyes following other headlights and people and wondering who they were, where they were going. As they wound their way out of the city and into the countryside, she reached out to Dan, in her mind and willed for him to make contact somehow. To let her know he was okay.

Making a decision on her way home, she asked the RAC man to wait for her outside Dan's house. Faith couldn't take it any longer; she had to take control of this situation. She couldn't lose her son. Feeling like an intruder, she let herself in using the key he had given her years ago, so she could check on the house if he was away. It had nestled on her keyring until now. Why hadn't she done this until now? *Because it's wrong,* she told herself, but went in anyway. The house was dark and quiet. She called his name. Nothing. Finding her way to the sitting room, she flicked the light on. Her heart leapt when she spotted the letter on the coffee table. She looked around again, and went over to pick it up. Still sealed. Faith put it in her jacket pocket. Her nerves frayed, she turned the light off and left, closing the door firmly behind her.

— — —

The man called Jacob sat in the same position, but smoking. He rubbed the lines of the bridge of his nose, and kept rubbing, as if he could somehow erase the ravages of time. His mind whirred with possibilities and implausibilities; of missed opportunities and despair. In trying to repair something, he knew, he had only made it worse; pushing it towards its logical conclusion. He stubbed his cigarette out and walked towards the bathroom. Aloneness seeping through his pores, like oil. What could be done? He must use up his last chance of redemption and if he failed, then so be it. He reached inside the small cabinet and pulled out his razor, carefully removing the blade. Quickly he made a small cut across the rim of his fingertip. It began to bleed immediately. He looked at the red liquid oozing out, a reminder of his fleshly status, and yet his impermanence in this place, this situation, how easy it was to become lost. The clouds outside parted, letting a shaft of warmth into the room, the edge of which rested on his left shoulder. He turned to put his face into the warmth. Sunlight casting pale on shadow, Jacob licked his finger and disappeared.

– – –

Dan walked without direction but his ears tried to track any unusual noise so that he could join the protest once more. He didn't know what else to do. After about 20 minutes, he realised the crowd had probably dispersed or gathered at the Fu Bar, the People of the Sun's usual meeting place. He headed in that direction. Above him, the clouds became denser until he felt the first few drops of rain. He had brought no coat, so sought shelter under the cover of a nearby office car park. Pulling his sleeves down over his hands, he wondered how it could have come to this. An immense sadness overtook him, and he found his eyes filling with tears. It was a blanket of grief, threatening to smother him then and there in that car park; grief over what might have been; the knowledge that he had been deceived and shared his life with a stranger; the realisation that his real father had never come looking for him. Faith had never expressed her total certainty of Jacob's death, which was partly why Dan had eventually bought into Ja...he stopped himself, what would he call him now? He settled on 'the imposter'.

Anyway, he now thought, it was Faith's ambiguity about the fate of Dan's father that had led him to be taken in by the imposter. Why hadn't she been straight with him? He had never asked much of her, and yet she had chosen to be vague about something as important as that. Didn't she value him enough to be honest about her past, to help him understand where he had come from? He felt the sadness being replaced, atom by atom, with bitterness and anger. By a stroke of pathetic fallacy, there was a clap of thunder and the sky turned even darker. Dan walked out into the storm, forcing his way through the pelting downpour and letting the raindrops mingle with his tears and wash them all away.

Later on, when the gathering had scattered, Dan was helping Simon and Ella clear up the flyers and general debris left behind by that amount of people crammed into a relatively small space. Ella found a £10 note and went to the main bar to buy them each a drink. Quinn was buoyed up, on his mobile and pacing around the room, stopping every now and then. Hs face was serious. Dan needed to keep busy. He did not want to let his mind drift back to earlier that day. Ella returned from the bar and gave him an uncharacteristic smile, biting her bottom lip. She had in her trademark bunches and suddenly he felt a pang of desire. He shoved the rest of the flyers he'd picked up and took a quick glance around the room, before taking the drinks off her and putting them down on a table. "Back to yours," he said. She looked at him and then over at Quinn. "He won't even notice we're gone. I'll text him and say we got waylaid. Come on."

They walked back to Ella's quickly, desire crackling about them like the first sparks of a fire. As soon as the front door was closed, Dan pushed her up against the wall and they had quick and feverish sex. The pleasure of it took him away from where he had been and away from his thoughts. After she'd come, she went down on him, there in the middle of the hall. He loved that about her; she didn't give a shit that her housemates could walk in at any time. For that matter, at that moment, neither did he.

An hour later, they sat, Ella talking about the protest and chain smoking, as she was wont to do when she was excited. Dan half-listened but his mind was elsewhere. He suddenly remembered his mum's letter. Where had he left it? What was in it? Did he even want to know?

At a pause in her spiel, Ella said, "What's up with you?"

Dan shrugged.

"Nothing."

She raised one eyebrow and shrugged herself, putting her cigarette out in her empty tea cup. "Don't be like that," he said. "You really want to know? I don't want to piss on your chips."

"Tell me," she said. He told her an abridged version of what had happened; about the first time he had met 'Jacob' and how he'd slowly been convinced that he was indeed his long-lost father, lost in Vietnam and come to find him after all these years. Thankfully, she didn't offer any advice but merely listened. He brought her up to date with the day's events, and she breathed out a long sigh and then offered him a cigarette. They were both quiet for a moment.

"You should call him 'John Doe'," she said, in the end.

"Oh," said Dan, who had been expecting some kind of urging to move on or put it all behind him.

"Or JD, for short," she continued, lighting his cigarette and then her own. He smiled.

"You're quite unusual," he said. Ella looked pleased. "JD it is then." They clinked imaginary glasses just as the doorbell went.

It was Quinn and Simon accompanied by the blonde girl he had seen at the very first meeting he'd gone to. It seemed like a lifetime ago. Quinn was carrying two bottles of champagne, and Simon held three more.

"Let's celebrate," Quinn said, grinning. "Ella, get some glasses will you, chick?" Dan was surprised that Ella didn't recoil at being called 'chick' as he felt sure she would if *he* had used such a term. She went off to the communal kitchen and came back with five odd glasses, placing them on her small glass coffee table. Simon got out a bag of coke and cut five generous lines on the glass. He asked around for a note, and they all had their share. The conversation inevitably turned to the day's protest. Simon and the other girl, whose name was Ruth and didn't suit her prettiness, were enthused about the message and kept praising Quinn for his speech at the post-protest gathering; how it had been rousing, to the point, and was sure to go down in history in years to come. Dan secretly thought they were going a bit far, but Quinn just sat listening, doing that half-smile of his. After they had come to a pause, he turned to Dan and asked,

"What did you think?" Dan chewed his lip for a brief moment, and replied "Genius." Quinn shoved him away as if to say *nah* but it almost looked, Dan thought, as if his opinion had mattered. Quinn gestured to Ella to move and she did so, swapping seats with him so she was next to Ruth. He leaned in close to Dan and said,

"What do you think of Big Ben? As a symbol, I mean? Of our movement."

Dan nodded. "It's a public symbol already. How about copyright? Can we use an image of it on our flyers or will we get sued?"

Quinn laughed. "I don't really mean it like that. I mean, we could use what it stands for to…make a point. You know, alert people all around the world to our message." Quinn looked briefly around him and said quietly, "Let's meet. Tomorrow. The park, say 2pm?"

Dan nodded. The conversation turned to politics as it inevitably did, and Dan sat back in his chair and let them talk.

The park was peppered with a few dog-walkers, and over on the other side, a running group stopped to check their heart rate and then began again, almost in unison. They looked the same except for their varying outlines. They moved together around the perimeter of the park and Dan watched them for a moment. He didn't notice Quinn until he was standing right beside him. They walked to the playground and sat on a bench. There were no children there yet, as school had not yet finished for the day. Quinn explained his plan in detail. He had some contacts who would put together a device for him which would stop the Great Clock of Big Ben at 10 o' clock precisely. Quinn would attend a pre-arranged tour, and hide the device in a designated place.

Dan would pose as a member of the team of the Keeper of the Great Clock, an engineer sent to wind the clock and make sure it was working properly. This happened three times a week so it was just a question of making sure that the real engineer was waylaid somehow, allowing Dan to replace him. It would be his vital role to affix the device to the correct part of the clock's mechanism. Quinn had already been in touch through a friend of a friend with someone on the security detail of Big Ben who would ensure Dan wasn't challenged at the gate.

Dan couldn't quite believe that the plan would work; he felt sure that such an important landmark and one so close to Westminster would have much more stringent entry procedures. Quinn reassured him that a phone call from the right people that morning, along with the correct contacts inside, as it were, would guarantee its success. He called it a clever prank – one in the style of the Joker from Batman, expect without the universal broadcast and ridiculous demands. It had one purpose and that was to wake people up and convey the 'time for a change' slogan of the People of the Sun. It would cause disruption and people to talk about it; open a dialogue between people that might otherwise not exist. Dan had to keep reminding himself that this wasn't a film, some Mission Impossible style caper; that he was playing an important (if illegal) role in a possible paradigm shift, or at least the beginnings of it. This could be the ripple that started the wave that brought change. There was no doubt we needed to change. Our lives had become so small, Dan thought.

He remembered something his mum had said to him when he was younger and not sure what to do with his life. *Think big,* she had urged him. *Don't waste your short time on this earth.* No, he decided then and there; he would not.

CHAPTER **TEN**

THE TWO BROTHERS HAD *gone out early in the hope that the storm had unearthed some new treasure not noticed the previous day. At worst, there could be fallen fruit, useful bits of rubbish to discover, or at best metal, or maybe even an old army supply box with candy in it. They had lost part of the roof of their house, and their mother had told them she could use just about anything. There were many trees down and the older boy, who was called Bao, which means 'protection', went ahead, true to his name, and cleared the way for the younger. Three year old Tam followed on his sturdy little legs, clambering over the branches that had been left behind by the storm and chatting to himself while he struggled to keep up with his older brother. The air was weirdly still and the animals in the forest eerily quiet, as if they were holding their breaths for another bombardment from the weather. Bao had just spied something interesting; a backpack, he thought, and was about to race over to retrieve it when he heard a high-pitched scream.*

"Tam!" He raced towards where the sound had come from, panic setting in that something had happened to his little brother and cursing himself for not being more patient and walking beside him as his mother had instructed. As he approached he saw that Tam was alright and still standing, but with his little hand pointing at something hidden from Bao's view. He was still screaming and Bao said calming words to him as he approached and held out his hands to the little boy, who came running into his arms. He stroked his hair and looked over Tam's shoulder to see what had scared him. His breath caught in his throat.

There was a man there, under the branches, not moving. He looked like a soldier, and his body seemed all bent. Just as Bao was taking all of this in and trying to contain his breathing, something unexpected happened. The man opened his eyes.

Huan was washing their clothes, their bedding and anything else which had suffered since the roof had collapsed the previous night. They had a bit of rice to last them the day but the rest was sat in a pool of dirty rainwater in the bowl in the corner. It had been a bad storm, and some of the older people in the community were calling it an omen; saying that it was God who was showing his displeasure at the Yanks for bringing death and pain to the land. Others cursed the Viet Cong for leading them into a war which they themselves wanted no part of. They said this in quiet voices, for fear that they would suffer a consequence for not showing their loyalty.

Huan knew not to believe these things; she had seen storms like this before as a girl and knew it to be nature reminding you who was in charge. Their village had escaped, so far, a chemical attack but she knew it could be just a matter of time. When you heard the helicopters go over, you had seconds to find cover. Huan had told her children they must go to the temple as quickly as possible, or find some other solid structure. They must not let the chemicals touch their skin. Living, as she did, with the fear of damage to her sons and herself, it was hard not to hate the Americans. They had brought so much suffering. However, she didn't care for theorising about the war and tried to give her children the most normal and happy life possible. She didn't want the boys to grow up in fear of other people or other races, or of what might be. Surely, she thought, this horror would have to end soon.

The boys' father, Cadeo, had been caught in some crossfire four years ago. He had gone to collect water from the spring and there had been a sudden spurt of gunfire. It was Bao who had found him. It had taken a long time to coax and encourage the boy back to his normal, daily life. Tam was born shortly afterwards and it was this event that gradually lifted him from his darkness. Huan knew that Tam had been her salvation too. She looked into his eyes and saw echoes of Cadeo, feeling that he was still with them in spirit and in the woods around them. They did not know who had fired the gun that had killed him, Huan simply wished there to be no guns at all. She tried to instil in Bao that talking was the best way to resolve situations. She smiled to herself as she thought of her sons and was brought quickly back to the moment when she heard shouting. Her heart sank as she dropped the garment she'd been holding and rushed out of the house. Her boys, thank you god, were both there, and Bao was carrying Tam on his back like an express package. He was out of breath and Huan lifted the younger boy off him, asking Bao what was wrong.

He caught his breath and simply managed to say that there was a man in the woods, alive but hurt. A soldier. Huan shooed them into the house and checked them quickly over before grabbing her father's old medical bag, which she supplemented with bits and bobs they had found in the jungle; a couple of stretch bandages, cotton wool, antiseptic wash, some tablets she couldn't read the name of, and a packet of plastic gloves. She filled her battered military canteen, another find from the forest, with water from the well. Instructing her sons to stay where they were, she threw a shout over her shoulder to her neighbour, Yen, saying that she needed to go out for a while and asking her to keep an eye on the boys.

As Huan followed the path into the forest, she could feel her heart thudding in her chest and her eyes flickered over her surroundings. She realised she had not asked the boys where the man was, but she could see their tracks well enough so kept going until they veered off the main path. The damage to the woods made them almost unrecognisable because some of the older trees, which she had used as landmarks, were down. She was just wondering whether to turn back when she caught sight of a backpack and she topped in her tracks. She scanned the debris and fallen branches until she spotted something that didn't quite fit. As she moved closer, she saw it was the tip of an army boot, and attached to that, the legs of an American soldier.

Huan approached cautiously, picking up a stick, aware of her vulnerability against not just this but any American, alone as she was. Despite Bao's warning, she still jumped when she saw the man's eyes open and looking at her. Yet it wasn't darkness in his look, nor the cloudiness of opium or hashish that she noticed in other soldiers, but fear. The man was bulky and lying in a strange position. Huan shuddered as she looked at one of his legs, which was twisted at a funny angle. His arms and hands weren't visible.

"I help you," she said to the man in a soft voice. She searched for the correct English words. "You speak?"

The man croaked but it wasn't recognisable at first, then on his next attempt, Huan heard a faint, "Yes."

"Where are you hurt?"

The man's eyes looked wildly downwards, and Huan gently pressed his chest and his ribs. There didn't seem to be any real blood there, just superficial wounds. She looked up at him again and his eyes pointed down. He managed to say, "Hand."

Hesitating, Huan lifted the branch that covered the man's arm and saw, to her horror, that the man's hand was gone. She felt acid in the back of her throat and tried to control her facial muscles so as not to betray her feelings, but when she looked at the man she could see he knew, for his eyes were brimming with tears.

"Nó sẽ ổn thôi," she said, softly. *It will be alright.* She touched his cheek, and then reached for her canteen, her left hand lifting his head up slightly so he could drink; she only let him have small sips each time, for fear of him choking. He didn't take his eyes off her as she got out a larger bandage from her bag and began to wrap his wound. His eyes glazed over, she knew it was causing him pain but she carried on, switching off that part of her that felt empathy. Methodical, she knew she must be; unfeeling, almost. *Stop the bleeding and apply pressure,* she told herself. The wound now bandaged, she undid her headscarf and carefully wrapped it around the stump of his wrist. She knotted it tightly below the wrist to act as a tourniquet.

As she worked, Huan wondered how long this man had lain here, guessing that he had been caught in the storm of the previous night. Her mind cast forward for solutions to the problem of moving him. She couldn't ask her neighbours; most were anti-soldiers and certainly would not want one in the village. Yen might help, but she was too old and crooked to take any weight, especially of this big man. If the Viet Cong found him, she would be putting her entire family at huge risk. She shook her head; it was not a decision to be made now – and went back to attending to his wounds. On closer inspection of his crooked leg, she realised that it was his boot which had become twisted, but his lower leg appeared intact. She gently removed the boot and then checked over the other leg. Looking in her bag, she pulled out the tablets. Huan had no idea what they were so she pointed at them and held them close to the man's face so he could read the name.

"Okay?" she asked, shaking the packet. He nodded. She put two in his mouth and gave him more water. Sitting back on her heels, Huan surveyed the scene once more and devised a plan. She leant over the soldier and looked him in the eye, saying,

"I come back." A flicker of fear passed over his eyes and she repeated her promise,

"I come back. Soon."

Gathering up her things, she looked around briefly to check there was no-one else nearby. She coaxed his injured arm up onto a clump of leaves and debris so it was raised. The she covered it in smaller twigs, and placed the fallen branches over him once again. She could not afford for anyone else to find him. She made the 'shh' gesture with her finger on her mouth.

As she turned to go, she heard him say, "Wait," his voice rasping.

Huan approached him and leant down.

"Your name?" he asked.

"Huan," she replied and smiled.

"Jacob," the man answered. And then, "Thank you."

Walking back through the undergrowth, Huan's breath quickened; not just because of the fast pace she had set for herself. She had promised to help the soldier but at what cost to herself and her children. When her heart explored the alternative, however, she knew there wasn't one. Her own father had been a doctor, of sorts, untrained but capable. He had learned most of his skills from books his uncle had passed along to him. His uncle, whose name was Quyěn, had lived in the city, and had formed an alliance with some American businessmen who didn't agree with the trade embargos in place at the time. According to her father, Quyěn dealt with all sorts of random goods, mainly building materials but sometimes medical supplies and old textbooks. Wanting his nephew Thu to benefit from some learning and feeling that he should better himself, his uncle passed on anything he felt would be of use. He knew the Americans would not miss a few books and he had felt, for himself, that it was too late to learn anything of substance.

Her father had liked the country lifestyle, poor as it was, but he had become an avid reader and on his uncle's death, he inherited other books as well as strange artefacts he didn't know the use for; some looking neither medical nor ornamental. Some of these turned out to be surgical instruments and some household implements to ease the role of the housewife. Huan's mother had laughed about them and displayed them on the crude shelf above her fire pit, where she and other wives from the village would gather and discuss what this or that could possibly be used for. These Americans, they would say. What would their women do if their skilled hands were replaced by metal things? What purpose would they have in the future?

Huan remembered, as a child, playing with a metal spring which walked by itself down steps. She went to the temple with it but the other children ran away when they first saw it, thinking it to be some kind of creature with a life of its own. When she showed them what it was, close up, they had all wanted to play with it. In the end, one older boy had broken it trying to pull it from her hands. She had cried for a long time. After that, she had hidden most of the other treasures her father had given her from her uncle's hoard.

Now, she carried her father's old medical bag back to the village. Her thoughts returned to the logistical problem of getting the soldier somewhere safe. Even if she managed that, how would she keep him a secret? There was no way that she could risk him being found. She knew from that moment that her life would change. She prayed that she and her family would be kept safe.

— — —

Prisoner 481 found himself in a white room. Not unpleasant. Not really anything at all. He looked down at his body, as if to confirm his own physical presence there. There were no visible lines to indicate the edges or the corners where wall met floor or ceiling, so much that he felt as if he were floating, suspended in nothingness, weightless. When he closed his eyes, his lids barely managed to block out the brightness, although there was some relief. He attempted to move his hands, but was unable to. *Ah,* he thought, *so I'm back here again.*

In this place, your senses held no purpose, he had found, so that you lost your sense of self, your sense of place and time. There were no indicators as to how long you had been there or how long you would have to wait. He remembered, as a young man, when cells were made of concrete, and bars over the windows let in chinks of light, and echoing corridors allowed you to hear other prisoners in their protests, their occasional joy, madness and even sometimes their bodily functions. A reminder of your physical presence in the world and of the boundaries created by the people who had decided you were no longer fit for society: pillars and bricks and noises, which told you when to wake up and when to go to sleep and when to do this or that. A way of counting down the days until you might get a sniff of daylight and the everyday air that all the other people on the other side of the wall breathed and shared.

He still carried the wound from a gang attack, when he'd been ambushed in the recreation area by the skinheads. They, like everyone else, thought he was a terrorist and one of them had managed to get hold of a carving knife from the prison kitchen, somehow. They went for his chest but 481 was quick on his feet and they caught his leg instead; sliced through a ligament in his right thigh. He was laid up for a few weeks. It never quite healed properly but he'd got used to the limp. In a way, it made him feel more at home; having a battle scar. When some newer prisoners started talking about how he'd got it, he just let them draw their own conclusions. He even started to believe he was that person; created a shell around his soul, it was the only way to survive.

He cast his mind back to that time; his first stretch after the 'crime'. When the courts had upped his sentence after supposedly finding new evidence, he had been moved to a high security unit. His mother had tried to see him several times when he had first arrived, when was that? Years ago. He had eventually written to her asking her not to come any longer, as he felt the decay and hopelessness of long term imprisonment seep into his dermal layers and spread through his veins and vessels, until he felt his very self was limp and pale and polluted with the bitterness and crime held within its walls. Years later, he wondered how she was; felt the pain of regret and yet felt too much time had passed for them to go back to how things had been.

And when he was even older, how old was he then? He had known at the time but now it the fact seemed to elude him. Forty-five, perhaps? Rumours had begun to circulate of an entirely new approach to prison and rehabilitation. Being 'inside', he had limited knowledge of the progress being made in the 'real' world, but had noticed an increasing lack of human presence in the prison and increased automation, until the inmates' meals were no longer served but were 'delivered' to their rooms through a kind of virtual dumb waiter. There was no longer any social interaction, and this was deemed 'for their own good' since in-prison crime and violence had reached epic proportions. It came that some days, 481 did not see anyone else nor talk to anybody.

Then one day, a very important and official looking man came to visit him. 481 had been overwhelmed by the idea that someone would be coming to see him. Dare he hope that this might be some kind of reprieve? After all, he had always considered himself a scapegoat, although he could no longer remember exactly how that had happened. And he thought he recalled at the time that there were some who had fought his corner, although he no longer remembered what their names were or whether they were friends or acquaintances or neither. He had no mirror in his cell so he made sure his teeth were clean and his nails as tidy as he could bite them down, and he used the starchy corner of his pillow case to clean underneath them. He was aware that his beard was unkempt, but *they* provided no way of shaving oneself; it was necessary to wait until the monthly grooming (which sounded like some kind of luxury but was terribly uncomfortable and left you smelling like a disinfected toilet unit). It was nice though, after those times, to feel your smooth skin again under your hands, to make believe you might be young again.

This man, this official-looking person, had even come into his cell. 481 had even been almost grateful that his hands were tied for fear he might reach out and crush this other body which stood there, this other human being, just for the sheer contact of it; skin not his own, a life from outside. He had so many questions and yet, when the man sat across from him, his demeanour indicated a closedness. His name was Mr Josephs, and he calmly explained that 481 had been randomly selected to trial a whole new method of rehabilitation; one whose progress could be tested and measured, and which, thanks to rapidly advancing technology, could prove one's ability to adapt once again to the rules of society. 481 had tried to interject, keen as he was to recall some details of what his life had been like before, but his efforts to talk were ignored. Politely so, and yet there was no question that he should be quiet. And so he was.

Mr Josephs went into further detail about the method of imprisonment, which they were calling the 'Ladder Project', and how it could lead 481 to complete his sentence in a shorter time, since it allowed for reflection and 'mind-space' within which to 'reinvent oneself'. In the end, that was what sold it to him, although 481 wasn't sure if he had much of a choice anyway. Just 10 prisoners had been chosen, due to the experimental nature of the methods and the expense to the government. He had placed his fingerprint on the dotted line and then he waited. When he'd left, Mr Josephs had not said 'goodbye'.

It was in this waiting period that he began to remember certain things, from long ago. Sitting eating his meal alone one day, he suddenly recalled the taste of peanut butter. Years before, peanuts had been removed from the prisoner's menu due to a rising number of allergy-sufferers, according to the chat of the prison guards, when you could still hear them chatting over their cups of coffee in the canteen. At this point, one of the other 'political' prisoners, as 481 was deemed to be although he no longer knew, had got hold of a newspaper and it seemed as though this was something which was happening in the world at large. Certain foods including peanuts and substances such as gluten and caffeine had been vetoed by the government and if you were found to be cooking with or consuming them, you would be punished. 481 had noted the use of the word 'punished', which seems more like a word to be used for naughty school children, not tax-paying, adult members of society.

On reading a few of the other articles before it had been confiscated, he'd seen no reference to conflicts, national or otherwise, and found himself checking the name of the paper. It was the Independent on Sunday. He had looked for a political column but found none. There were no real clues about what it was like for people outside the prison walls. Every face was a smiling one and all of the headlines held a positive message. Could it be that things had changed for the better? What had made this so? Surely, we were human and thus destined to be at odds with each other some of the time. Wasn't that what life on earth was all about?

And now – this funny memory of peanut butter. He could almost feel the glue-like stuff on the inside of his teeth, and he rubbed his tongue against them. Another time, during grooming, he had felt a small shudder along his spine and after a moment recognised it as a feeling of pleasure as he experienced the strong and sudden recollection of someone's fingertips on his neck. To his delight he found that afterwards, he could summon this feeling at will. He was not sure whose fingers they were, but they were cold, not unpleasantly so – and gentle, as they brushed the tips of his hairline away from the skin. It had awakened something in him, which he recognised as bordering on sexual desire, and yet what he found in those hands was the comfort of a person who cared for him. Perhaps even loved him.

Then one day, they came for him. He had not expected to be taken so roughly, since Mr Josephs, although distant, had treated him with a degree of respect. He was marched along corridor after corridor, and then he found himself in a tunnel, ascending what looked like the steps to enter an aircraft. His suspicions were confirmed when he found his ears popping during the journey, although it was like no flight he could remember; smooth as it was, like butter. He wished he could see the plane they were in. At the other end, men and women in clinical clothes took measurements of him; his body itself and many of his bodily processes. He enjoyed it, the contact, despite their gloved hands. Finally, after being prodded and inserted with various instruments and being asked to change clothes into a bright white overall, which reminded him of old Daz adverts from his past when he had watched the TV, he was given an injection into his arm. He remembered this quite clearly, for it was a female who had delivered it, and before he had lost consciousness, she had removed her face mask and smiled. He was so puzzled, as his mind drifted away, that when he awoke, he still remembered it vividly. Her teeth were very white, and at the right-hand corner of her lips there was a tiny dusting of dried toothpaste. Why had she waited until then to smile at him? What did it mean? Was it a smile of affection or one that said 'I know where you're going and you deserve it'? He thought of the latter some time later, of course.

The image of that smile was all 481 had seen, etched in front of his eyes like a negative, for the longest time; until it had faded and all that lay before him was this white. He'd wondered if he had gone blind; or if they had killed him. That would have been a pretty cost-effective solution to the prisoner crisis, but he had a sense of his heart beating, although his actual physical presence seemed to shimmer. It was not an unpleasant feeling but after while he had tested out his voice to see if he was still there or was just some disembodied mind like in one of those old sci-fi B movies. His voice had worked, and therefore he surmised there must still be a voice box attached and the other physical elements needed to make a bodily, oral sound.

He wanted to move but seemed glued to the spot, although there was nothing visible to explore, he wanted to check if this was really some kind of limitless cell. Where did it begin or end? How could he come from a condition so confined and now find himself in a seemingly endless space? He had sat there for some time, a lot of time perhaps. He had not felt thirsty or hungry. He had not become aware of any discomfort, such as you would expect from sitting in the same position for a long time. He was wondered if this would be it, forever. Then something happened. Like a projector, except it was all encompassing, an image flashed up in front of him. When he moved his gaze, he discovered it moved with him, like the eyes of an old painting following you around the room. At first it was unmoving, the face he looked upon. After a while, he began to notice small twitches or little changes. It was all he could stare at, there was nothing else, and it allowed him to study the face closely. He did, indeed, strongly recognise the face, although it wasn't one he had looked upon in many, many years. Slowly, flickers of memory came back to him: of book shelves; a turquoise scarf; the noise of a bus; the thud of music in his ears; the smell of roll-ups. As he remembered more and more things, the face before him became slightly smaller and yet more concentrated, as if additional pixels were being added with each recollection he made. Until after who knew how much time, a picture had formed around it, a whole person, a scene of life, and the picture began to move. And 481 looked down and he saw his hands, and when he tried to move he felt his body working. He breathed in the smell of a city, alive. And when he'd looked around, as if his mind was creating it, he'd found himself on a familiar street, staring in through a window, at the face of the boy who was so familiar and yet, who he had never thought to see again.

He had watched for a moment. What a young face. This must have been before...things started going wrong. 481 then wondered where he would go from here, although he'd suddenly known his exact purpose. He'd wondered if he had any money, and if so, where it was. In a bank? In his pocket? He'd looked down at what he had been wearing and again, this looked vaguely familiar. He had felt his face and it was rough with hair. Without thinking, he'd sniffed one of his armpits. It had been so odd to smell again after the sterility of the white room. As he was pulling a face, he noticed a woman walking past him, staring. He'd looked away, embarrassed. He became aware that he was carrying something on his shoulder. It was a small rucksack. When he looked inside, he found a wallet, which to his amazement held about £160 in cash. It had been so long since he had seen or handled money that it felt bizarre and he almost wanted to rip it up, because it had lost its meaning. There was also an old book, a journal of sorts. He read the inscription inside, and closed it again, putting it away. Rummaging further, he had discovered a packet of tobacco, rizla and a couple of tubes of filters. In the outer pocket was a small, compact camera. The sudden and burning desire to smoke washed over him like an unexpected wave. *Think practically, man.*

Prisoner 481 had walked purposefully away from Macklin Street, towards the more residential area which led up to the old mill. He was looking for a sign, anything, such as 'Rooms to Let' or a B and B. Turning down Junction Road, he spotted a small notice outside a terraced house: *Studio lets, low prices, short-term available.* He rang the bell. An old lady answered. She was not unfriendly, and yet she did not welcome him either. Not looking him in the eye, she showed him her two available rooms. He quietly explained that he needed very little, and would be willing to pay a retainer, but for the future he asked if she would be willing to take payment in the form of other jobs she needed doing. Could he help her with maintenance? Decorating? He did not say the whole place could do with a lick of paint. She shook her head at first, and then when he insisted, she disappeared into a small room off the hall, which he guessed must be her living quarters or her office. She handed him a ledger book, with a list of names, addresses and two columns beside it, some with ticks and others with red dots.

"I'm getting too old to collect the rent. My husband used to do it but he's...he passed on last month. These foreigners – "

She looked at him again, as if to confirm he did not fall into that category. "They have funny tempers. It's too much for an old woman. Perhaps you can do better?"

The names were almost all Eastern European by the looks of things, and 481 realised the landlady had a good thing going on with potentially illegal immigrants and what looked like several properties dotted around the city centre. Was he about to break the law again? He'd only just arrived. But what choice did he have? He needed a roof over his head. He took the book off her and said, "Leave it to me." She showed him to a room on the second floor. It had cracks in the windows but there was a small kitchenette and a tiny bathroom. Through the dirt on the windows, the sun shone, and it gave him a feeling of optimism.

"Give me enough to cover your electricity and gas, say £20 a week?" she said, as she handed him the keys. Her hands, he noticed, had that waxy quality that comes to aged skin. She made her way slowly down the stairs, as he watched her, which he imagined creaked to the time of her bones. She did not, to his relief, ask for his name or for a reference. What was he to call himself, in this world?

Sitting down on the beaten up and solitary old armchair, he took out the journal from his back-pack. It was empty; some pages had been ripped out. There was a pen attached to a string in the old lady's ledger book. He gnawed through the string with his teeth so he could detach the pen and use it to begin his plan. The first thing he had done was to formulate an alternative history. He would become Jacob, the lost father. If he could convince the Dan of today of that, then the rest of his plan might fall into place. God help them if it did not. 481 had sensed a dangerous glimmer of something at the edge of his heart, which he recognised as hope. Like a germ, it had begun to spread through his soul, leaving him no real choice but to succeed and believe that there might be another way.

Now, sitting back there again, on the invisible cushion of

numbness and emptiness, the hope that he had felt then on his first attempt, had faded and become crumpled like parchment, battered down by the reality. He refused to believe he had failed. He could not, surely, be given that chance, and have experienced that world again without clutching at the possibility of living within it once more.

He thought of his mother, and wondered if she could help, but it had been so long since he had seen her that all he could conjure up was an image of her younger face; it must have been from a photograph. She had her hair up and was smiling, but not looking into the camera itself. As the image appeared before him, details began to paint themselves around it. She was in a grey place, but it was busy. Now, 481 could hear the noises in that place, announcements, the low rumble of chatter, wheels on tiles. He felt almost as if all the molecules in his body were vibrating. He shut his eyes, and became aware of his feet touching something solid. He opened them once more as if from a deep sleep, and found himself in an airport. There were people close to him, nearly touching him but nobody turned around. They wore browns and greys. There was a distinct lack of families and children. And women. He looked around at the people standing at the baggage carousel, and then he saw her, about 5 metres away, waiting. She was much younger, and when he looked more closely he saw that she was pregnant. His mind could not compute that this was possible, and he knew it was a mistake. He had to go back. Just as he turned to go, she looked directly at him. There was a challenge in her expression. It was a second before he realised she would not see *him*, who he *was*, just some stranger. They did not know each other, now. She turned away, spotting her holdall and grabbing it. He watched as she walked away. He wondered if she would change anything about her life or if she could sail away like that, through the mist of time. Locking himself in a free cubicle, he dried his face with toilet paper.

He sat on the toilet seat and shut his eyes, screwing them up tight. He pictured a candle flame, burning. Staring into it, he let his mind become a vacuum, as if he had no memories, no past, no future. About an hour later, the toilet attendant tried the door several times, and opened it to find it empty, save a screwed up bit of loo roll on the floor.

Once more in the white room, Prisoner 481 tried to empty his mind, to start again, to make it as white as the space around him. *No more lies,* he thought. *Lies will not work.* There were too many variables at stake, and too many reconciliations that needed to happen. He had watched it all again and wanted to cry out in anger. And Fiona: a brief touch in the bookshop, and then the hope that Dan might introduce them again, but he had not. The joy of having her close at the cinema; and yet how pathetic he had felt, an old man lusting after a younger woman. Oh, the wasted opportunities that youth could ignore, and with hindsight, the pain of watching love thrown away, desolate, like an empty punch thrown yet missing its mark. He had no need of a face now to transport him back to that time. He had raw and delicious and painful memories, a longing that he had forgotten how to feel, or perhaps he never had. Passion. Desire. Enough to make the trip back without much effort at all, but all the while the unspoken knowledge that this was his last chance. Who will I be? He thought, as he materialised in front of the bookshop once again. Not Jacob, and not a prisoner anymore. A speaker of the truth. A traveller through time.

— — —

Quinn had two journeys to make that day. He walked out of his flat and locked the door behind him, pulling his cap over his head. The first place he headed for was about a mile away. As he walked up the hill towards Juror's Corner, he fiddled with the key ring in his pocket. It was a metal one in the shape of a guitar, which doubled as a bottle opener. He rubbed one of his fingers along the metal edge as he walked, creating a rhythm in his mind, which calmed him. As he rounded the top of the road, he once again went through the speech he had made after last month's protest. The crowd, what was left of them, had piled into back room at the Fu Bar, and the atmosphere had been charged with excitement and purpose. Quinn had grabbed a chair and stood on it, holding his arms out for quiet.

"People of Britain!" A cheer. *"People, from wherever you hail! Here we are — together and united!"* Another roar from the crowd. *"Today we have shown how, to paraphrase a singer I admire, we can start a revolution with a whisper, and that whisper can grow into a shout, which demands to be heard!"* Cheers and applause. *"Only we can change the world and it is way past the time for non-action. We know how to make the world listen, we need to take drastic measures, it's the only way!"* Some whooping and fists in the air.

"We are the People of the Sun, we call ourselves that because we recognise the need for a new dawn in society; an awakening. Too many people live with their heads buried in the sand, going about their daily business, like everything is just peachy, am I right?" *"Yes!"* shouted the

crowd. *"Today we have given them a wake-up call – a shake up! (Here, he raised his voice) A slap round the face!"* The crowd went wild.

"And across the rooftops of this town, we may shout at the top of our voices, as we have done, and will continue to do, that it is time for a change, time for a change – " Quinn began to pump his fist in the air, and the crowd joined him. *"TIME FOR A CHANGE!"* they cried with one voice. *"TIME FOR A CHANGE!"*

He couldn't help but grin to himself at the energy recaptured, at the thrill of it. He was on Cromford Avenue now, and walking past a row of terraced Victorian houses. It was like many other streets in the town; red bricked, wheelie bins outside with white painted numbers on. Every other house had an alleyway, and sometimes you would look down them and see a random object; a shopping trolley from Sainsbury's, an old telly or a pile of bottles and cans, the remnants of a house party, perhaps.

Quinn checked which number he was at and saw it was the next house he wanted. He took a look around him as he approached. There were a few cars further down the road, an old transit van parked across it, and a moped further down on this side. No-one was around. He knocked on the door three times, and waited a couple of seconds, then knocked again once, waited again; then eight knocks. This was what they had agreed. After a couple of moments, he heard the latch being lifted, the door was opened, and he walked inside. Two hours later, Quinn exited the house carrying a bulky looking backpack. He glanced around again, and saw that the van was still there but the moped had gone. It didn't matter anyway, he thought; it wasn't a crime to carry a bag down a street. He strolled off up the road the way he had come, slightly slower this time, and yet still with purpose.

Later, having been home, he called round to Ella's where he knew he would find Dan. When he arrived, the two of them were eating a take away and watching some crap on TV; he tried to hide his distaste. Ella had immediately switched it off when Quinn had come in, and put her plate on the side, but Dan had carried on eating. He asked Ella if she could give them some privacy and she did, but gave him a look, which he ignored.

"I'll get straight to the point," Quinn said to Dan, watching him closely and waiting for him to put his fork down. "We're on for next month; what we talked about. Everything will be in place. You know your role?" At this, Dan did put his fork down. He didn't swallow the mouthful he'd been chewing straightaway, but nodded first.

"Let's liaise, keep in touch. I need to make sure you're on point with the plan. It's a once in a lifetime chance to make such a bold statement." At this, Quinn stood up and reached out his hand to Dan, who wiped his own on the arm of the chair in which he sat before he took it. They shook.

"Great stuff," Quinn said, and turned to go.

"Quinn," Dan said before he'd reached the door. Quinn turned his head. "You can count on me." In response, Quinn gave a wink and a half-smile. He pointed his index finger up in the air, and fired a pretend gun into the atmosphere. Dan smiled.

Outside the door, Ella tried to look nonchalant as Quinn approached her. He reached out and cupped her chin in his right hand, leaning in close to her face. "See you soon, beautiful."

She watched him go, and stood for a moment later, looking after him and seeing the shape of him in the mottled glass getting smaller and smaller. She reached up to touch her chin.

CHAPTER **ELEVEN**

INSIDE THE BIG CLOCK, a small mechanism waited patiently for the right time. Dan sat at a nearby coffee shop people watching. Quinn was right, of course. Life needed a shake up, people in the city seemed like matches in a pile, and they needed throwing up in air so they fell in a different way; into a better way. His was a greater purpose.

A shadow cast across his vision and he looked up. A man who looked vaguely familiar, in a shabby coat, looked back at him.

"JD?"

The man smiled. "Call me that, if you like."

He looked searchingly into Dan's eyes as he sat down across from him. The metal of the chair rasped against the concrete paving as he pulled himself closer.

"Whatever you think of me, or whatever you think you know, we must talk before it is too late. I know what you've come here to do, and it won't have the outcome you seek."

Dan's anger began to bubble but he did not want JD to see it. He did not want to be distracted from his purpose.

"There's nothing you can say," he said through gritted teeth. "You can't know what I feel, or what I've seen. You're not even my dad, so you can't claim rights over me."

"But I do know what you're feeling," JD's voice sounded suddenly weary and he rubbed his eyes.

Dan spat back: "How can you possibly know? Why do you

keep interfering with my life? Haven't you done enough?"

A waitress appeared. "Can I get you something, sir?"

"Yes, please, a coffee would be great," said the older man. "Thank you."

He sat back in his chair and looked around him. He saw the city of his misspent youth, and old memories like shadows passed across his face. The sun shone through gaps between buildings and through the criss-cross of the wrought iron table, making patterns on the floor.

Finally he turned to Dan, and said: "I'm not who you think I am."

"I don't think you're anyone, I don't think you're anybody, why are you here?"

"Sorry to make you angry." JD looked down at his feet and sighed, which infuriated Dan even more.

Dan banged on the table, shouting, "How did you even find me?" and a few customers turn round uncomfortably.

JD didn't reply.

Dan looked puzzled, suddenly. "Where's your beard gone? You look…"

"I wanted a clean start," JD said. He rubbed his chin, and took a breath.

"Why did you say you were my father? Why make me believe that?" asked Dan, his voice breaking.

The older man leaned forward: "Because I knew you'd want to get to know me, and then you would let me into your life."

Dan's temper was beginning to fray.

"How? How the fuck did you know that?"

"Because…" He looked down at his hands on the table.

"Because I know you better than you know yourself. I know you then, after, I've always known you and I always will."

"Oh, this is bullshit!" Dan scraped his chair back furiously and scrabbled in his back pocket for some change.

"Wait, Dan! Look, I know what you're up to," JD continued, raising his voice.

Dan's stomach lurched and he stopped in his tracks, but he maintained his cool exterior.

"I'm just having some time out," he said, quietly seething. "Some time to reflect."

JD looked out at the square again and back at Dan, fixing his gaze.

"We both know that's not true, Dan. You came here on a mission, I understand, I know that group you've been hanging around with. I need you to listen to me. You must know before it's too late…"

He paused and said, almost to himself, "This is the turning point…"

"What? Bring it on, old man, I can take it!" Dan sat down again, and spread his hands out to welcome the words, but inside he felt a pang of guilt for calling JD 'old'. It seemed demeaning somehow. He didn't look so old anymore. Even so, he continued, "I'm stronger now! I'm not the person you met two years ago."

JD sighed.

"Dan," he closed his eyes.

"Hang on, how did you find me here? Only Quinn and Mum knew I was coming to London …and how did you know *exactly* where I was?"

"Well, that's what I need to tell you, in a manner of speaking…"

Dan stood up, his voice rising uncontrollably.

"Why did you say you were him? Everything I thought about you… I imagined we might have some kind of future together!"

"Daniel, we do – "

"How did you know?" He shouted. "How did you know I would believe you? Be so stupid as to believe my dad had come back from the dead?" A tear burst from his right eye and he quickly rubbed it away.

"Because… I've always known you and I always will. I'm…a visitor, a traveller. I took some wrong turns, we took some wrong turns, and I've come to make it right. I need to steer you back on course, Dan, for everyone's sake."

Dan looked at the man before him, the way he sat there with his hands clasped, his eyes older and yet…suddenly familiar in the true sense of the word, reminding him of a face he'd studied a thousand times. His own.

In his head, a key turned, a lock clicked, and inside the big clock, the timer ticked.

— — —

Faith sat staring out of the window of her bedroom. Against her better judgement, she had braved the ladder to the loft and dragged down her memory box, although it had nearly fallen on top of her on the way down.

Dan would be so cross with me, she thought, smiling sadly. He had seemed very distant when they last spoke, but she had been so grateful for the contact. Deep down, she knew she had been a coward stealing back the letter; stealing back the truth from under his nose, but she had been so afraid. He told her he was going to London but had been vague about the reasons why. Faith was worried that this group were leading him astray. She felt the name was more that of a cult than an organisation of activists, although she understood these days it was important to be catchy. Pithy. She liked that very English sounding word, wrapping her tongue around it. She loved this country, but at the same time, it made her feel old. It hadn't always been that way, but now her youth seemed trapped like wet sand in an hourglass, trapped in the dust on the street in New York where she had lived. Memories were frozen in echoes of songs, the smell of weed she caught sometimes as she walked back from the local shop, the feel of wooden floors under her bare feet, like the one she had in her apartment. *Their apartment*, she corrected herself.

Her memory box was made of brown leather, and reminded her of a treasure chest. Jacob had bought it for her on their first Christmas together. She couldn't quite believe that was nearly 40 years ago. Inside it, he had put a big bag of Hershey's kisses, a bottle of wine and the new Jimi Hendrix album. He'd separated the kisses so she had to find them amongst a load of shredded paper.

Faith shook her head, as if to shake off the memory and yet she knew it was waiting for her. Judy had once said to her that she, Faith, looked for pain. She said it seemed like Faith did things to hurt herself on purpose. Faith couldn't explain that it wasn't so much she enjoyed the hurt, more that she knew it was coming and wanted it on her own terms.

"Bring it on, life!" she used to say into the mirror. "I can take it; do your worst!"

So now, the memory box, yes – back to that. Her old bravado resurfacing, she braced herself, and opened the lid.

Nothing jumped out and took a bite out of her, at least. There were some bundles of letters, an old musty envelope which she remembered contained some old photos from her youth, her Bob Dylan tickets from '71 and a few cassette tapes. She blew the dust off one, turned the tiny wheel spokes with her index finger to make sure it still ran, and walked over to the stereo that Dan had bought her for her birthday a few years before. She had insisted on having a record player and a tape deck, despite his assurances that CD's were here to stay. She couldn't believe that; they only lasted five minutes. He always told her off for leaving them out of the box but surely your music collection should be built to last. She still had her Jr Walker LP 'Roadrunner' from '66, the first album she'd ever bought. It still played fine, with a few scratches, which she'd grown used to and had adjusted her singing accordingly to accommodate.

Underneath the letters was a frame, face down. She let her hand rest on it for a few minutes and closed her eyes. The tape was playing 'Don't think twice, it's alright'. She let her mind travel to that place again to see if it was safe. She thought about him again just to see what would happen. She had buried those feelings somewhere, enwrapped with cells like emotional scar tissue, enveloped in her heart. She tried to visualise what lay inside; she thought it would be hard like the earth's core, made of iron and impenetrable, all those layers of time around it.

Faith suddenly had the strong urge to call Dan on his mobile, to see if he was okay. He'd said he'd gone to London for a book fair but Faith wasn't sure if she believed him. She knew 'The Blank Page' was struggling and, from what she had heard about Phil, the owner, he certainly wouldn't be readily forking out cash for a 'jolly', as Dan called it.

She dialled his mobile and waited, but it just went through to voicemail. She didn't know what to say so she hung up. *Stupid woman,* she told herself. *He's not a kid anymore.* Yet she still couldn't shake the feeling of unease, which had taken root in her belly and was permeating her consciousness like a creeping mist.

— — —

Dan was standing a few metres away from the wrought iron table with his hands clenched into fists and yet unmoving. He was staring at the older man sat at the table, while the older man stared back at him, unflinching. He began to mutter under his breath and he shut his eyes and began to sway.

The older man stood up, placed a five pound note onto the metal plate on top of their bill and went towards Dan, gently reaching out to touch his arm.

"You need to come with me, Dan" he said softly.

La la la, said Dan, in his head. He laughed out loud. This was insane, utterly insane. The breeze caressed his hair and he no longer knew where he was, only that he could smell London in all its concrete and culture and fucked-upness and possibility. Strangely, he felt light, as if his feet were no longer touching the ground. He opened his eyes, confused. A bright white light filled them to start with, and then he began to focus. He was aware of someone holding his arm and when his eyes had adjusted, he saw that it was some kind of policeman, but wearing a visor and with a riot shield in his other hand. There were several, more than several actually, and as he tuned in to his surroundings, he could hear sirens. Everyone was looking at him.

"What..." he said to the policeman holding him, who ignored him and led him to a van. He put up no resistance. "Excuse me," he said to the policeman as they were walking. "What's happening?"

The man shook his head in disbelief and pushed Dan into the back of a police van. There were dogs barking. He cuffed Dan to a pole inside the vehicle and gave him a look almost of pity, although he quickly masked it.

"Wait!" Dan shouted to his back as he climbed out. As he did so, another man climbed in and sat down across from Dan. He was grey haired and had eyebrows which flared out, giving him a slightly eccentric look. He brought in a smell of cigarettes, which made Dan want one. He decided not to ask.

"Daniel Anderson, I'm arresting you on suspicion of Manslaughter and Acts of Terrorism," he said. "You do not have to say anything. But it may harm your defence if you do not mention when questioned something you later rely on in court. Anything you do say may be given in evidence.»

Dan stared at the floor while he attempted to piece together his situation. How had he got here? Just moments ago, he'd been talking to... and before that...The bomb. Quinn had said it was only designed to stop the clock though; something must have gone wrong.

"Who are you?" he asked, his voice suddenly timid like a child's.

"I'm Inspector Gillow," he said, removing a small recording device from his pocket and setting it on his lap. "It's now 11.03am on 7th July 2005. I have here with me one Daniel Anderson." Dan found himself nodding and he started to speak but the man took no notice and continued.

"An incendiary device went off at 10 o'clock this morning inside Big Ben," he said, to no-one in particular. His voice was deep with a hint of an accent, although Dan couldn't quite place it. "The explosion dislodged one of the clock hands, which fell and crushed a woman to death on the ground."

The Inspector then looked Dan right in the eyes.

"We have reason to believe you were responsible, and that you have connections with the other terrorists at large in the city."

"Other *terrorists…*" Dan couldn't understand what he was hearing. He started to feel slightly sick. A woman killed. Because of what he'd done? He closed his eyes.

The van was moving now but the windows were all blacked out, so he had a strong feeling of disorientation; as if he was being swept along by dark waters. He remembered going through a cave on a boat once, and having to lean down so his head didn't touch the roof. He felt like that now.

"A sequence of attacks," continued Inspector Gillow sternly, "on the tube, on a bus. We don't believe it's just a coincidence."

Dan looked at the recording device, then up to the man, searching his eyes for a connection, some kind of hope, or a sign that this was all just a mistake.

"I don't know about any of the other...attacks," Dan's voice was croaky and he cleared his throat. "We just wanted to make people think, just to make people change...just...if people could maybe..."

Inspector Gillow cut him off:

"So you're saying that you have no terrorist connections, you were unaware of the other attacks, that your motives were independent?"

"Yes, "said Dan emphatically. "Yes! I'm part of a protest group. We just wanted to...make the clock stop to make a statement, to show people it was time for a change...that was our slogan."

The man raised his eyebrows.

"So you are admitting that you were responsible for planting the device?"

"I was trying to take social action," Dan replied, but as he said this he slumped back into his seat, hearing how he must sound to the inspector; reversing in his head, back to earlier that morning when he had connected the device, believing in his stupidity that it was a brave and anarchic statement they were making; the People of the Sun; thinking of his mother and how she would find out; Quinn could speak up for him, or Ella... maybe it could all be sorted out.

Dan shut his eyes. Inspector Gillow was talking, and waiting, and the motion of the van, driving him somewhere unseen and unknown, made him feel oh, so tired. There were shapes moving behind his eyelids and he felt very far away. It reminded him of the time he'd tried acid at university; the detachment from oneself. After a while or not very long at all, the engine stopped.

He felt a rough hand on his shoulder and a voice waking him. *It was a dream,* he said to himself and opened his eyes hoping to find himself in his bed at home. Instead he saw another police officer standing before him, who uncuffed him from the pole and re-cuffed him so his hands were in front of him. He felt blinded by the midday sun as he walked out. It was quiet there, high walls and fences, eerily still although Dan felt the weight of a thousand invisible eyes judging, misunderstanding and condemning. He was led inside, putting one foot in front of the other, stopping to have his fingerprints taken and to watch his belongings being handed over. He walked on with his head down, the policeman still holding him in a cold embrace, until finally he found himself in a small cell with a metal bed, a sink and a urinal. He lay down on the bed and slept.

— — —

He was woken by a rapping on the cell door, and the entrance of a familiar figure, although not one he welcomed. It wasn't all a dream, then. It was that Inspector from before. Dan wasn't so sure what time of day it was or how much time had elapsed since he had been put in here. He was flanked by a uniformed police officer.

"Daniel?"

He nodded.

"We need to go through your statement from yesterday. Come with me," said Inspector Gillow, letting the officer cuff Dan's hands together once more and leading him out into the corridor.

"Where am I?" Dan asked, almost under his breath.

"You're at HM Prison Belmarsh until we decide what to do with you."

Dan recognised the name, but had no idea what this meant geographically. They were pacing through corridors. He could hear low noises and every now and then a shout or a whistle from a cell as they walked past.

They turned into a rather bland looking room with three chairs and a table. Dan was put down on one of the chairs and the Inspector sat across from him. Another man came in, he was quite round, and dishevelled looking. This man actually shook Dan's hand. It almost broke his heart; in that small moment of normality he was taken back to his life. His *normal* life, the one he had before today; where even strangers smiled at you sometimes, and you could make conversation about the weather.

After an hour of questioning, Dan felt exhausted and even more detached from reality. Connections were being made that he didn't understand. They had placed before him a photograph of the woman who had been killed by the clock hand; she was about his mother's age. Then they showed him a picture of Quinn visiting a man who they claimed had known links to an extremist group. Dan admitted that he knew Quinn, he told them where they had met and what they had talked about. He'd explained it wasn't about race or religion – just a higher state of consciousness. He insisted he wasn't a terrorist and didn't believe Quinn was either. Could they bring Quinn in to corroborate his story? The two men looked at one another, expressionless.

The large man, who had introduced himself as David Pike, looked at him quizzically and asked questions like, *how did you feel when you planted the bomb?* Dan didn't have the energy to lie so he told them the truth: that he had felt excitement about changing the world for the better. Inspector Gillow then reminded him about the woman he'd killed and he felt the darkness of realisation clog up his head and all his membranes and he had started to tremble. He placed a photograph before him, but Dan couldn't look at it. All he had seen was a squashed straw hat. Somehow this made it worse. David Pike signalled something to the Inspector and the interview was terminated until a later time.

"There's someone waiting to see you," David explained. "Since we don't believe you pose an immediate threat you're allowed 10 minutes through the separation wall."

Dan couldn't imagine who would want to see him if he actually was this person they said he was; if he was really responsible for what they claimed had happened. He shuddered. They walked through another door and he found himself in a room with chairs and windows facing outwards.

"Number 3," said the escorting officer, and Dan felt him let go of his arm. It was like being at a bank, sort of, waiting your turn, waiting until your number came up. As he reached window 3 he saw her, sat with her hands clasped and up to her mouth, wearing a red coat which he hadn't seen before, her nails painted to match.

"Mum…" He sat down in the chair and looked across at her.

"Dan," she put her hands up to the window.

"What happened, hun? What did you do?"

He shook his head; he couldn't look her in the eye.

"Something bad, Mum…I didn't mean it," Dan suddenly

felt like a child again, remembering a time he had broken one of Faith's LP's and brought it into the sitting room, crying. He had been terrified of her response and just like then, she now said,

"I know, it was a misunderstanding, it'll be okay." But Dan could hear the shudder in her voice and he realised that Faith was scared.

"How can I fix it?" he asked, his eyes filling with tears.

"We'll get through it together," she replied. "Dan, I… I feel like somehow I'm to blame."

"Mum, no – " he began, but it was clear Faith had made up her mind and wanted to talk.

"You've been asking so much about your father and I've told you so little, I've always pushed it away, maybe you need to know about the past…"

Her voice trailed off and he said,

"My dad was a soldier."

She looked at him, and down at her hands which she had put in front of her almost as if to steel her from a blow.

"That was Jacob," she said, quietly. "Dan, I'm sorry but… he's not your father."

Dan felt a weird sensation of recognition which tickled at the back of his memory but wouldn't present itself clearly for him to examine.

"You mean JD…the man who said he was Jacob? I know he's not my father. I found him out."

She shook her head but looked puzzled. "JD? No. I mean the real Jacob, my Jacob. He's not…" She seemed to run out of breath and ran her fingers around the collar of her coat.

"Jesus, mum, why are you telling me this now?"

"Because I want to help you," she said, "because maybe if you can accept the past and know the truth you can feel stronger, you can take what's ahead, and fight – "

"What happened to that letter, Mum??"

Her face reddened. Angry, he carried on. "The letter? The one you gave me? What did you do with it?"

She was silent. Dan felt a wave of rage build up within him, a red mist in front of his eyes as he heard himself shouting at her.

"What the fuck kind of good does this information do me *now*, huh? Tell me you can sort this out Mum, for fuck's sake, or just GO! Get OUT!" He was standing now, his heart in his throat, his face full of the white heat of his words, which shot out like bullets.

"HELP me or FUCK off, you lying BITCH!" He roared at this woman, who he suddenly felt he no longer knew.

Faith, visibly shaking, grabbed her bag and almost ran from the window at the same time as an officer walked swiftly to Dan and grabbed him, restraining him as, for the first time since he'd been taken in, he resisted and fought to break free.

Back in his cell, he stood against the wall, taking deep breaths, but relentlessly the anger bubbled away, gnawing at his insides. He felt betrayal like a twisting knife in his guts, by Quinn, by Fiona who loved Quinn, by his own mother who had given him a false history and thanks to whom his whole life felt like it had been a lie.

As the bitterness swirled and tumbled around him, enveloping him in a whirl of malevolence, he sat down on the bed and somewhere in his mind a switch flicked. He began to sing a song in his head to help him focus, one he remember from school, about thorns and lies. He didn't remember all the words. *La la la,* he thought and lay down on his side, pulling the rough grey blanket over his legs and allowing the welcome escape of sleep to drag him in.

– – –

He had barely closed his eyes when a feeling of fresh air and outdoor city aromas made him open them again. He could feel an arm around his shoulders and he looked sideways to see JD standing there. They were outside the café. Dan's heart was thudding in his chest and he knew he was having a panic attack. He put his head down and tried to breathe.

"What did – you – just do to me?" He said, between gasps. Without giving him time to answer, Dan began to walk. He walked quickly, trying to contain his breathing within a step, one step at a time, counting along with his feet. Not seeing the people walking past him, not noticing that he had dropped his phone in his haste. As he paced forward, Dan tried to focus on the rhythm of his feet as they pressed down on the pavement, but he could not stop the pounding in his head; his heart felt as though it had relocated to the mid-point of his skull. He turned a corner and in his line of vision registered some green; the tops of tall trees, so he headed for it. Crossing a busy road in a daze, with a throng of other solitary souls, he approached St James's Park. He entered through the large wrought iron gates and paced along the smooth asphalt footpath, which was lined with neat and indeterminate shrubbery. He still couldn't seem to slow his breathing. As the path turned a bend, he spotted a bench a few hundred metres away, under a tree. He crossed onto the grass and found it, plonking himself down and clutching the wooden rungs which held him, as if trying to connect once more to the earth and to reality.

His eyes closed against the world, he finally managed to take in some oxygen. He formulated a simple thought. *I am here.* The solidity of the wood felt reassuring against his body. *But where was I just then?* Fiona popped into his head. He wondered where she was at that moment. He recognised a sick feeling, but could not identify it. Regret, perhaps. Or love.

A few metres from the café, his phone was vibrating, a cursing Quinn on the other end. He was leaving his third message, his cool slipping a fraction.

"Dan, man, dude, we need to touch base. I need to know everything's in place. I saw Fiona this morning. Plus, where the fuck are you? Hey fella, call me back as soon as humanly possible."

Dan's breath was slowing. Opening his eyes took some effort, and his vision was blurred at first. On the huge lake in the middle of the park were gathered a collection of geese and smaller birds he guessed must be ducks or grebes. He began to take in his surroundings. There was a collection of people in the park, some groups with a picnic, a few dog-walkers. The sunshine gave everything a shimmering quality. *I am here,* he thought again. He reached for his phone, but it wasn't in his pocket anymore. *Shit.* He fumbled around and found, in his jacket, an old packet of Embassy with two sad looking cigarettes in it. He felt a rush of relief; a temporary reprieve. He thought about the film 'Back to the Future'. Rules for time travel: don't intervene. He felt like Marty at the 'Enchantment under the Sea' dance, clutching his fading photograph.

He looked around again and saw a woman on her own standing on the path from where he had come. She was holding a city map and kept looking up and back down again. She caught him looking at her, and walked over. The dread he felt at having to make everyday conversation was overridden by his hope that she might possess a lighter of some kind. He stared straight ahead of him. She sat down at the edge of the bench.

"Do you mind?" Her voice was husky and reminded him of an English actress from a US TV series, he couldn't remember the name. He shook his head.

She sat quietly studying the map again.

"I don't suppose you know where I can find the Abraham Lincoln statue? I seem to be going round in circles!" She laughed as if embarrassed at her own incompetence. Dan began to apologise but then he gently took the map from her and cast his eye around the park.

"It looks like you might need to head over to that side and, yeah, you should come out near the statue. I could be wrong. I'm not from London."

"No," she replied. "I suspect not many of us are." She gestured at the other people frequenting the park.

"I don't suppose," Dan asked, his voice laden with hope, "by some small miracle, you happen to have a light?"

She fished around in her pocket and pulled out a box of matches. He weakly offered her the other Embassy and lit it for her.

"I've tried so many times to give up," she said, "but in the end I just think, life's too short."

He took a long deep drag and held it in. She carried on talking, as if to fill the silence.

"You must think I'm silly getting lost around here, what with so many landmarks to navigate from. I thought if I could find Big Ben I'd be okay but – "

A stab of reality. The sharp injection of a memory. Dan's eyes shot to her face and then immediately to her wrist.

"What time is it?" He asked, with breathless urgency, standing up.

She took what seemed like an age to fumble with her sleeve so she could see her watch.

"Ten to 10," she said. "Cowboy time…"

She had smiled at her own joke, but Dan did not see it. He had bolted. Across the grass he ran, a wind like quality to his limbs, and he looked up to the sky, towards the big clock tower, dodging the passers-by and willing himself onwards through time.

The woman shrugged and tried to make sense of what had just happened. She put the city map into her bag, and pulled out a floppy straw hat. The sun was toasting her neck and she resolved to walk in the opposite direction for a while. She had all day, after all. Exiting the park over there would take her towards Westminster, she thought, and towards the height and splendour of Big Ben.

– – –

Dan stopped, leaning against the railings and looked up at the clock.

"Shit, shit, shit!" he said out loud, and a few tourists passing by gave him a nervous look. He had two minutes to get up there. He scrabbled onwards, through the turnstiles, flashing his fake ID at the tour guides, one of whom recognised him from earlier that morning and looked at him questioningly.

"Forgot something!" Dan shouted in response, smiling and dashing off. She smiled faintly back and was immediately distracted by a garishly dressed tourist with an urgent question about the next chance to view the Houses of Parliament. He raced into the small wooden door at the bottom of the structure and began to scale the chalky steps two at a time. Looking up made him feel dizzy and he yearned for the air to push him up faster and higher; what the hell had he been thinking? He slipped on a step and banged his knee, cursing, and sped onwards. His heightened breath, in, out, and the repeated taps of his ascent, both formed a rhythm that pulsed with adrenalin and regret. He passed the prison room and felt an icy stab of memory shudder through him, then he became aware of a soreness on the palm of his hand from the friction of the wooden banister; his vision was becoming slightly blurred and his running dropped lower to the ground as he gasped at the air. Suddenly there was a loud noise; the chime had begun, he wasn't even halfway up. Something in Dan's head began to let go, and his body began to slow down as if no longer under his control. He struggled onwards, yet something beneath his feet pulled at him, dragging him towards it. He was on his knees as the great bell struck and he threw his arms around his head, the cold alabaster step rising to greet his forehead, his painful intakes of breath bringing with them the taste of chalk and sweet aroma of 1000 earthly footsteps. As the sound of Big Ben reverberated around his skull, a picture formed in his head, as if drawn upon his eyelids by an invisible hand: a door with a small barred window and a face looking through it; a photograph of a woman lying dead. Awaiting what he knew must come after, Dan became lost in the echo of each formidable clang, which enveloped him like a twister; in it he saw figures, just like Dorothy in the Wizard of Oz; there was his mother on a bike with a headscarf on, and behind her was Jacob who was looking at his watch, and then came Fiona, who reached her hands out to him pleadingly.

CHAPTER **TWELVE**

DAN WAS WALKING ON the cycle path by the river. The cars on the nearby dual carriageway zoomed past, blending into the general stillness of the water. He thought about JD's disappearing act. He still had to call him that, for what else could he do? Was what had happened in the clock tower all in his imagination? No. JD had succeeded in stopping Dan from following a destructive path, but Dan still felt like there was something missing. What was to stop him fucking it all up again? And yet, to know that in all of that chaos, he had some control over himself, albeit with hindsight; it felt like progress. His mind revisited the dark place; the place in which he had been harbouring bitterness and he found, thankfully, some peace, but still, a vacant part of his soul lay bare, waiting to be filled.

He crossed over the metal footbridge, pausing to look out over the changing city. Suddenly, he noticed a heron, standing very still on the river bank just a few feet from him. He stopped to look, and soon found himself transported back to the previous day; a day that seemed a lifetime ago.

There at the edge of the bell room, he collapsed on the top step, awaiting the big bang. The noise was deafening up there, the huge bell sounding one ring after the other; heralding the start of a new hour as it had done countless times before. Dan tried to cram his sleeves into his ears and cup them with his hands as the blast of metal upon metal took over his senses. After the tenth deafening clang, there was nothing left but the memory, reverberating around his skull. His eyes closed, he had waited for it to subside.

When finally there was silence, muffled even further by his temporary deafness, he opened his eyes and crawled to his feet. Climbing the final few steps, his legs like lead, he saw a shaft of sunlight as it hit the shape of a man he knew quite well. His outline was clear, as if drawn in charcoal, and he turned to face Dan, smiling. As Dan watched, all the molecules that made up the man appeared to vibrate, in such a manner that his face and body morphed before Dan's eyes into a bright, almost blinding light. Amidst the reality of the bell room, almost liquid now, he was lifted and melded and elevated until there was nothing solid there anymore, but a whisper of white. And then, that too had disappeared.

Knowing suddenly what he must do, Dan removed the empty back pack from behind the huge bell mechanism where he had stashed it, and picked up the obsolete device, which had been disconnected and lay there alone, a mesh of metal and wires and plastic. He placed it carefully in his bag and put it over his shoulders, walked shakily down the steps and out into the sunlight. Although he could hear the security guard's radio somewhere, the man himself was no-where to be seen, so he walked swiftly away.

He found that the tube was closed; listening in to conversations it sounded as though some terrorist attacks had occurred across London, and the news made him shiver. He walked across Westminster Bridge seeing the signs for Waterloo Station. Not knowing if he could travel from there or not, he resolved to get a train in the general direction of home, or at least out of the city as quickly as possible. His heart was thumping as if it was expanding and he had the sensation that his rib cage would crack. He stopped and put a hand out to rest on one of the pale green walls which lined the bridge. Breathe, he reminded himself, shutting his eyes.

When his mind had cleared and his breathing had slowed, he opened his eyes once more and looked tentatively around him. He could see the Houses of Parliament in the direction from which he had come, and ahead of him, the Millennium Eye which was, at this point, unmoving. He tried not to let himself think about what could have been. Letting his eyes travel and rest on the water, the grey Thames as it flowed through the heart of this city and took with it all its inhabitants hopes and dreams, he removed the rucksack from his back, and swiftly checked there was no-one nearby. The city was unnaturally quiet, as though people had retreated in fear, into the safety of their houses, of their lives. As quickly and silently as he could, he dropped the bag into the river. It sank almost straightaway. He looked around again. No-one had seen him or paid any attention. There were no cameras that he could see from here. A man without baggage, he walked, ahead and away from the city and into a different future.

After an hour and amidst the chaos of the train station, Dan finally managed to get hold of a ticket to Basingstoke, where he felt sure he could make his way up country and home. He had misplaced his mobile, possibly in that cafe, who knew – so he looked around the station for a payphone and called his mum. Beside herself, she explained she had been trying to get through to him but all the phone networks were jammed. She kept saying, "Why today? Why of all days?" and then she would respond to herself, "But you're okay, you're alive!" She insisted he come to see her as soon as he could; that there was something important she must talk to him about. She told him that she had called Fi to find out if she knew anything, but that Fi hadn't even realised he was in London – weren't they friends anymore? He didn't answer, but asked his mum if she would let Fiona know he was okay and of course, she had agreed.

Now Dan found himself back in the present moment, thinking about Fi. Everything was raw and it felt like a clean slate again; a tabula rasa. He thought maybe in time he could forgive himself for losing his way so utterly and almost completely, and wondered if she could too. As he stared into the middle distance, he became aware of movement. The big bird gradually unfolded its wings and almost in slow motion, alighted from the bank and set off on a low flight to who knew where.

He thought about his mum and the important thing she had to tell him. Deep down he felt he might already know, but he needed to hear her say it; needed to hear her explain. He still couldn't understand why she hadn't told the truth. He looked again, for the anger he had felt at that prison window, but he found only a twinge of disappointment. Standing there watching the heron fly away, he suddenly became aware that he was wasting time – time he had been gifted, time which so easily could have been taken away. Turning away from the railings on the bridge, he broke into a run in the direction of the town centre, and the bus station.

– – –

Faith woke up in her armchair with a start. The TV was still on, some kind of chat show or self-help garbage. She heard someone was banging on the door, pummelling, in fact. She had just been having a semi-dream about Jacob, where he had taken her dancing, but to some old fashioned place, like a tea-dance. The music was 20's and Jacob had spread his hands out smiling and was saying, "Look baby, I'm all here!" Everyone was gawping at them, and he'd looked so handsome.

What time was it? She shot up, realising it was Dan and at that moment she heard a familiar voice shouting, "Mum! Open up!"

She rushed to unhook the latch and pulled the door open, her son almost collapsed into her.

"Oh thank god, Dan! Thank god you're home!"

She pulled him in and put her arms around him. "My Daniel," she said quietly and wouldn't let go. After a moment, he managed to prise her arms from around him and she apologised. Dan found he couldn't speak; he was suddenly overcome with emotion, and crumpled down onto the floor of the hallway. She crouched down next to him. She grabbed his face and made him look at her.

"Are you alright?" Faith looked quickly at the door to make sure she had set the latch again.

"Please Dan, are you okay?" She realised he was crying, and again went to put her arms around him; this time he didn't try and curb her embrace and they sat like that for some time, until he calmed down.

Softly Faith said, "I was so worried, I thought I'd lost you."

Dan looked up at her, and gave her a slight smile; his eyes still puffy and a solitary tear running down his cheek.

"I had a lucky escape," he replied.

They were quiet for a moment.

"You want some tea, sweetie?" Faith reached into her sleeve and blew her nose on a crumpled up tissue. She took a deep breath in.

"Yeah Mum," he sniffed. "Yeah, that'd be great."

In the kitchen, Faith took some more deep breaths to calm herself. The kettle came to a boil. She listened to the noise and for a moment forgot Dan was in the hall. This seemed to happen a lot at the moment; she'd be doing something and she'd just drift off. She turned around but he hadn't come in; it was strange he hadn't followed her into the kitchen.

She made tea and stirred his for longer than necessary. She planned what to say when they had sat down together; there was a feeling in her belly that she knew to be her instinct kicking in. Something afoot, a change in the air. She had known it was coming though; who was she kidding? *But thank God I've got the chance to tell him now*, thought Faith.

She walked back into the hall but Dan wasn't there anymore.

"Hun? Where are you? Dan?" She walked into the living room but nothing was disturbed. Then the house creaked and she knew he was in her bedroom, and heard the dragging of a box across the floorboards. She knew, then, what he must have guessed, somehow. She put their tea down and looked at herself in the hall mirror at the bottom of the stairs. Faith pushed some strands of hair behind her right ear. That person who looked back was getting old. How does that happen? Who can say what right time has to do that to you? But then again, all of the things she had worried about didn't matter anymore; if she could've spent more time being happy as a teenager instead of wanting to be someone else, wow, what a different time she might have had. But she wouldn't have had Jacob, and she wouldn't have had Dan, and she wouldn't have had the pleasures and the pain, and all the goddamn life.

She smiled.

"Bring it on then," she said quietly.

— — —

There were so many questions Dan wanted to ask JD. As he turned into the entrance of the park, he saw impressed into the path some paw prints, presumably of a dog, which must have walked on the wet concrete and then it had dried like that. He wondered how long they had been there. The asphalt emitted a baked smell, and the insects and birds and all of nature carried on regardless of the city streets which surrounded the park. A train passed over the nearby bridge and sounded its horn, which scattered a flock of gulls who'd been feasting on someone's picnic remains.

In his pocket, he fiddled with the letter he had received that morning. It had been written in a familiar hand; more neatly than in the journal he had invaded, and yet still sloping and now, in hindsight, immediately recognisable. It was a short note, asking him to be in a certain place at a certain time; telling him that it was important, please. It had been on his doormat when he'd arrived home from his mum's the previous evening. He had to trust the author of it, for whom can we trust if we cannot trust ourselves? Fiona would meet him the following day. He had said he would go to her flat so they could talk properly. He felt, within, an excitement and the sweet anticipation of something good: something right.

He thought about his mum. She had finally told him that Jacob was not his father; that he had been the product of a 'one night stand' when she was in a bad place, but that as soon as she had known she was pregnant she had wanted him, she had loved him. He had asked who the man was, but she had merely said: it didn't matter. She told him about how she had felt for those first few years; how her only solace had been to relive the good times with Jacob and that she had convinced herself of the lie almost as much as she had convinced other people, even her closest friend, Judy. He couldn't contain his curiosity and his frustration at not finding out his father's identity, and he had questioned her and pressured her until she had broken down and left the room.

It was as though she wasn't the person he'd always thought she was; and on top of that, neither was he, himself, Dan anymore. And yet, he thought, who was he before? Are our identities fixed, bound by our parents and our forefathers, tied to the roots that we leave behind, those roots that we leave severed, trailing in the distance? Can't we begin again? He didn't know why he was here today but he had felt compelled; like he owed it to himself. It wasn't that he didn't think he could forgive Faith, but more as though he felt she needed to know he wouldn't just accept it. And yet, he felt ashamed. After all, what was the point of it, when all was said and done? All those years she could have told him; but she had done her best. Whatever had been said by either of them, though, it didn't change the fact that he was fatherless now, and if Jacob wasn't his dad, then who was? And why did JD want him here anyway, at this particular time?

He rounded the corner and spotted the entrance to the Peace Garden, where the letter had asked him to go. A crisp packet danced before him in the breeze and he watched. These were moments; one after the other, gone in a flash like dust. He found himself at the garden's iron gates, which squeaked in protest as he pushed them open. The path before him forked into a circle around a decorative fish pond in the middle. He had expected to find people there, even wondering in the back of his mind whether this could be a secret meeting place for gays or drug dealers. He inwardly laughed at himself for having such middle-aged thoughts.

Who was he supposed to meet here? What was he supposed to see? Would he be visited again by his future self, like some angel to Mary? He decided to walk the outer border of the garden and see if JD was hidden from view by the tall rhododendron plants which were in full bloom. Suddenly, as he turned one corner, he saw a man sat on a bench, right in front of him. As he got closer, he realised this man was familiar, although it wasn't the face he'd expected to see. The man looked up, he looked at first troubled and then shocked and confused. They looked at each other for a brief moment before Dan spoke.

"Aren't you…my mum's friend…aren't you Christopher?"

The man nodded and slowly put out his hand to Dan.

"Daniel," he said, and they shook.

Dan sat down next to him. There didn't seem to be words for the situation they found themselves in, because it was just so unlikely and Dan was still wondering if JD might be nearby, and how on earth Christopher was here, when it dawned on him that if you could travel in time, then there was no such thing as a coincidence.

Christopher seemed just as astonished. He was leaning forward, his hands placed evenly on his knees as if to steady his position. Dan noticed his watch; it had a distinctive green face.

The older man caught him looking in the corner of his eye and it seemed to shake him out of his stunned state.

"Unusual, isn't it?" he said. "Your mother gave it to me, strangely enough, when we lived opposite each other." He smiled.

"You lived opposite each other...oh, she never told me." Dan looked down at his own hands, as if some answer could be found there. "In New York?"

"That's right," the man replied. "We were good friends. It was when she worked at the watchmakers, she always said green was my colour." Christopher laughed quietly and ran a hand through his greying hair.

"What was she like?" Dan said, resting his elbows on his knees and leaning forward onto his hands as he suddenly felt like all of his energy had gone.

Christopher looked sideways at him, raising his eyebrows questioningly.

"She was...her own person," he said. "She was the life and soul, you know? If you went to one of their parties, hers and Jacob's..." He paused, as if not sure whether he should mention this name. Dan nodded, encouraging him to continue.

"Well, everyone wanted to talk to Faith, she was like this light we all danced around like moths, hypnotised by her." He screwed up his eyes now, and leant forward so he was level with Dan.

"He loved her, Jacob, he did, but getting drafted to 'Nam, well it just about finished them, even before he'd left."

"How do you mean?" asked Dan, leaning back and letting the sun get in his eyes so he saw bluish light at the corners.

"He didn't want to let go of her, and I think he knew what

would happen if he went, not that she would stop loving him but that he would change and maybe they could never be the way they were." Christopher stopped abruptly, and Dan realised he was crying.

Dan sat for a moment and let things arrange themselves again in his head, before pure instinct made him reach to Christopher's arm and squeeze it.

"A few days after he'd gone, I buzzed her apartment," Christopher continued. "She was real upset, and she'd been drinking. I made her a coffee and we sat for a smoke, I remember she was so quiet. She just wanted a friend really, you know? But Jesus, I was so…I was…in love with her." His voice broke. "Things just happen sometimes, don't they, and you wonder how and you spend your life going over them and then…" He looked directly at Dan, "weird coincidences or a twist of fate or whatever it is brings you to now."

Dan shut his eyes. He imagined his mother just as another girl, sitting in her apartment with all her stuff and her heart broken. Somehow her face became that of Fiona too, with her misspent weekends burning a hole in her while she tried to move on, to be different. Something hard and like stone, something that had been inside him for the longest time, that for some unknown reason he had been clinging on to, began to crumble away, and in his chest, a lightening, a warmth. He realised he was crying but it didn't matter. He heard Christopher take in a breath, and then he felt an arm around him, an arm in a crumpled army coat.

And there, the two men held each other; like children, like lovers, like best friends, like brothers. Like father and son.

— — —

Faith hasn't moved in a couple of hours. She is staring at her hands, but not really looking at them. She is playing with the ring she wears on her right hand, the one Jacob gave her before he went away. In her mind, a replay of the conversation she last had with Dan is revolving, on a loop. Try as she might, and she does, she cannot stop hearing his reproaches. They pile up inside her, like dirt, and she adds them to the self-loathing she has tried to keep hidden over the years. Now she basks in it, wallows in the murk. "Perhaps I will just drown in it and let go," she thinks. What has stopped her before is Dan, his love and respect, but now she isn't sure if she has lost that anyway.

It's dark outside but Faith hasn't turned on any lights, so when a car pulls up outside, the headlights penetrate her stony gaze and she looks up, her head spinning slightly. She doesn't think it's anyone for her, and barely hears the key turn in the lock of her front door. Shutting her eyes, she leans back in the chair and rests her weary head, the skin of her cheeks and neck pulled taught with drying tears.

When a hand touches her shoulder, she starts, as if brought back from another place; as if being awoken from a strange dream. She sees Dan before her, and yet she doesn't believe it, even more so when another man comes into view. They stand before her, as if waiting. What for? Her approval? She nods for she doesn't know what else to do; doesn't know what the situation requires nor how they have come to be here together.

"Hello again, Faith," says Christopher, softly. He comes towards her now, crouching down and pulling her into a gentle hug. She allows herself to fold into it, the warmth of it, the comfort and hugs him back tightly. She feels like a child again. As he backs away, she begins, "I don't understand, why are you here?" She says this to both of them. Dan kneels down and takes her hand.

"I'm so sorry, Mum." She breaks into tears at the sheer relief of the words.

"No, Daniel, I'm the one who should be sorry," she says, and sobs. "I should never have lied. I was just...scared. Stupid woman."

She kisses the top of his head and the tears run down her chin again, in the same rivulets as before but somehow newer and more poignant because they fall onto Dan's hair, anointing him in her emotion.

In a muffled voice Dan says, "I think I understand why you did lie, but will you tell me please?"

"Tell you what?" Faith says, willing to tell him anything.

As if in answer to her thoughts, Dan replies, "Everything."

Some hours later, Christopher is snoring slightly, collapsed in Faith's old armchair. Dan and Faith sit on the floor, surrounded by photographs and letters. Dan leans forward and tops up his mum's glass. She rubs her eyes, exhausted, but with no intention of going to bed yet.

"So, when did you know...I mean, that Jacob wasn't...?" Dan asks, taking a sip from his glass.

Faith smiles, "Things hadn't been great between us the month before he left. He didn't want to be alone with me. I knew in my heart when they told me my due date. Your fa...I mean, Jacob – he had been gone a few weeks anyway. Then when you started to grow into a little boy and you were no longer a baby, then I could see little things that reminded me of Chris, but I couldn't accept it even though I knew it was true."

"But why? I mean, I thought you were friends?"

Faith sighs, "Because, Dan, I loved Jacob with all of my heart. I couldn't reconcile myself with what I'd done. And then when…" Her voice grows quieter. "When he went missing, I believed he'd had my letter and that was the last thing he'd read before he…well, before whatever happened, happened."

Dan crosses his legs and leans back against the sofa.

"But what did happen?"

Faith looks at him longingly, as if she can't face another telling of it, but then steels herself. After all, she thinks, it's different now. They are talking to each other like fellow human beings, not just mother and son. She must be honest and true. He deserves that.

"Well, I can't remember what I've told you in the past, but you know he hadn't been out there very long, just a couple of months. He was one of the last people to go on the draft. I used to wonder about that, but all I ever come back to is that if he hadn't, I wouldn't have you.

"Anyway, something happened to him and his group. The locals had said it was a storm but the US army suspected it was an attack. The only two that survived couldn't really remember what had happened expect that it was sudden. They looked for Jacob but they never found him, but they found…one of his hands."

Faith shudders, even now, at the memory as she casts herself back to that day, when she read the letter. She looks up and saw that Dan's face has gone slightly pale. "That's how I knew that...that man wasn't him. Sorry hun, do you really want to know?"

Dan nods and Faith reaches over to take his hand.

"I can remember how I felt, even now, when I read the words, Missing in Action. All that went through my head was, *It's my fault, it's my fault, I sent him to his death.* I sunk into this darkness that I couldn't get out of. Chris wanted to talk about what had happened between us, but I never let him get past his first question. He knew I was pregnant, of course, but after a while he let it go and I guess he did exactly as I did, convinced himself you were Jacob's. We pretended like it was all fine and I let him be my friend again."

At this, Faith shakes her head. "Gee, it makes me sound so shallow, or so...full of my own importance... I *let* him."

Dan clears his throat, "He said to me, in the park, that he was in love with you."

Faith looks ashamed. "I guess I knew that, and I recoiled from it. Stupid girl. But you can't force your own heart.

"The only thing that lifted me out of the dark place was the news that I had a home in England, a place to start over, with you, a blank space in which I could etch my own future...*our* future, as a family."

Dan stands up and walked over to the window, looking out at the darkness of the garden and the three quarter moon, which sheds partial light over the familiar objects. He examines them as if with new eyes. The watering can on the step is full of flowers, and the old rope he used as a swing when he was little, hangs from a branch of the crab apple tree, withered and frayed.

Faith takes a deep breath. "I need to tell you, Dan, that you've met Chris before."

Dan turns to look at her, confused.

"I don't think you remember. We went to the seaside when you were little, about one and a half. Chris was over on business and he had called and called until I agreed to meet up with him. It was the first time you'd seen the sea – you weren't afraid one bit!"

She laughs at the memory, and this softens Dan, who smiles and says, "I can't' remember."

"And it was freezing," Faith continues, "but you didn't care. I held you in the waves and you laughed and laughed. When I put you down on the sand, you toddled back towards the sea again."

As if he has some glimmer of recognition, Dan twists his face quizzically and frowns. Faith almost knows what's coming, and lets him make the discovery himself. He slowly walks over to the mantelpiece and picks up the old photograph of himself and his mother on the beach. He lifts it up in a gesture that asks, *this time?*

"Yes," Faith replied, looking at him and then at Chris. "You never asked me who took it."

– – –

Sitting and looking through the holes in the mosquito net at what remains of the forest, the American (for that was what they called him) allows his mind to skirt around his memories. The netting lends everything a hazy quality, like if you can't face the sharp edges it is some kind of relief. He can hear his neighbours chatting and is able to make out some of the gist of it; what price for flour, that there was bánh cooking and they couldn't be long but did you know so and so's son was getting married and his family was moving to the city? And so it went on. It was pleasant. The pace of this life had gradually soothed his wounds and gone some way to healing his soul.

Huan enters the room softly and pulls at the cord of the netting, letting sunlight into the room. Dust particles danced around in the warm air. She looks at the familiar yellowing envelope with the red and white stamp and the small 11c in the corner. The folded letter peeping out, creased with the re-reading and in that delicate, spidery hand.

"Some tea?"

He nods and clasps her hand briefly when she puts the cup down. She sits down between him and the window, and takes his hand in her own.

"You remember now?" she asks, her eyes slightly brimming with tears.

"I do."

She gives his hand a squeeze and gets up, walking over to her small wicker desk and removing a pen from the straw pot. She then brings over the round drum to act as a small table. She places a sheet of writing paper down and holds it steady for him, and with his good arm lent across the drum and the pen clutched carefully between his fingers, Jacob begins his reply.

— — —

Somewhere else, somewhere far away, another man screws up his eyes, and then opens them again, as if to confirm that things are not as he left them. It is a neat room, where he now finds himself, and he looks out upon a view of not just other concrete blocks like his, but one of the sea. The window is large, and open, and the sliding caress of waves on pebbles soothes his mind immediately. He stares at this for a few moments, adjusting to its beauty and basking in the inevitable and reassuring repetition of it.

On a small table are a battered looking notebook and an equally ravaged old watch. He thinks he may recognise it. He turns around to see a small kitchen and notices there are more windows and the sun, streaming in, is making patterns on the cool, tiled floor.

He notices now that his feet are bare and looking down at them, suddenly becomes aware that his leg no longer hurts. He reaches down to rub it and then observes something else; that his arm is clean. There are no numbers cruelly etched upon his skin. He stands up, straighter this time, and his heart begins to lighten. He looks for the heavy, dull pain which has been a part of him for so long and finds nothing. Suddenly, he thinks he hears a faint noise somewhere else in the building. Could it be...? And then as if in answer, a familiar voice, slightly gravelled with the passing of time and yet as familiar and comforting as a warm embrace, calls,

"Dan, are you there?"

Fiona.

He smiles and turns quickly, walking towards her, pulled with a force made from the invisible steel-like threads which tie us together through time with love, and the absolute knowledge of one thing; that he is finally home.

ELIZABETH MACBAIN was born in London and now lives in Derbyshire. She has had a variety of jobs to date, but writing has always been her true passion. *'The Heart Ladder'* is Elizabeth's debut novel.

Urbane Publications is dedicated to
developing new author voices, and publishing
fiction and non-fiction that challenges, thrills and
fascinates.

From page-turning novels to innovative
reference books, our goal is to publish what
YOU want to read.

Find out more at
urbanepublications.com